FEARLESS HEARTS

Acclaim for Radclyffe's Fiction

"Medical drama, gossipy lesbian romance, and angsty backstory all get equal time in [*Unrivaled*,] Radclyffe's fifth PMC Hospital Romance…[F]ans of small community dynamics and workplace romance without ethical complications will find this hits the spot."—*Publishers Weekly*

"*Dangerous Waters* is a bumpy ride through a devastating time with powerful events and resolute characters. Radclyffe gives us the strong, dedicated women we love to read in a story that keeps us turning pages until the end."—*Lambda Literary Review*

"Radclyffe's *Dangerous Waters* has the feel of a tense television drama, as the narrative interchanges between hurricane trackers and first responders. Sawyer and Dara butt heads in the beginning as each moves for some level of control during the storm's approach, and the interference of a lovely television reporter adds an engaging love triangle threat to the sexual tension brewing between them."—*RT Book Reviews*

"*Love After Hours*, the fourth in Radclyffe's Rivers Community series, evokes the sense of a continuing drama as Gina and Carrie's slow-burning romance intertwines with details of other Rivers residents. They become part of a greater picture where friends and family support each other in personal and recreational endeavors. Vivid settings and characters draw in the reader…"
—*RT Book Reviews*

Secret Hearts "delivers exactly what it says on the tin: poignant story, sweet romance, great characters, chemistry and hot sex scenes. Radclyffe knows how to pen a good lesbian romance."
—*LezReviewBooks Blog*

Wild Shores "will hook you early. Radclyffe weaves a chance encounter into all-out steamy romance. These strong, dynamic women have great conversations, and fantastic chemistry."
—*The Romantic Reader Blog*

In **2016 RWA/OCC Book Buyers Best award winner for suspense and mystery with romantic elements** *Price of Honor* "Radclyffe is master of the action-thriller series…The old familiar characters are there, but enough new blood is introduced to give it a fresh feel and open new avenues for intrigue."—*Curve Magazine*

In *Prescription for Love* "Radclyffe populates her small town with colorful characters, among the most memorable being Flann's little sister, Margie, and Abby's 15-year-old trans son, Blake…This romantic drama has plenty of heart and soul." —*Publishers Weekly*

2013 RWA/New England Bean Pot award winner for contemporary romance *Crossroads* "will draw the reader in and make her heart ache, willing the two main characters to find love and a life together. It's a story that lingers long after coming to 'the end.'"—*Lambda Literary*

In **2012 RWA/FTHRW Lories and RWA HODRW Aspen Gold award winner** *Firestorm* "Radclyffe brings another hot lesbian romance for her readers."—*The Lesbrary*

Foreword Review Book of the Year finalist and IPPY silver medalist *Trauma Alert* "is hard to put down and it will sizzle in the reader's hands. The characters are hot, the sex scenes explicit and explosive, and the book is moved along by an interesting plot with well drawn secondary characters. The real star of this show is the attraction between the two characters, both of whom resist and then fall head over heels."—*Lambda Literary Reviews*

Lambda Literary Award Finalist *Best Lesbian Romance 2010* features "stories [that] are diverse in tone, style, and subject, making for more variety than in many, similar anthologies… well written, each containing a satisfying, surprising twist. Best Lesbian Romance series editor Radclyffe has assembled a respectable crop of 17 authors for this year's offering."—*Curve Magazine*

Applause for L.L. Raand's Midnight Hunters Series

"Raand has built a complex world inhabited by werewolves, vampires, and other paranormal beings…Raand has given her readers a complex plot filled with wonderful characters as well as insight into the hierarchy of Sylvan's pack and vampire clans. There are many plot twists and turns, as well as erotic sex scenes in this riveting novel that keep the pages flying until its satisfying conclusion."—*Just About Write*

"Once again, I am amazed at the storytelling ability of L.L. Raand aka Radclyffe. In *Blood Hunt*, she mixes high levels of sheer eroticism that will leave you squirming in your seat with an impeccable multi-character storyline all streaming together to form one great read."—*Queer Magazine Online*

"Are you sick of the same old hetero vampire/werewolf story plastered in every bookstore and at every movie theater? Well, I've got the cure to your werewolf fever. *The Midnight Hunt* is first in, what I hope is, a long-running series of fantasy erotica for L.L. Raand (aka Radclyffe)."—*Queer Magazine Online*

By Radclyffe

Romances

Innocent Hearts
Promising Hearts
Love's Melody Lost
Love's Tender Warriors
Tomorrow's Promise
Love's Masquerade
shadowland
Turn Back Time
When Dreams Tremble
The Lonely Hearts Club
Secrets in the Stone
Desire by Starlight
Homestead
The Color of Love
Secret Hearts
Only This Summer

First Responders Novels

Trauma Alert
Firestorm
Taking Fire
Wild Shores

Heart Stop
Dangerous Waters
Fearless Hearts

Red Sky Ranch Novels (With Julie Cannon)

Fire in the Sky

Wild Fire

Honor Series

Above All, Honor
Honor Bound
Love & Honor
Honor Guards
Honor Reclaimed
Honor Under Siege

Word of Honor
Oath of Honor
(First Responders)
Code of Honor
Price of Honor
Cost of Honor

Justice Series

A Matter of Trust (prequel)
Shield of Justice
In Pursuit of Justice

Justice in the Shadows
Justice Served
Justice for All

Visit us at www.boldstrokesbooks.com

FEARLESS HEARTS

by

RADCLY*f*FE

2025

This Trade Paperback Original Is Published By
Bold Strokes Books, Inc.
P.O. Box 249
Valley Falls, NY 12185

First Edition: July 2025

Credits
Editor: Stacia Seaman
Production Design: Stacia Seaman
Cover Design by Tammy Seidick

Acknowledgments

Like many of my series, this one began by accident in 2007 when I published *When Dreams Tremble*. That story takes place at a resort on Lake George based on the one where I worked during the summer between graduating high school and starting college. Nat Evans was introduced in that book, and I always meant to tell her story—now I have, and I hope you enjoy it.

Enormous thanks to editor Stacia Seaman for finding an embarrassing number of details I mangled—I am obviously comma impaired. Stacia has been editing my books for over twenty years and has yet to complain. I swear I use a grammar checker, but nothing will replace a human editor. Kudos to Stacia and all the BSB editors for making us look better. Thanks to Sandy Lowe for story input, keeping the shop running while I'm writing, and too many essential things to name.

And to Lee, amo te.

To the vets and staff of the Upstate Veterinary Specialists hospital, who have saved three of my dogs and thousands of other animals

CHAPTER ONE

The ringing phone jarred Vic O'Brien from restless sleep. She fumbled for it, the screen's glow stabbing at her groggy eyes. Her cousin. Her pulse kicked up. She hadn't heard from Charlie since the funeral.

She swiped to accept, her voice cracking. "Charlie, what the—"

"Hey Vic, listen..." He sounded maddeningly chipper for the middle of the night. "We've got an unexpected vacancy in the sheriff's department. One of the summer hires backed out. We could really use you here—like tomorrow. You're not committed to anything right now, are you?"

"Wait, what?" Vic sat up, still fuzzy-headed. The two hours she'd been down had been about the longest she'd slept in one go since before the funeral. She grasped at hazy memories of the wake. The whole thing had been a blur. She hadn't seen her older cousin in years. Maybe he had mentioned a job. Maybe she'd just been too gutted to register it.

"What kind of job?"

"In a boat—look, I gotta tell the Cap if you're coming. You've got your license, and all your academy paperwork is in order, right?"

"Sure, but—"

"Okay, then. I've got a place for you to stay. Can you get here yesterday?"

Vic rubbed her face and glanced around the rented room—a by-the-week place she'd taken after letting the apartment go. A sparse, utilitarian space meant for short stays, with faded beige walls that reflected the dullness of too many tenants passing through. Thin carpet covered the floor, worn at the edges from years of foot traffic. A small nightstand sat beside the narrow metal-framed bed, cluttered with a chipped lamp and a half-empty bottle of water. The place was clean, though, and that was enough. She hadn't planned to stick around long anyway. She just hadn't figured out where the hell she was going next.

And maybe that was the problem. She had nothing holding her down.

For weeks, she'd been drifting—untethered, directionless. The thought of leaving Cutler gnawed at her. Moving meant leaving behind the last traces of her father—the smell of salt air, the creak of the docks, the hum of the boat engine beneath her feet. Could she really step away from that? If she did, was there anything left of the person she used to be?

She stared at the darkened room around her. There was nothing keeping her here anymore. Not really. Charlie offered her…something. A few months in a new place to figure out her life. And no one to care if she left Cutler behind for good.

"Sure, yeah, I'm in," Vic said, sitting on the side of the bed. Four a.m. Five hundred miles. No problem. "I'll start packing."

"Great—I'll text you the address." He laughed. "Gonna be a great summer, kid."

Kid.

She was a lot of things right now—practically homeless, hurting in a place nothing could heal, and uncertain what she was going to do with the rest of her life—but she wasn't the fourteen-year-old Charlie remembered.

❖

Vic hadn't intended to fall asleep in a stranger's driveway, but she hadn't been planning on driving five hundred miles without stopping or starting a new job with two days' notice either. The sharp rap on the glass of her battered Dodge pickup brought her jerking up in her seat.

"Fuck!" She blinked and looked out the window into eyes a deeper shade of blue than the Atlantic in high summer, framed by waves of dark brunette hair. A face, verging between beautiful and handsome, that she recognized—and a name Charlie had neglected to mention.

Natalie Evans.

Caught off guard, she fumbled for the start button, managed to hit it, and lowered her window.

"Are you lost?" Natalie asked, her voice an even alto, tinged with irritation.

"Only part of the time," Vic answered without thinking. When the faint look of irritation blossomed into surprise, she added quickly, "I don't think so. Not lost now, I mean."

She checked the mailbox reflected in her side view mirror. Right address. Forest green Jeep Wrangler with the DEC logo on the side. Natalie's slightly rumpled, matching green uniform with badge and patches indicated she belonged to the vehicle. Yep. She was sitting in her long-ago camp counselor's driveway. "I think I've got the right place. If this is the place with the room to rent?"

"I didn't expect you until tomorrow," Natalie went on in a flat, oddly weary voice, all the surprise having disappeared. She shook her head and briefly pressed a hand over her eyes. "I might've gotten my days mixed up."

Vic opened the door and climbed out, searching for some sign Natalie recognized her. Nothing. Not even a flicker of familiarity. Natalie didn't remember her. Vic's disappointment was quickly followed by relief. There was no reason Natalie should remember one teenager out of the dozens she'd instructed over the years at the DEC camp. Just because Vic had been fascinated by her at thirteen didn't mean Nat had ever noticed her at all.

For an instant, Vic saw beyond the weariness. Fifteen years had passed since the last time she'd seen Natalie, when Natalie had been just a couple years older than Vic was now, but the years had only added to her attractiveness. The shadows in her eyes were new and spoke of sadness that Vic had been too young to notice, or that hadn't been there. But then, they were both different people now.

"Sorry, I'll come back another time," Vic said quickly.

"No, that's ridiculous. You're here now." Natalie took a deep breath and stepped back. "That is, if you're Charlie's cousin Vic? He didn't mention the Vic was short for Victoria." She studied Vic for a beat longer, then muttered, "Not that I'm disappointed—never mind. I'll show you the place."

"That's because it's not Victoria," Vic said, rolling her shoulders. "It's Victory."

Nat's eyebrows shot up. "Really."

"Yup."

"I like it. I guess you must've been a special baby."

Vic blinked, surprised and weirdly touched. "You're right, at least that's how my dad always told it. But most people just make some kind of joke about it."

"Well, most people can be dickheads."

Vic laughed. When was the last time she'd laughed? Or thought about anyone as…well…interesting? Had to be because of the weird coincidence. "That kind of day, huh?"

"You have no idea." Natalie held out her hand. "Sorry, I'm not usually such a misanthrope. I'm Natalie Evans—Nat. And you're catching the tail end of a bad day, so I apologize for the attitude."

"Listen, I've had days like that myself." Vic hesitated, then said softly, "Rough one?"

Natalie—*Nat*—fell silent.

"Never mind," Vic said hastily, feeling the blush rise on her neck. She wasn't a redhead like her dad, but she had the fair skin that telegraphed every damn feeling, especially when she didn't want to. "I get it."

"Actually, I guess you probably do, if you're joining the sheriff's department. We spent the last eighteen hours searching for an eighty-year-old man with dementia who wandered away when his caretaker went into the house to get him a sandwich. We just found him."

The tightness in her voice told Vic everything she needed to know. Not a rescue. A recovery. "I'm sorry."

"Yeah." Nat blew out a breath. "Thanks."

She probably wouldn't've told anyone who wasn't on the job what had just happened, and maybe not even then. But for some reason, she felt this stranger who'd dropped so unexpectedly into her day might somehow understand. Maybe it was the business with her name, or the fatigue in her eyes. And beneath that, loneliness she recognized.

"Are you sure I shouldn't come back in the morning?" Vic said. "To be honest, I wasn't really thinking about anything except getting here. The whole thing blew up faster than a summer squall. Charlie called and said I needed to get here, and I…I had no reason to hang around."

"Where did you in come from?" Nat said. "Charlie didn't say."

"Cutler. It's a little fishing village on the coast of Maine."

Nat nodded. "That's a haul. You drive straight through?"

Vic nodded. "I didn't think that you might not be expecting me. I'm sure there are motels or something available nearby where I can stay tonight. It is Lake George at the start of the season, after all."

"Exactly. And the prices have already doubled. Come on." Nat gestured for Vic to join her. "I'm not about to send you off hunting for a room when you've got a place right here."

You've got a place right here...

The words hit Vic hard, even though she knew Nat didn't really mean them the way they sounded. How long had it been since she'd had any place that felt like hers?

Given no choice and too damn tired to protest, Vic followed Nat along a rough stone path that wound around the side of a neat, white clapboard cottage. A wide porch spanned the entire width of the front along with several well-cared-for flowerbeds flanking the walkway. At the end of the crushed stone drive, a grassy backyard stretched to the forest at the foot of a towering mountain. A log cabin with its own deep porch, smaller than some garages, nestled into the far end of the clearing. Two windows on either side of the door, a stone chimney rising on the right side, and several small flowerbeds framing the steps. Welcoming despite the isolation.

"That's a house," Vic said, hesitating. "Charlie said room."

"It's mostly one room." Nat laughed, her tone lighter.

Vic liked her laugh.

"It's small," Nat said, opening the door, "but it's got a fireplace, which I recommend using for heat, although there is a propane space heater for the winter months, a small kitchen, and a fully functioning if somewhat tight-quartered bathroom."

"I don't need much," Vic said, "but this is...awesome."

"I lived in the cabin for five years after I bought the land," Nat said. "It needed some work. Old hunting shack—cabin would have been a generous term at the time." She switched on a light that glowed above a small oak table sitting in one corner of the room. The ceiling rose a half story above the main room where a skylight let in the last of the evening sun. No dust swirled in the air and the windows sparkled. What looked to be a day bed rested against one wall.

"Sorry, no separate bedroom," Nat said, following Vic's gaze.

"Like I said, I don't need much, and this, trust me, is more than I expected. I'll take it."

Nat laughed again, a rich warm sound. "I haven't mentioned the rent."

"I don't care. It's just...okay, this is going to sound weird, but it feels like home."

The way Vic said *home* struck Nat with that sense of longing again, and the unexpected reaction had her stepping back a pace. Her nerves— no, not her nerves, *all* of her—felt raw and just a little vulnerable. She named a price, and Vic nodded.

"I'm a temporary hire," Vic said, "so is a six-month lease or whatever okay? I'm not exactly sure if I'll be there that long."

"Month to month is fine," Nat said. "The key is on the hook by the door."

"Listen," Vic said quickly, "if it's okay with you, I've got my gear—" She shrugged, looked slightly sheepish. "Actually, everything I own is in the pickup. So if it's okay with you, I can send you the payment right now, if you're sure about me staying here tonight."

"I take it there's no furniture in your truck? Are you storing all that or sending for it?"

Vic winced. "Neither. It's all been sold—what there was worth selling." She looked away and took a long breath before meeting Nat's questioning gaze. "Believe it or not, I lived at home until about two months ago. Things have changed, and I let the place go."

"A big change," Nat said carefully. The flatness in Vic's tone warned her there was more to the story, which she didn't feel she could ask about.

Vic nodded. "It's, well, not where I want to be now. So when Charlie talked to me about applying for a job here, I didn't really think anything would come of it. Didn't really think about it at all until he called, and here I am."

"Have you eaten?" Nat said suddenly.

Vic blinked. "Um, does a fish sandwich on the highway for breakfast count?"

Nat waggled a hand. "I can't say that I haven't had that at times, but I was thinking more along the lines of exceptional burgers, fries if that's your thing, and excellent draft beer. If that's also your thing."

Vic turned, brows lifting slightly, like she hadn't expected the offer. "Yeah. That's my thing."

For a second, Nat considered backpedaling— playing it off as politeness, maybe even saying she was too tired after all. But something in the way Vic answered, a flicker of relief barely masked under her casual tone, made her persist.

Nat exhaled. Well. No taking it back now. "Good. Forty-five minutes?"

Vic hesitated, just for a breath, and Nat saw it—that moment of resistance, like she had second thoughts. Then, finally, she nodded.

"I'll be there."

"Alright then, just come on up to the house when you're ready. The back door is open." Nat held out her hand. "And welcome."

Nat hurried up the path to her house. What the hell was she doing? Why had she invited Vic out? She should've given her the key, walked away, and let her settle in. She wasn't in the habit of offering dinner to strangers. Especially not ones renting her cabin. And yet, something about Vic—about the tiredness in her eyes, the way she'd looked around the place as if it was the first thing in a long time that felt right—had made her say it before she could stop herself.

❖

Vic pushed her duffel into the corner by the day bed. She could unpack the rest of her clothes in the morning. After a quick glance around the cabin to be sure all was secure, she crossed the expanse of grass to the rear of Nat's house. At the top of the back steps, she hesitated. Nat had said to go on in, but entering a stranger's house on her own, even when she'd been invited, seemed too personal. And if Nat looked out and saw her standing there like a confused squirrel, uncertain whether to jump left or right, she'd feel like an idiot. So, inside it was. She slipped through the back door, leaving the cool night air behind. A light glowed from a single ceiling light hanging inside a pale peach fluted glass shade. She wasn't sure why, but its graceful elegance reminded her of Nat. But then, Nat was a beautiful woman—physically, sure, but also in the way she exuded warmth and self-assuredness. Drawn back again to when she'd been that impressionable thirteen-year-old teenager, away from home for the first time, away from everything she knew including the sea, she'd been drawn to Nat's confidence, her obvious skill and strength, and probably most of all, her patience and ability to put a gaggle of disparate teenagers at ease. A little embarrassed now, remembering her adolescent fantasies, she settled against the counter, shoved her hands into her jeans pockets, and took in her surroundings.

The kitchen was a study in practical minimalism. Mostly bare, wood-grained countertops provided space for a few essential appliances—a coffee maker, microwave, and blender. A square oak table with four matching chairs centered the room. A solo potted herb of some kind sat on the windowsill above the sink. Pretty, and practical.

The casual order of the room reminded her of her dad's galley aboard the *Nightingale*—everything in its place, all safely stowed in case of a blow, he used to say. Her chest ached, remembering, as his deep voice echoed in her heart.

At the sound of footsteps, Vic straightened. Her breath caught as Natalie walked in. She'd traded her forest ranger uniform for slim black pants that lightly hugged the curves Vic hadn't fully appreciated earlier, paired with stylish black boots that gave her an inch or so on Vic's five-nine. A red silk shirt added a bit of relaxed sophistication. Vic caught herself tracing the path of a delicate gold chain that dipped down from Nat's throat into the vee exposed by the open buttons of Nat's shirt, and quickly jerked her gaze upward.

To find Natalie watching her with undisguised amusement.

Damn it, she was blushing. Obvious much?

"Hi," Nat said, smiling softly. "Find everything okay in the cabin?"

"Yes." Vic cleared her throat of the sudden hoarseness. "Everything's fine. You look great, by the way."

Nat tilted her head, her expression still amused. "Thank you."

Vic mentally rolled her eyes. What the hell was wrong with her? She didn't even know this woman, and she was acting like a twelve-year-old on their first date. And this was so not—that. "I might be a tad underdressed."

"I like the T-shirt," Nat said.

Vic grinned. The *I Heart Fish* was a favorite.

"I have a friend, an environmental biologist," Nat said, "who once told me in all seriousness that fish are people too."

"Well, sure."

Nat laughed, the sound warm and inviting. "I suspect you'll meet her at some point before the summer is over." Nat paused, her gaze lingering on Vic's before she grabbed keys from a shallow dish on the table. "The shirt suits you. Ready to head out?"

Vic nodded, following Natalie's lead. As they stepped outside, the scent of pine wafted on the cool breeze. Vic took a deep breath. "That never gets old."

"It doesn't, does it," Nat murmured.

"I remember the first time I smelled the forest, how amazing it was. Like the sea, so alive. It calls to you—that scent in the air."

Nat slowed by the side of the Jeep and studied her. "You're a sailor, aren't you?"

"Born and bred." Vic looked away quickly to hide the moisture suddenly filling her eyes. Damn it.

"Well, let's get to town," Nat said softly, sliding into the Jeep and starting the engine.

Vic walked around to the passenger side, appreciating the time to get her shields back in place. And appreciating that Nat had given her the space to do it.

She wasn't used to being so vulnerable, and she definitely wasn't used to anyone seeing it. She ought to have been embarrassed, but Nat seemed to know just what she needed. That was new.

Chapter Two

Nat tightened her grip on the steering wheel as she resisted the urge to glance over at Victory—*Vic*—who'd been quiet since they'd left. Maybe Vic was as surprised by the dinner invitation as she was. Her impetuous suggestion that they go out for dinner was decidedly unlike her. What she really needed to do was get a few hours' sleep, but she'd seen her own weariness reflected in Vic's eyes. Maybe neither one of them wanted to be alone.

Well. No taking the invitation back now.

The silence wasn't uncomfortable, and she let the beauty of the drive that she never tired of ease some of her sadness. Sunlight filtered through the evergreens that crouched along the narrow road leading from her small compound back to the highway, and with the windows down and the scent of the forest filling the car, she could almost shake the images of anguish and despair that would haunt her until they too faded along with so many senseless tragedies she'd witnessed over the years. *Sometimes*, she had gently tried to remind the family of the lost man, *even when we did everything we could, it wasn't enough.*

Vic shifted, stretching her arm lazily against the doorframe, her fingers tapping a quiet rhythm against the window.

Nat glanced over, just for a second. Strong hands, a scar cutting faintly across the top of one knuckle, muscles flexing under sun-browned skin. Her collar-length chestnut-colored hair fluttered in the breeze. Their eyes met and held for a second, and Nat's stomach did an odd little flip.

She wrenched her gaze back to the road, irritated with herself. Vic O'Brien was damned attractive, especially lounging in the passenger seat with the wind tousling her hair and the sunlight making her face glow. Her lean, rangy body, looking strong and fit, just added to her appeal. Nat mentally shook her head. She didn't go around getting stirred up by women she barely knew, especially not when she had an easy twenty years on them.

Not who she should be noticing. Not at all.

"So you grew up in Maine?" she asked, searching for a little distance.

"Yep," Vic asked. "How long have you lived out here?"

"I grew up in Bolton Landing." Nat noticed the quick change in subject. Okay, nothing too personal. Message received. "About twelve years ago."

"Did you build the house yourself?" Vic asked.

"How did you know?"

"The house—the whole place—just feels…intimate. Personal, I guess."

Nat nodded, a little taken aback by Vic's perceptiveness. "I had help with the big stuff, but most of it."

"That's impressive."

Nat laughed. "Thanks. How about you? What made you decide to take a job in Lake George? It's a long way to come for a change."

"Part of it was Charlie pushing for me to think about the job here," Vic said slowly. "I really wasn't sure what I was going to do. I thought I'd like small-town policing, but spending my days in a patrol car, not so much. And…" She hesitated, and when Nat looked over, she blushed.

Inwardly, Nat sighed. Okay, so Vic could be even more attractive than she had been before. And *she* really needed to find her brain instead of letting her body drive the bus. "And?"

"Would you believe me if I said I've been here before?"

Nat raised an eyebrow. "Where? The lake?"

"Not exactly. When I was thirteen. DEC summer camp at Thunder Ridge Lodge." Vic felt the blush deepen. "I discovered I loved the mountains almost as much as the sea. I think that was as important as the job offer in my decision to come."

"Wait a minute," Nat said slowly. A hazy recollection of a gangly, quiet girl with a mop of unruly brown hair, who knew more about water safety than some cadets, formed in her mind. "I think I remember you. You were in my group for the water rescue session, weren't you?"

Vic's face lit up. "I can't believe you remember that."

"I didn't until you mentioned it. That had to be—twenty years ago." Nat did the math in her head and winced. A very long twenty years ago it felt like now, sitting next to a young woman who affected her far more than she should. "I can't believe I forgot the name Victory, though."

"You didn't," Vic said. "I was thirteen, in a new place, and I didn't want to seem weird. I told everybody to call me O'Brien, which sounded cooler."

"Of course," Nat said, as the memories crystallized. "You were the one who aced all the exercises first time. And you swim like a fish."

Vic nodded and gazed out at the passing scenery with a wistful expression. "You know, I never forgot this place. It always felt like…I don't know. Like I could belong here, somehow—and no place on land has ever felt that way."

"You've spent more time on the water than on land, I'm guessing."

"As much as I could."

Nat heard the longing in Vic's voice and wished she could offer some comfort, not even knowing the source of the sadness. "We've got plenty of water around here—not ocean water, I know, but Lake George is thirty-eight miles of some fine, pretty water."

Vic glanced over, her smile returning. "That's what I'm counting on."

Just knowing some of Vic's pain had subsided eased Nat's worry. What kept her on edge was the way every damn thing about Victory O'Brien triggered sensations she didn't have a clue how to handle.

❖

Nat parked in a long, narrow lot opposite Lake George Harbor. Despite being early in the season, the harbor buzzed with activity. Several multi-decked tourist boats, their brightly painted hulls gleaming under the setting sun, lay at anchor along the docks. Flags flapped in the breeze, and kiosks at the end of the docks advertised scenic lake tours and sunset cruises. The air carried the mingled scents of lake water, diesel fuel, and food wafting from the restaurants overlooking the harbor. Along the shore, a steady stream of visitors paused to take photos or hurried to corral excited kids running down to the water's edge, their laughter echoing over the rhythmic pulse of the waves breaking on shore. The sound of a distant boat horn and the occasional cry of gulls circling overhead punctuated the chatter.

"It's a little cool out," Nat said as they walked to one of her favorite waterfront restaurants. Barney's exuded rustic charm, its weathered wood and stone construction echoing the natural beauty of the lakefront. A large, wraparound verandah fronted the building, offering sweeping views of the harbor and the long stretch of Lake George disappearing into the distance. Hanging baskets of bright flowers and lantern-style lights gave the impression of a cozy lakeside retreat that carried through to the hardwood and polished stone interior. Fishing nets and vintage oars adorned the exposed-beam ceiling, giving the space a nautical touch. Rustic pendant lamps above each table cast a warm, golden glow over the wood-paneled walls, while large windows offered a view of the sweeping vistas.

"They've got the tables out on the verandah. Are you up for some outdoor dining?" Nat asked as they waited to be seated.

"Totally."

Nat knew the menu by heart and leaned back in the web-backed patio chair while Vic studied hers. When she realized she was watching Vic's hands as she flipped through the pages on the clipboard, she quickly looked away. Okay. Enough. Just stop.

A sandy-haired young guy bearing a friendly smile and a pad and pen—probably one of the hundreds of college students who flocked to the area for summer work every season—appeared to take their order, rescuing her before she embarrassed herself by being caught staring.

"So," Nat said after they'd ordered, "tell me about this new position. From what you said about sitting in cruisers, I take it you're not planning on highway patrol."

Vic's face came alive. Her smile transformed her from ruggedly attractive to downright captivating. She waited a minute while their server slid food and drinks onto the table before saying, "Nope. I'll be joining the Water Patrol unit on the lake."

"Really? I don't know why I didn't make the connection right away. That's a great position, especially for a water rat."

Vic laughed. "It helps I have my captain's license."

"Now *I'm* impressed," Nat said, meaning it. "You...ah..."

"Don't look old enough?" Vic said when Nat faltered.

"Ah, I *was* going to say that. I guess you hear that a lot."

"Not where I'm from. I've been on a trawler since I was three and piloting it long before I was old enough for a license."

"Which is when?" Nat asked.

"For a craft over sixty-five feet? Eighteen." Vic shrugged.

"Although the craft I'll be piloting on the lake will be quite a bit smaller."

"I guess that's why Charlie thought to call me about the cabin, since we'll be working together." A mix of excitement and apprehension swirled in Nat's chest. Working together meant more time spent in Vic's company, a prospect that both pleased and unnerved her. "Charlie is often long on enthusiasm and short on details."

"Really?" A crease formed between Vic's brows. "Not that I'd mind, but, uh, am I technically working for you?"

Nat laughed. "Not even a little bit. Our jurisdiction overlaps with that of the WPU in that the lake is an integral part of the environment, and that's the DEC's main focus. We'll often work with the WPU if there's a situation that impacts local laws—that's your bailiwick—and the safety or integrity of the waters."

"I see," Vic said, her expression relaxing. "I'm glad to hear it!"

"We'll usually liaise with your unit a few times a week, share reports, and provide backup during complicated situations."

Vic sipped her beer. "You're right—they've got good beer. Sounds like we're going to be busy this summer."

"The lake can get pretty wild during tourist season," Nat said. "Campers and day-trippers on the islands, more speedboats every year—those damn Jet Skis everywhere." She stopped. "Now I'm showing my age."

"Not from where I'm sitting," Vic said, her eyes intent as she looked at Nat.

Nat's throat tightened. Vic had to know she was close to two decades older. She'd been a ranger for half a dozen years already when Vic was a teenager at camp. She couldn't possibly be flirting. "Well, I...thanks."

"I'm twenty-eight," Vic said casually and reached for her burger.

Not quite twenty years' difference in age, then—but still more than half of Vic's lifetime between them. A world of different experiences, to say nothing of the fact that she was still in good shape but far from being in her twenties. That dose of reality was just what she needed. Nat stepped the conversation back to the safe and friendly. "So you captained for your dad?"

"Yeah." Vic's expression grew distant, her voice softening. "I worked on the boat from the time I was old enough to learn boat safety. Weekends during the school year—and sometimes a few missed school days thrown in here and there. And then full-time after high school."

"Those sound like great times," Nat said.

"Pretty much the best," Vic said.

"What made you switch to law enforcement?" Nat sipped her single beer of the evening.

A shadow passed over Vic's face, there and then gone in an instant. "Well, it wasn't exactly planned. Dad lost the business to the big fishing corporations a few years back. He'd never known anything but fishing. When he had to sell the *Nightingale*, he—well, he lost a bit of himself, I guess." She took a deep breath. "He died suddenly about two months ago."

"God, that's awful," Nat murmured. "I'm so sorry."

"I needed to work, and I never would have made it in some kind of inside job all day. So I entered the academy, and here I am." Vic finished her beer and pushed the empty glass away along with her plate. "And that's pretty much the whole story."

Nat's heart clenched at the undercurrent of loss in Vic's voice. Instinctively she started to reach for her hand and abruptly pulled back. "I can't really imagine what you've been through, but I hope being here is a good change for you."

Vic's smile was a mix of determination and vulnerability. "I wasn't kidding when I said there's something about this place that just feels right. I'm glad to hear we'll be working together some too."

"So am I," Nat said.

As their eyes met, warmth spread through Nat's chest. For a moment, she had a glimpse of the spirit that had kept a young woman going when her world had tragically changed. When the father she obviously adored had died. When she was uprooted from the sea she loved and all she'd cherished. Nat appreciated Vic's resilience, muted by loss but there beneath the surface. A remarkable woman, for all her youth.

Nat raised her glass in a salute. "Here's to unexpected partnerships, and fewer motorized vehicles on land *or* sea."

"I'll drink to that, Ranger Evans." Vic laughed, but as her smile faded, the sadness returned to her eyes.

A pang of regret twisted in Nat's throat. Softly, she said, "I'm sorry. I didn't mean to bring up painful memories."

Vic blinked, refocusing on Nat's face, and shook her head. "No, it's okay. It's just…sometimes it hits me all over again."

Nat dealt with loss all too often—frequently was the one to bring the news that would change someone's life forever. Like that family she'd had to inform earlier that their loved one had died. She hesitated, then reached across the table, her fingers lightly brushing Vic's hand. "Loss has a way of doing that. I hope it gets better as time passes."

"Thanks," Vic said, letting her hand stay a moment beneath Nat's before pulling it away. "You had a rough day too. I guess we should get back."

"You're right." Nat pushed back her chair. "I'll stop and pay on the way out."

Vic pulled out her wallet. "Here, let me."

"I've got it," Nat said. "Consider it a house gift in lieu of the obligatory bottle of wine."

"Next time is on me, then," Vic said, rising.

Nat doubted there would be a next time, but nodded as they walked back inside the restaurant.

The drive back to Nat's was quiet, the earlier ease replaced by a tense awareness. Nat's mind raced with conflicting emotions—sympathy, respect, attraction, discomfort. She stole glances at Vic, who sat stiffly in the passenger seat, staring out at the dark night. As they pulled up to the cabin, Nat cut the engine, the silence suddenly deafening. She turned to Vic, searching for the right words, but none came. "Good luck at the new job."

Vic nodded, her hand already on the door handle. "Thanks for dinner. And the cabin."

As Vic stepped out of the car, Nat called out impulsively, "Vic?"

Vic turned, her silhouette backlit by the porch light. "Yeah?"

Nat wanted to tell her she'd be around if she needed to talk, if she needed...what? A friend? Was that what *she* wanted? "Just...welcome to Lake George."

"Good night, Nat," Vic replied softly, before disappearing down the path to the cabin.

"Good night," Nat whispered as a pale-yellow glow from the cabin's windows signaled Vic had gone inside. For some reason, that made her irrationally happy.

Nat made her way upstairs to her bedroom, uncertain what to make of Vic O'Brien. What was this unexpected pull she felt toward her? And why did their parting leave her feeling so unsettled? The answers eluded her as she walked to the window and stood in the dark, watching the flickering light from the cabin.

CHAPTER THREE

The scent of pine needles and damp earth filtered through the slightly open window, sharp and foreign. Vic blinked at the wooden ceiling, disoriented, the sky outside still dark, her mind still foggy with dreams of open water and salt spray. For a second—just a second—she expected to hear the hum of the *Nightingale*'s engine. The creak of ropes. The slap of salt water against the hull.

But the only sound was the whisper of wind through trees.

No low-slung bunks. No gentle rocking beneath her.

She exhaled slowly, her chest tight.

This was her life now.

The quilt pooled around her waist as she sat up, running a hand over her face. She'd crawled into bed the night before, exhausted from the long drive and the ache of loss that had ridden her hard with each mile she'd put between herself and her old life.

She should feel rested, but instead, she felt like a ship unmoored.

One step at a time, then.

She stood, stretching, muscles aching from yesterday's long drive. The pine floorboards were cool against her feet. She found coffee beans in the tiny fridge, and as she watched the dark brew drip, thought about the strange night before.

Dinner with Natalie.

They had talked for what felt like hours, but had probably been barely one. Still, she had said more—shared more—than she had with anyone in years. Even before her dad had withdrawn into himself, when he'd still been the laughing, vigorous man who didn't know the word *quit*, she'd rarely spoken of personal things with him. Not that she thought he wouldn't care or understand, but their language had always been that of silent communication as they'd worked side by side—hauling in lines, off-loading catch, and sharing a quick look of satisfaction after a good day's work. With Nat, the words had poured out, like water from an overflowing cup. She couldn't remember the last time she had opened up to someone so completely, so effortlessly. Being so revealing, so exposed, wasn't like her at all. Maybe it was the fatigue—or the memories of that golden summer she'd spent at camp when life had looked so bright and she'd felt the pull of her first crush.

She'd hated the camp when she arrived—the towering mountains, the vast wilderness—so foreign to everything she'd known. And she'd missed her dad so much. She'd never been away from home before. A pang of sadness struck as she recalled her father's words. *A few weeks away will be good for you—give you an idea of what the rest of the world is like.* The sound of his voice in her mind, as clear as if he was in the room, hit her like a physical blow, stealing the breath from her lungs. He had been her anchor, her true north. Losing him was like being set adrift in a storm, no land in sight. She knew what he'd say to that too. *Turn her into the wind, Vic. We'll ride out this storm.*

He'd been right then. Gradually she'd adjusted and found new things to learn, even made new friends. And there'd been Nat. She smiled ruefully at the image of her younger self, waking with excitement and anticipation for Ranger Evans's arrival on the days she led the wilderness training sessions. Looking back, she could still feel Nat's magnetism and the quiet strength and patience that had drawn her in. Just like last night, apparently.

She shouldn't have remembered so much about her. It had been years since that summer at camp, but the images were still sharp in her mind. Nat in the firelight, eyes bright with laughter. The steady confidence in her voice when she taught them how to navigate the woods.

And now, last night—that same steadiness, that same quiet command.

She should let it go.

Vic dragged a hand down her face. It didn't matter.

She wasn't a teenager anymore, looking at her counselor with wide-eyed admiration. This was different. They were different.

Shaking her head, she headed for the shower. She couldn't afford to get lost in the past, not today. It was her first day at a new post, and she was determined to make a good impression. She had a job to do, a purpose to fulfill. Maybe then the aching emptiness inside her would start to feel a little less vast.

She showered quickly, dressed in navy chinos, a light blue polo, and a black belt and boots. She climbed into her pickup, programmed the address of the sheriff's department in the map, and headed out. As she drove, her thoughts kept drifting back to Natalie. She couldn't explain the instant connection, and that was as confounding as it was nice. She'd spent so much of her life holding people at arm's length, never letting anyone get too close. Relationships, even most friendships, were something she avoided. She couldn't do justice to either, not when the sea was always calling her away. The women she might have wished to be friends with, or even more, deserved time and attention, neither of which she could provide when the *Nightingale* and the sea commanded most of her energy.

And she'd never minded. Oh, sure, when her hormones had burst onto the scene and she'd realized girls were who turned her on, she'd wanted to connect with someone to explore those feelings. She'd quickly learned that she needed to actually be available to develop any kind of connection and had made her choice. The sea and chasing the next catch called to her more than other people. But Nat was different, had somehow pulled her in with kindness and empathy. With her, Vic felt seen in a way she never had before, as if all her carefully constructed walls were made of glass, transparent and fragile. Nat's sympathy had been genuine, just as her understanding of how nothing—not words, not a new place, not a new job—would ease the pain of all she'd lost.

Still, the thought of letting someone close, of being vulnerable, of failing like she always had, made her stomach twist. She rounded a curve just as the sun crested the mountaintops, setting the forest aglow. Flaming red and orange, like fire in the sky, just like on those magical mornings that long-ago summer. Vic took a deep breath, steadying herself. She wasn't sure of what path lay ahead for her, but she was certain of one thing: This was the place where she would find out. And if she had a chance to explore what she'd passed over in another lifetime, she might take it.

❖

Vic hesitated at the threshold of the station. Once she stepped through that door, she had to commit to it. No half measures. No turning back.

Then again, wasn't that the whole point of leaving Maine?
Squaring her shoulders, she pushed inside.

The familiar scent of yesterday's coffee instantly eased her nerves.
The duty sergeant, a balding, middle-aged guy whose dark brown skin
showed the weathered lines of a lifelong outdoorsman, looked up as she
approached the desk.

"Help you?"

"Morning," she said. "I'm looking for Charlie Thompson. I'm—"

"Victory," a gruff voice called out.

With a mental eye roll, aware of the instant attention from every
other officer passing by, Vic turned just in time to brace herself as her
cousin swept her up into a bear hug.

"Thought you'd be lost at sea forever," Charlie boomed, letting
her go abruptly, as if he'd surprised himself as well as her.

"Nope, all smooth sailing," Vic said.

Half a head taller and half again her weight, he smelled of
aftershave and fresh air. His enthusiastic if cautious greeting reminded
her a little of her dad, who was quick to praise but rarely physically
affectionate beyond a rough hug. She hadn't realized until just that
moment how good it felt to have family, even though she hadn't seen
Charlie in over a decade—other than the one day he'd been in Cutler
for the funeral.

"Thanks for this, Charlie. And, uh, thanks for announcing my
arrival to the whole station."

"Nothing to thank me for. We're getting the bargain." His
cornflower blue eyes grew serious. "How are you doing? You make it
to Nat's place okay?"

"I'm good. I got in late yesterday." She shook her head. "You
didn't mention the room was a whole cabin."

"You don't like it?"

"It's great. I don't think she's charging me enough, though."

"Probably not." He shrugged and grinned a little sheepishly. "I
don't think she usually rents it out. I knew she had it and asked her
about it."

Vic stared. "You mean you put her on the spot? Crap—maybe I
should look for another place, then."

The idea of leaving Nat's bothered her more than it should. The
cabin was great, sure. She already felt at home there. But what she
really liked was knowing she'd see Nat a lot more if she lived there.

"Why?" He frowned. "Nat wouldn't have rented it out if she

didn't want to. When you get to know her, you'll see she's not going to let anybody push her into something she doesn't want to do."

"I met her last night. We had dinner together."

Charlie gave her an odd look.

"What?"

"Nothing," he said after a second. "So you need a few days to get settled?"

She braced her shoulders and stepped back. "Thanks for the offer, and no, I'm ready to go."

"Good." Charlie gave her arm a quick squeeze. "Let's get you squared away. Hold on...hey, Phee!"

A woman about Vic's age with collar-length, dark curly hair and light brown skin stopped and shot Charlie a questioning look.

"Meet our new recruit. Vic O'Brien," Charlie said.

Phee, a sergeant by the stripes on her uniform sleeve, approached with a friendly smile, her brown eyes warm. She held out her hand. "I'm Phee Gomez, team leader of the Water Patrol unit. Welcome aboard."

Vic shook her hand, impressed by the firm grip and the air of confidence Phee exuded. "Thanks. I'm glad to be here."

"Come on, I'll show you around. We'll get out on the lake after roll call."

Phee led Vic through the bustling hallways, pointing out the locker rooms, the equipment storage, and the briefing area. The layout was new but the atmosphere familiar. Station houses were homes away from homes, and the officers who filled them sometimes had as much family there as any they might have outside working hours. Vic hadn't had much time to make those connections back in Maine, but she had learned the importance of the trust and camaraderie that linked the tight-knit group.

As they walked, Phee kept up a steady stream of conversation, her voice light and teasing. "So, you're Charlie's cousin, huh? You're a lot better looking."

"Thanks. I won't mention you said that."

Phee grinned. "Oh, he probably already knows. Not being blind and all."

In the locker room, Phee leaned against the bank of lockers, arms crossed, with an easy confidence that made it clear: She ran this place.

"So you just got in?"

"Last night," Vic said, exchanging her street clothes for the uniform the supply clerk had provided. She tucked in the crisp shirt, willing it to feel familiar. It didn't. Not yet.

Nothing much felt familiar. Even Charlie was practically a stranger.

"You settle in okay?" Phee asked, tilting her head.

Vic nodded. "Cabin's nice. Quiet."

Phee's mouth twitched. "Charlie said you're not much for crowds."

Vic blinked. She wasn't used to people knowing things about her.

"Don't look so surprised," Phee added. "Charlie talks a lot. Mostly about himself, but sometimes about family." She gave Vic a quick once-over. "You look like you can hold your own, though. That's good. We need steady hands."

Something about the way she said it made Vic straighten. Maybe this wasn't just a job to Phee. Maybe it meant something.

And maybe—for the first time in a while—she wanted something that meant something too.

❖

At just after seven a.m., Nat pulled up to Alma Quince's pale blue gingerbread cottage nestled among the towering pines, the facade covered with pink flowering vines. As she stepped out of her Jeep, Alma, her white hair carefully pinned up in a bun, emerged from her front door, her step brisk and her flushed face etched with a combination of alarm and outrage. She wore a floral dress and a summer green cardigan, the colors faded but still vibrant. She held a grizzled pug who must be nearing twenty clutched to her chest. Alma and Hugo were fixtures around town. Everyone knew the pair, especially since almost all the locals had had Alma Quince for high school English, including Nat.

"Thank goodness you're here, Natalie," Alma said. "That fox, it just wasn't right. Prowling around my yard in broad daylight, looking all mangy and disoriented. Why, he could have attacked my Hugo if I hadn't been out here to run him off."

Nat offered a reassuring smile. "You did the right thing by calling, Mrs. Quince. Can you show me where you last saw it?"

Alma led Nat around the side of the house, gesturing toward a cluster of mountain laurel. "The darned varmint was right over there, pacing back and forth like it was lost or something."

Nat surveyed the area, scanning for signs of the animal. "I don't see any tracks, but that doesn't mean it's not still around. Best to keep Hugo inside for now, and if you spot the fox again, give me a call." She paused, knowing her old teacher well enough to avoid risking insult by suggesting she couldn't handle one little fox. A potentially rabid fox. "It's best I trap him so we can get him to the animal center and see if he's sick."

Alma scowled. "Well, I'll be walking Hugo when he needs to go outside, but we're not letting animal or human threaten us on our own land."

"Of course not." Nat handed Alma a card with her personal cell number. "Call this number—day or night. Then wait for me if you see him, if you would."

Alma pursed her lips and sighed. "I will. And thank you for coming out so quickly."

Nat touched a finger to her hat. "Anytime, Mrs. Quince. You take care now."

As Nat climbed back into her vehicle, letting the engine idle while she started work on the incident report, her thoughts drifted to the dinner with her new tenant. The surprisingly easy connection kept coming back to her, along with the way Vic's face had glowed as she'd talked of her times at sea…and the sadness that lurked so close to the surface in her eyes. She'd rarely been so comfortable with someone she barely knew, and that was enough to put her off balance. Maybe their long-ago interactions at the camp had something to do with it. They shared some memories and a love for the mountains, even if Vic was a child of the sea. Nat shook her head, mentally chiding herself. She was making too much of a chance encounter.

Nevertheless, as she radioed the other rangers about the location of the possibly rabid fox sighting, she found herself heading toward Thunder Ridge without having planned to stop in until the campers arrived. The camp opened soon for the summer season, and once the sixty-plus teens arrived, she'd be spending a fair amount of time there leading the DEC wilderness training sessions. Might as well take advantage of the quiet to check in with Sarah and find out just how many of the training sessions Chase Fielder had managed to get out of doing. Although she supposed having a four-month-old infant earned Chase a few more months of half-time work.

As she crested the rise to the lodge that sat at the base of the mountains capped by Thunder Ridge, glimpses through the towering evergreens of the shimmering lake that carried the same name greeted her. The sweeping, three-story log building boasted a broad timber front porch that wrapped around both sides of the massive structure like huge arms. A dozen smaller log cabins, crouched like baby ducks around their mother, sat tucked within cozy little clearings in the forest to the right of the main building. She pulled up to the lodge, surprised to see another DEC Jeep already parked there. A quick mental rundown of where her rangers were deployed left only Chase as the obvious choice. Sure enough, as she climbed out of the Jeep, Chase walked out the wide front door with a mug of coffee in hand and a grin on her face.

"Starting early?" Chase called down to her.

"Not hardly." Nat strode up the steps to the broad, plank-board porch. Chase looked good—if she was tired, it didn't show. Her sandy hair was shaggy in a completely unstudied way, her blue eyes clear and, as they had been for the last two years since she'd met Lily Davenport, free of the old pain that had haunted her. "Just came to see what Sarah has in store for me—unless you're planning to take some of the sessions."

"Nope—I'm happy to stick to patrol."

Nat shook her head. "Whatever happened to rank and privileges and all that?"

"Just a myth."

"Apparently." Nat tilted her head toward the mug. "Is there more of that somewhere?"

"Yep. Clara made some fresh when I got here."

"She's still spoiling you, I see."

Clara, the longtime chef at the camp, had always had a soft spot for Chase. Maybe because Chase had been coming to Thunder Ridge since she was ten and her sister Sarah had been a camp counselor. Now Sarah ran the year-round DEC programs out of Thunder Ridge. "I'll be right back."

Chase settled into a rocker with a sigh. "I'll be here."

After a quick chat with Clara, Nat settled beside Chase and sipped the rich, dark brew.

"Why can't coffee always taste this good?"

"Because Clara didn't make it. She does something to it that will remain a secret for all eternity."

Nat laughed. "So how is Will? Sleeping through the night?"

Chase grimaced, but the warmth in her eyes belied any irritation. "Not so you'd notice. We've been trying to get him on some kind of sleep schedule, but he's a lot like Lily, never seems to get tired."

"It's a good thing both of you are still part-time, then."

"For which I am grateful every day." Chase studied Nat for a moment. "So what brings you out here besides wanting to torture yourself with whatever Sarah has planned for you?"

"You know," Nat said, "I don't mind doing the camp sessions. In fact, I enjoy them."

"That must be why you're the regional director," Chase said wryly.

"And that must be why you're still patrolling."

"True enough. So what's the other reason? Too much paperwork in the office?"

Nat looked down toward the lake that spread out from the narrow beach and seemed to extend to the horizon in every direction. For a moment, she could see the young campers gathered around her as she talked about water rescue, safety procedures, and what to do when a kayak capsized. Picturing it in her mind, she could see a young Vic O'Brien, and the memory was bittersweet. A child from her past who had somehow returned a grown woman. A very attractive woman.

"You're not going to remember this, because you were a few years younger, but a camper who was here years ago is renting my cabin now."

Chase frowned. "Someone from here?"

Nat nodded.

"Who?"

"A young woman named Victory O'Brien. I don't suppose—"

"Sure, I remember her. Who could forget somebody named Victory. That was the last summer before—" Chase looked away.

"I'm sorry," Nat said quickly. That was the summer when Chase and Sarah's mother had died. How did she keep bringing up those painful memories? First with Vic and now Chase. "I didn't think."

"Nothing to apologize for," Chase said quietly. "I was just thinking about how great that summer was. Anyhow, O'Brien is staying at your place now? How did that happen?"

Nat lifted her shoulder. "I wish I knew. Charlie Thompson said his cousin was moving to the area and needed a place to stay, and before I knew it, I'd offered the place."

"Sounds like Charlie," Chase said with a grin. "He could talk the paint off one of our Jeeps, and you know that stuff is practically indestructible. So what is she doing?"

"She's joining the Water Patrol unit. She's a sailor."

"Navy, you mean?"

Nat laughed. "No, ocean. She grew up on a fishing trawler. Captained one for a while."

"Interesting." Chase tilted her head and smiled slightly. "So, she sounds interesting."

Nat ignored the warmth creeping up the back of her neck. "I guess."

Chase chuckled. "I guess she is."

Nat exhaled sharply. "Absolutely not."

"Straight?"

"I have no idea."

"That doesn't always matter, you know."

"It would to me, and besides that, she's practically a child."

"Well, she's got to be of legal age if she's working on the patrol unit," Chase said reasonably.

"Yes, of course," Nat said, knowing she sounded defensive. Double damn.

Chase snorted. "Oh, please. How young?"

Nat sighed. "Twenty-eight."

Chase arched a brow. "And you're what? Forty-eight?"

"Forty-five," Nat corrected, but even saying it made her stomach tighten.

"Right," Chase said, grinning. "Because three years totally makes a difference."

"Does to me," Nat said under her breath.

"Sorry? Didn't catch that."

Nat scowled. "It's not just that."

Chase leaned in, eyes dancing. "Then what?"

Nat hesitated. For a second, Vic's face flashed in her mind— stormy gray eyes, sharp wit, that quiet strength beneath the surface.

No. No, this wasn't happening.

She forced herself to shrug. "It doesn't matter. I'm not looking for anything. Not with her. Not with anyone."

The words felt solid, final. She needed them to be.

"Who are you trying to convince?"

Nat sighed, realizing she'd let her guard down more than she intended. "It's nothing, Chase. Really. I just met her a few days ago when she moved in. We had dinner, that's all."

Chase's eyebrows shot up. "Dinner? On her first night here?"

"It wasn't like that," Nat said quickly, feeling flustered. "I was being friendly. She'd just driven hundreds of miles and needed to eat, that's all."

"Uh-huh," Chase said, a hint of teasing in her voice. "And how often do you have dinner with your tenants on their first night, or any night?"

"I don't *have* tenants—" Nat felt her cheeks warm. "Look, it's not—" Nat sighed, running a hand through her hair. "It doesn't matter. She's just renting the cabin, that's all."

"I get it." Chase paused. "That must be why you're out here at the crack of dawn, avoiding your office and talking about her."

"I'm not avoiding anything," Nat said, but even to her own ears the protest sounded weak. "And it's not the crack of dawn. I had a call about a possibly rabid fox, and I thought I'd swing by here on my way back."

"Right," Chase drawled. "Because Thunder Ridge is totally on the way back from Alma Quince's place."

Nat stared. "How did you know it was Alma?"

Chase grinned. "Who else would call about a fox in their yard at six a.m.?"

Nat stood up abruptly, needing to change the subject to anything but Vic O'Brien. "I ought to go find Sarah."

Chase's eyes twinkled with amusement, but she nodded. "Sure thing. Tell her I said hi."

"Sarah?"

"No—Victory."

Nat scowled. "You know, you can be a right pain in the ass."

"Yep. It's part of my charm."

"Charm apparently only Lily can see," Nat muttered.

As she walked into the lodge, she vowed to push thoughts of Vic aside. She had no business thinking about her that way—in any way at all. And if the occasional image of Vic popped into her mind?

Well, that was no one's problem but hers.

CHAPTER FOUR

N at stared at the duty roster, realizing she'd entered the wrong shift times. Again.

She exhaled sharply, rubbing a hand over her face. This was ridiculous. She had plenty to do meeting with new summer hires, overseeing a prescribed burn when one of her senior rangers called out with a family emergency, and tending to the endless paperwork. What she didn't have time for was thoughts of Vic O'Brien.

And yet—her mind kept circling back.

To Vic's laughter, low and easy over dinner.

To the way her eyes crinkled when she smiled.

To how animated she had become talking about her time at sea.

Never mind the nights *she'd* had to resist walking down to the cabin to ask how Vic was settling in.

She scowled, grabbed the roster, and diligently reentered the shift times correctly. It didn't matter. Vic was her tenant. Nothing else.

So why the hell was she acting like a teenager with a crush?

Finally satisfied she'd at least conquered her to-do list, she decided to call it a day. Maybe some quiet time would help clear her head. When she rounded the bend to home, she spotted Vic just pulling into the drive. Her heart did a little flip in her chest.

No. It did not. Of course it didn't.

Nat exited her Jeep just as Vic got out of the pickup.

Vic called, "Evening."

"Hey there," Nat said, aiming for casual. "We finally crossed paths."

Vic leaned against the fender of her truck, her arms casually crossed over her chest, her booted feet crossed at the ankles. She wore the khaki Water Patrol uniform today, the emblem on her shoulder and a name tag on her chest. She looked good in a uniform, but then she'd looked good in jeans and a T-shirt too. Just then, though, with the slanting sunlight catching the angles of her face, highlighting the sharp cut of her jaw, and the wind ruffling the edges of her dark hair, she was striking. Nat swallowed. Noticing. That's all it was.

She blamed the uniform.

"How are things going?"

"Oh," Vic said casually, "the usual rookie hazing. First my cousin embarrasses me in front of everyone by announcing my given name, which I don't usually use on first meeting, and then my shift commander informs me I am taking the team out on our first run. Fortunately, I've never run into a motor or a boat I couldn't pilot."

"Surprised them, did you?" Nat grinned. Everyone broke rookies in with a little good-natured teasing. She did it herself, although true hazing, and rightly so, was a thing of the past. Getting the new guy up to speed and integrated into the team as quickly as possible benefited everyone. She could imagine that Vic's crewmates underestimated her skills, considering how young she looked. How young she *was*.

"I think I disappointed them that I didn't panic when the crew piled in and Phee told me to take her up the lake to Dome Island."

Nat laughed. "Did some homework, did you?"

"Well, sure. You don't set out on the water without having studied the navigational charts."

Nat chuckled, but she was also impressed.

She'd seen plenty of new recruits struggle their first few weeks, trying too hard, overcompensating. Vic, though—she was steady. Comfortable in her skin.

That kind of confidence only came from real experience.

"Sounds like you passed the test."

"We'll see. Jury's still out." Vic shrugged. "Phee is a good chief. Exactly what you want on a mission. I plan to live up to the expectations."

Nat inclined her head, not doubting that Vic would succeed. "How did you like the lake?"

Vic's eyes lit up the way Nat was coming to recognize when Vic was happy. The look suited her. "It's not the ocean, mind you, but it's pretty water. And the Whaler's big enough to do it justice. Plus, the tech is a major upgrade from what I was used to."

Natalie couldn't help but return the smile. Vic's easygoing charm somehow erased the disconcerted feeling she'd had all day.

"How about you?" Vic asked. "You've been getting in pretty late yourself."

Nat started. Vic had noticed when she was getting home? Why did her heart give a little leap? Silly. Just an innocent remark that meant nothing.

"Oh, you know. Rescued a few hikers, fought off a bear or two. The usual."

Vic laughed, the sound sending a pleasant shiver through Nat's limbs. "Sounds like your week was more exciting than mine."

"That will likely change pretty quickly. And actually, I mostly did paperwork—a necessary evil."

"I'm glad Charlie gets stuck with all of that," Vic said.

Nat hesitated as they walked down the gravel path leading to the backyard. "I was thinking about having a beer. Feel like one?"

"God, yes," Vic said. "I'd offer to provide something to go with it, but I, ah, haven't been grocery shopping."

"How do you feel about cold pizza?"

"I feel extremely positive," Vic said.

Nat laughed. "Then I'll bring supplies, and you provide the porch chairs."

"Done," Vic said. "I just happen to have two handy."

"Give me a minute to change," Nat said.

"Take a few. I could use a quick shower," Vic said.

"I'll see you soon, then," Nat said, steadfastly *not* thinking about whether her desire to spend a few minutes with her new renter was a wise decision.

Twenty minutes later, Nat settled onto the cabin porch, the tranquil evening sounds of the forest a familiar backdrop. She balanced the pizza box on a small table between two Adirondack chairs. When Vic came out in loose black sweats and a pale blue tee decorated with a school of iridescent fish, Nat handed her a beer. And did not even think, even for a second, about how good Vic looked.

"Thanks," Vic said, settling into the other chair.

Nat pointed to the pizza. "Help yourself. Hope you don't mind vegetarian."

Vic popped the top on the can of beer. "Are you? Vegetarian, I mean?"

"No," Nat said, "but I try to keep my pizza sins to a minimum."

"There is never sin attached to pizza," Vic said reverently and lifted out a slice.

"Tell that to my waistline," Nat said lightly, taking a slice for herself.

Vic shot her a look. "Can't see any problems there."

Nat gave thanks that the gathering dusk hid the blush that flooded her cheeks. The stirring was back in her midsection, and she knew damn well what it was from. She quickly reminded herself that Vic was good-looking and charming, but that didn't mean she was flirting.

Taking a sip of her beer, she retreated to safe ground. "So, other than the usual rookie rituals, how did you find your crew?"

"The WPU deputies are great. Experienced but laid back. Like I said, Phee knows her stuff, for sure."

Nat nodded neutrally. Phee Gomez. There'd been a time she'd thought something might develop between her and Phee, but they hadn't had the same picture of what they wanted, and she could only do casual for so long before the emptiness of it all returned. No hard feelings for either of them. She liked Phee and respected her as a professional, and she could see how Vic would find her attractive, if Vic leaned that way. The idea unsettled her. So did the picture she couldn't help imagining of Phee and Vic together.

"Phee's great," Nat said, hoping her voice sounded normal. "You're in good hands with her."

Vic studied Nat in that way she had of making Nat feel like Vic could see into the places she usually had no trouble hiding.

"I guess most everyone on the job around here knows each other," Vic said evenly, "and you mentioned you worked with the patrol."

Nat nodded, her throat suddenly tight.

Vic's eyebrows rose when Nat didn't offer anything further, but she didn't press, which Nat appreciated. Instead, Vic took a long pull from her beer, her gaze drifting to the mountaintops as the sun settled behind them. "It's so beautiful here. I can see why you love it so much."

Natalie followed Vic's gaze, a sense of peace washing over her. "It's my haven. My place to escape from the world."

"I get that." Vic hesitated, seeming to wrestle with her next words. "Charlie mentioned…he said you don't usually rent out the cabin."

Natalie's heart skipped a beat. She wouldn't have brought it up, but leave it to Charlie to do it instead. "He's right. I don't."

Vic looked worried and unexpectedly vulnerable. "Then why did you?"

"Honestly, I have no idea. Charlie asked, and for some reason, I just said yes." Natalie swallowed hard, the words sticking in her throat. "I surprised myself at the time, and now that you're here, I'm glad that I said yes." She laughed, trying for a teasing tone. "Apparently I just have a soft spot for wayward sailors."

But Vic didn't laugh. She held Natalie's gaze, the air suddenly charged. "I'm really glad you do—have that soft spot," she said softly. "This place...I couldn't have planned it so well if I'd tried."

Natalie's heart swelled at the words, a fierce protectiveness rising inside her. "Good, because I want you to stay," she said, the words escaping before she could think better of them. "As long as you want. The cabin's yours."

"Are you sure? I don't want to impose."

"You're not," Natalie said firmly. "I want you here."

The words hung in the air as if neither of them quite knew what to say next. Or perhaps feared to say anything else. At last, Vic reached out, her fingers grazing Natalie's hand.

"Thank you," Vic whispered, her voice thick. "For the place, and the welcome."

The touch sent sparks racing up Nat's arm, her skin tingling. She just nodded, not trusting herself to speak. Vic stirred feelings she wasn't sure how to decipher—excitement, tenderness, and a whole lot of warning bells she really needed to heed. She carefully slipped her hand away from Vic's and immediately registered the sense of loss. Oh, yes, plenty of warning bells now. She took a long breath as the sun finally dipped below the horizon, painting the sky in shades of orange and pink.

"I should probably head back to the house," she said. "Early morning tomorrow."

Vic nodded, rising to her feet. They stood face-to-face, the moonlight casting shadows across Vic's face. Vic's eyes dropped to Nat's lips.

"Right. Phee said we'd have a joint meeting tomorrow." She laughed softly. "Introductions."

For a breathless moment, Nat had the foolish notion that Vic might kiss her. The anticipation coiled in her stomach and, thankfully, sanity returned. She took a quick step back.

"You'll get a chance to meet everyone from the local teams then. First of June means lake traffic will quadruple overnight. We'll be working together for the rest of the season."

"I'm glad to hear that," Vic murmured, her voice husky. "Good night, Nat."

"Good night, Vic," Nat whispered as Vic turned and headed inside.

The cabin door closed softly behind her. Heart racing, Nat hurried up the path to the safety of her house. When the kitchen door closed behind her, she took a long breath. Whatever had just happened, she needed to remember that nothing *could* happen between them.

❖

After a quick shower, Vic stretched out on her bed in a tank top and loose sweats. She should have been tired, but her mind was alive with the memory of sitting on the porch with Nat. When she closed her eyes, trying to calm her racing thoughts, all she saw was Nat's face in the moonlight, her eyes shimmering with an intensity that made Vic's breath catch. She recalled the way Nat's lips had parted slightly when their eyes met, as if she too had felt that magnetic pull.

Rolling onto her side, Vic hugged a pillow to her chest, inhaling deeply. The scent of pine brought the image of the soaring mountains enclosing them in their own private oasis, reminding her of Nat's closeness on the porch. She couldn't shake the feeling of Nat's fingers brushing against hers, that brief contact sending electricity coursing along her nerve endings.

Alone in the dark, she could admit she'd wanted to kiss her.

"Get it together, O'Brien," Vic muttered to herself, but her body wasn't listening. Heat pooled low in her belly as she imagined what might have happened if she'd given in to the urge to kiss Nat. Would Nat's lips be as soft as they looked? Would she kiss her back with the same kind of hunger that stalked Vic now? A hunger she couldn't remember ever having before. Would Nat welcome her touch?

Vic's hand drifted down her body, slipping beneath the waistband of her sweats. She gasped softly as her fingers found the heat and the hard edge of her need. It had been so long since she'd felt this kind of desire, this aching urgency to touch—and be touched.

As she stroked, Vic imagined Nat's eyes glazed with hunger, heard Nat's voice whispering, "I want you to stay."

The pressure built, and Nat pressed her mouth against Vic's throat, murmuring, "I want you."

Vic pumped her hips against her hand, her breathing growing ragged. The fantasy was so vivid she could almost feel Nat's body pressed to hers. She imagined Nat beneath her, their legs entwined, Nat's hands roaming over her back, caressing her ass, pulling her closer until they rocked into each other. Vic moaned, picturing Nat's lips on her neck, the piercing jolt of teeth nipping her collarbone. The ache between her thighs grew, a pounding deep inside drawing a moan from her in the still, warm room. As Vic slipped her fingers into Nat's welcoming heat, Nat cupped her, pressing her palm rhythmically into Vic's clit. So close now—so good.

Vic bit her lip, fighting back a groan as the dam burst and pleasure roared through her. Her back arched, waves of sensation, intense and all-consuming. For a few blissful moments, she was lost in the fantasy, every nerve ending alive with pleasure.

As the aftershocks subsided, reality slowly crept back in. She opened her eyes, her chest still heaving as she caught her breath. A sliver of moonlight lanced across her face. The cabin was silent save for the soft chirping of crickets outside her half-open window. She was alone.

The images had been so real, the pleasure so intense. The need lingered still, an unsettled roiling in her depths. If she touched herself again, she'd come in a heartbeat. She sucked in a shocked breath. "Fuck."

She'd never fantasized about a woman like that before—never come as hard with anyone she'd been with.

A mix of emotions swirled within—satisfaction, longing, and a twinge of undeniable desire to make the fantasy a reality. She rolled onto her back, staring up at the shadowy ceiling. What was she doing? She barely knew Nat. And even if there was an attraction there, Nat hadn't given her the tiniest indication she was even interested. And why would she be? Vic wasn't exactly someone an accomplished, successful, impressive woman like Nat would even notice. For all Nat knew, Vic was just a summer hire, passing time while she figured out her life.

And wasn't that the truth? Wasn't that why she'd taken this job? To get away from the pain every time she looked out to sea and knew that that life was gone? Just like her dad. She had nowhere to be, and here she was.

Nat wasn't the kind of woman to jump into bed with a practical stranger—that much Vic felt sure about. She sighed, rubbing her hands over her face. She needed to get her head on straight and stop thinking about Nat as anything other than a friend and colleague.

Still, she couldn't deny the pull she felt toward her. It wasn't just physical attraction, although there was certainly plenty of that. Nat's quiet strength, her obvious love for this place and the work she did here stirred feelings that Vic thought had died along with her father and their fishing business. Sharing the quiet and beauty of the night with her, talking easily about her day and the work they had in common was the most connected she'd felt to anyone in years. The hunger for more surprised her, even if the chance of more was wishful thinking. She was still grateful for the reawakening, even if Nat only offered friendship.

But as she drifted off, she couldn't help but wonder if Nat was lying awake too, thinking of her.

CHAPTER FIVE

The next morning dawned crisp and clear, the air heavy with the scent of pine and damp earth. Vic stretched as she stepped onto the porch, coffee mug in hand. The forest was alive with birdsong and the rustle of small animals in the underbrush. She took a deep breath, savoring the peace of the moment. From where she stood, she could see Lake George through the trees. The early morning light painted the surface in shades of silver and rose. A thin mist hovered over the water, the ghostly veil swirling in the cool breeze. The air carried the faint tang of the lake, crisp and clean, mingling with the rich aroma of dew-drenched leaves. Trees along the shore stood sentinel over the still-quiet water. A sailboat skimmed the surface in the distance as somewhere a loon cried its mournful call.

Sipping her coffee, Vic glanced over to Nat's house. No sign of movement yet. Her breath fluttered at the thought of seeing her again. As quickly as the feeling rose, she pushed it aside, reminding herself of her resolution from the night before. Friends. Colleagues. No reason to expect anything more.

But as she finished her coffee and was about to head back inside, Nat emerged from her house and walked toward her Jeep. She was in uniform and carried a travel mug in one hand. When Nat looked her way, Vic waited a beat before raising her coffee cup in salute. "Morning."

Nat paused, as if deciding whether to linger, and finally walked back down the path to the cabin. "You're up early."

"Back at you," Vic said, trying to keep her voice casual even as her stomach flipped at the sight of Nat in uniform—focused, capable, and frustratingly distant.

"Restless night," Nat said, shrugging, though the shadows beneath her eyes told a different story.

"Yeah. I know the feeling." She'd had plenty of those nights after her dad died. Of course, the night before had been very different. She'd tossed and turned thinking about kissing the woman who was studying her now from shadowed eyes. The weight of unsaid things hung thick as the morning mist over the lake.

Vic hesitated. The temptation to invite Nat inside flickered—a cup of coffee, a conversation, maybe a chance to break through whatever wall Nat was rebuilding. "Want to come up for a fresh cup?"

Nat glanced at her watch, then back at Vic. Something flashed in her eyes—hesitation, maybe longing—before she shook her head. "I can't. Early start. But…thanks."

"Another time, then," Vic said, trying to keep her tone light. She probably should have let it go—Nat obviously wanted to leave, but something inside pressed her to ask. "Everything okay?"

"Fine," Nat said, her fingers tightening around her travel mug.

For a moment, silence descended, the morning air thick with more than just pine scent. Vic wanted to offer some word of comfort, for what, she wasn't even sure—just *something* to ease the gulf between them. The silence stretched.

"I should go," Nat said finally, gesturing vaguely toward her Jeep.

"Right," Vic said. "I'll see you at the meeting, then."

Nat smiled briefly. "Yes. Duty calls."

Vic watched for a moment as Nat strode to her Jeep, climbed in, and pulled away. Vic watched Nat's Jeep disappear down the road, the hollow ache in her chest sharp and sudden.

Right. Friends. Colleagues.

Nothing more.

The words sounded hollow now.

She drained the last of her coffee and set the mug down with more force than necessary. Why did it matter so much? Why did Nat's distance feel like rejection, when they'd barely crossed the line to begin with?

Because it wasn't just about attraction.

Nat had made her feel like she belonged—like maybe she wasn't completely adrift after all.

And that was dangerous. Too dangerous.

❖

On the drive to the regional DEC headquarters in Bolton, Nat tried to shake off the remnants of her restless night. She couldn't remember much of her dreams, just flashes of dark eyes, the heat of a near touch, and the gnawing sense of something unfinished.

This wasn't supposed to happen.

She hadn't expected to see Vic in the morning, but now the image of her in sweats and an old T-shirt, hair tousled from sleep, wouldn't leave her alone. Vic didn't seem to have any idea how attractive she was, which was another reason Nat liked her. Found her intriguing. Damn it. She pushed the picture of Vic leaning against the porch railing, all loose-limbed and a little rumpled in a decidedly sexy way, out of her mind. She had a meeting to run. She did not need to be daydreaming about a young stranger sleeping fifty feet from her back door. Losing sleep over her was bad enough.

Nat exhaled, long and slow, forcing her jaw to unclench. Why couldn't she let this go? Why did every glance, every brush of proximity feel like the start of something she couldn't afford? Had Vic really wanted to kiss her? Had she wanted Vic to?

By the time she pulled into the lot, her shoulders ached from the tension. She needed to focus. She had a meeting to run. Responsibilities. A life that didn't involve tangled thoughts of Vic O'Brien.

But even as she cut the engine, the ghost of Vic's smile lingered in her mind—unwanted and entirely unavoidable. Determined to put unanswerable questions aside, she headed inside.

"Hey, Nat," Megan Oloff called. "Hold up!"

Nat turned to see Meg jogging toward her, the warm smile that was rarely absent shining brightly. Her blond hair was pulled back in a stubby ponytail, and she wore her Bolton FD blue uniform. As Meg reached her, Nat couldn't help but notice the way her shirt clung to her curves. For a fleeting second, she wished she'd been dreaming about Meg the night before. Life would be so much simpler.

"Hi," Nat said. "You got tagged to represent today?"

"Yep," Meg said, slightly out of breath. "Always happy for an easy assignment. Have you got all your summer replacements yet?"

Nat nodded, trying to focus on the conversation and not the memories of their last intimate encounter. Which had been—weeks ago? But that wasn't unusual. They both had busy schedules and had never defined just what their relationship was, other than friends first and sometimes-lovers second. "We're still looking for a couple more, but we've got most of the positions covered."

"What about Chase—still half-time?"

"Yes." Nat laughed. "Chase is loving baby care, apparently. Plus with a reduced schedule, she can spend all her time in the field and avoid community events."

"Just the way she likes it." Meg grinned. "I'd be envious, except not for the wife and baby so much."

"That's because you enjoy playing the field as much as you enjoy patrolling it," Nat teased.

"True—and speaking of," Meg said, taking a quick look around, "it's been a while since we've had some personal time together. What do you say we get together soon, maybe this weekend if you're free?"

She reached out and lightly touched Nat's arm, her fingertips grazing Nat's skin.

Nat hesitated, feeling a strange twinge of discomfort at the thought of being intimate with Meg again. Not that she didn't enjoy their time together—she did. But something felt different now, like a shift had occurred within her. Struggling with too many emotions she couldn't decipher, she tried to keep her tone casual.

"I don't know, Meg. Camp opens soon, and I'm not sure yet where and when I'll need to fill in on shifts. Can I leave it at maybe for now?"

Megan narrowed her eyes before her smile returned. "Sure, no worries. I understand. Just let me know whenever."

"Count on it. Thanks." Nat opened the door to the converted boathouse on the edge of the lake that now served as their regional headquarters as well as the launch site for the DEC patrol boats. She had a small office on the upper floor next to the conference room—and tried to spend as little time as possible in either of them. Hopefully this meeting would be quick.

"See you upstairs," Meg said as they parted ways just inside. "You know how I feel about sitting around in small, crowded spaces."

"Ten minutes," Nat said. "I'll save you a seat."

When the rangers from her district and the six-man crew of the Water Patrol unit filed in and got settled, rangers on one side and deputies on the other, Nat walked to the front of the conference room. She scanned the room, taking in the assembled group of DEC rangers and Water Patrol officers. Her gaze landed on Vic, sitting next to Phee Gomez in the back row. Vic smiled when their eyes met. Nat's pulse quickened and she quickly looked away, annoyed by a twinge of completely uncalled for and totally out-of-place irritation at how comfortable Vic and Phee looked, sitting with their shoulders almost touching. She took a breath to refocus.

"Morning, everyone. We've got a few new people, so let's get introductions out of the way first. I'm Lieutenant Nat Evans, the regional director for District A. Rangers, want to sound off?"

The ten rangers followed suit with their names, and then Phee Gomez stood up.

"Sergeant Phee Gomez, crew chief on the Water Patrol craft *Bayside Betty*"—which drew the usual laughter—"and our officers."

The deputies, most of whom Nat knew, stood one by one, and she tried to avoid staring at Vic when she rose to speak. Meg shot Nat an amused look as she stood to introduce herself as the Bolton FD liaison.

"Right," Nat said, not thinking at all how good Vic looked in her navy-blue uniform. She pointed to a Google satellite image projected on the wall, the dark blue ribbon of Lake George cutting through a sea of green.

"This," she began, tapping the screen, "is Lake George. Thirty-eight miles long, two to three miles wide, and over two hundred feet deep in places. They call it the Queen of American Lakes for good reason. It's pristine—one of the cleanest lakes in the country—and it's our job to help keep it that way."

Happy to see she had everyone's attention, she traced a finger along the shoreline. "It's surrounded by the Adirondack Park, six million acres of protected land. Think of the lake as its sparkling crown jewel. Up here in the north, you've got the Narrows—a cluster of over 170 islands, most of them accessible only by boat. It's a favorite spot for campers, but that also means it's a hot spot for issues like littering, illegal fires, and the occasional party that gets out of hand.

"Down here," she said, tapping the southern extent of the shoreline, "is Lake George Village. This is the tourist hub. On a summer weekend, the population here swells from a few thousand to tens of thousands. You'll see everything from kids on paddleboards to speedboats buzzing around like they own the water. It's beautiful, but it can be chaos."

Nat stepped back and gestured to the surrounding parklands. "Now, all of this—the forests, the trails, the campsites—is under DEC jurisdiction. The lake is a key part of an ecosystem. The streams and wetlands feed it, the mountains shelter it, and its water gives life to everything from bald eagles to fish that you'll hear people bragging about catching. The WPU provides law enforcement on the lake and along the shore, and where our responsibilities intersect, including search and rescue, we work together."

She made eye contact with each recruit, but even the veterans looked alert and focused. She loved that about her rangers—they cared about the land and lake they served, as well as the people who arrived to enjoy it.

"You'll see things here that'll take your breath away—sunrises over the water, the stars mirrored on its surface on a calm night. But you'll also face challenges: weather that turns dangerous in minutes, boating and hiking accidents, and all too frequent illegal activities. All of it is ours to protect. Questions?"

Nat fielded questions, keeping the meeting on track, but even when the topic turned to scheduling—what everyone wanted to know about, considering the three holiday weekends during the height of the season. As she wound things down, she was acutely aware of Vic's presence, like a gravitational pull. When the meeting ended, the attendees filed out, chatting amongst themselves.

Meg joined her as she stored the AV equipment away.

"So—interesting new group," Meg said nonchalantly.

"Pretty much the usual," Nat said, only half listening as she watched Phee and Vic leaving together.

"Oh, I don't know about usual." Meg lowered her voice. "That new Water Patrol officer, Vic—she's pretty hot, huh? You think she's single?"

Nat tensed. "I wouldn't know. It's not like we discussed our personal lives."

Meg gave her a curious look. "You know her, then?"

"I wouldn't say I know her." Nat really wanted to avoid the issue of Vic's attractiveness. Or Meg's interest in her. She had no exclusive agreement with Meg about anything personal, and she certainly had no hold on Vic. "She's a tenant, that's all."

"Wait a sec. Tenant?"

"She's renting my cabin."

"When were you going to tell me that?" The edge in Meg's voice wasn't like her. Easygoing defined her, and that made their personal relationship work. No expectations, no demands, and no territorialism.

"We haven't exactly had much time to catch up lately. It didn't occur to me that I needed to make an announcement," Nat said, leading the way out into the hall.

"Okay, I get it," Meg said, her tone indicating she thought she got more than was actually being said.

Vic, who'd been leaning against the opposite wall, straightened up when Nat and Meg approached. She held out her hand to Meg. "Hi. I'm Vic O'Brien."

"Megan Oloff," Meg said. "Welcome aboard."

"Thanks." Vic's smile flashed, and damn it, Nat got butterflies again.

Just then, Phee came around the corner and paused when she saw them. Her gaze flickered to Nat, something unreadable in her eyes, before she smiled. "Nat, good to see you again. Hi, Meg. Vic and I were just about to grab some lunch before our patrol. Care to join us?"

The invitation hung in the air, but Nat knew it was merely a polite formality. She forced a smile, ignoring the way Vic's gaze lingered on her, a silent question in her eyes. "Thanks, but I need to get out to Thunder Ridge."

"I'll take a rain check too," Meg added.

"Some other time, then." Phee glanced at Vic. "All set?"

"Yep." Vic looked at Nat. "Have a good one."

"You too." Nat watched them walk away and clenched her jaw, angry at herself for the irrational reaction.

Meg gave a low whistle. "Well, Phee Gomez seems awfully interested in the new rook."

Nat shoved down the sudden flare of possessiveness. "Phee can do what she wants. They're both adults."

"Geez, touch-y! It was just an observation." Meg held up her hands in mock surrender.

Nat sighed. "Sorry. Just a lot on my mind."

Meg's expression softened. "I've got a date with *my* rookie partner—who is cute but seriously married—so I've got to run too. Call me?"

"I will—soon as things settle down a little."

"Ha—hope you don't wait till October," Meg called, hurrying away.

Nat paused on the steps outside, watching Vic's retreating figure as she walked with Phee toward a cruiser. They laughed about something—an easy, familiar sound that hit Nat harder than it should have. Their camaraderie was obvious and effortless—a kind of comfort Nat hadn't been prepared to see, much less feel jealous of. Her jaw tightened.

She had no claim on Vic. No right to feel this way. And no desire to feel any way at all.

Logic didn't help.

❖

"Barney's has great burgers," Phee said." And with our boat launch right up the block, super convenient if we have to leave in a hurry."

"I've had the burgers," Vic said. "No argument from me."

Phee shot her a look. "Then you've already hit one of the highlights in town."

Vic laughed. "I had dinner here with Nat the night I arrived. At the time, anything would've tasted great. I'm definitely ready for a repeat, though."

As they took a table not far from the one she'd shared with Nat that first night, Vic recalled the way they'd talked. And then again when they'd shared beer and pizza at the cabin. How easy it was to open up to her, something she'd never done with anyone else. Maybe it was just the newness of the place, so different from home, but she didn't think so. She thought it was Nat.

"So you and Nat," Phee said after they'd ordered, "friends of the family or something?"

"Not exactly," Vic said. "Charlie and Nat are friends, and he arranged for me to rent her cabin."

Phee's eyebrows rose. "I didn't know that. So the two of you are neighbors."

"I guess you could say that." The memory of Nat's lingering gaze that morning flickered uninvited into her mind. She cleared her throat. "I was lucky to get the place."

"Mmm."

Phee didn't say a lot, and said a lot in the silence. Vic sensed there was more beneath Phee's curiosity but didn't press. She didn't want to think about Nat and Phee's shared history—or the way her stomach twisted at the idea.

"So what's our route today?"

Phee liked to keep the day's patrol route to herself until the crew came aboard, a little test, maybe, of Vic's readiness to navigate the new waters. Since she'd had plenty of free time in the last week or so to study the boating channels, she could chart their course pretty quickly once Phee gave her their destination. In another few days she wouldn't need the GPS. They weren't on the Atlantic, after all, although the simplicity of the red and green buoys that marked the boat channels was essential for the safety of the casual boaters and even the experienced captain when a storm blew in and obscured visibility. Nothing like the gales at sea that she and her dad had navigated by instinct, but maybe that was the point. Maybe she was meant to leave the vast, merciless waters behind and learn to navigate something smaller, quieter. Setting out onto the lake with the WPU wasn't about survival, but teamwork and public service.

For the short term, at least, this was her life.

"We'll swing up to the lower islands today, check out the camp-sites. They should be filling up, and we may do some permit checks. Also boating and fishing license checks."

"The North Shore, then," Vic said. "Nice route through the Little Sisters. The Narrows will be fun."

Phee grinned. "A-plus, Rookie."

"It's not *that* big a lake." Vic took a bite of her burger—as good as the first time—and said after a moment, "How much actual policing will we be doing—as compared to service type calls?"

"It varies, and we have to be ready for anything every day. More law enforcement on the holiday weekends, for sure," Phee said. "A lot of alcohol out on the water and at the campsites, and too many people who decide they need to pilot their craft when they're three sheets to the wind."

Vic grimaced. "Yeah, that's a recipe for disaster."

"I imagine you saw a little bit of that in your fishing days."

Vic shook her head. "Not on our boat. Oh sure, everybody hit the bars once they made the dock and unloaded the catch, but at least on the *Nightingale*, no alcohol."

"That was your boat? The *Nightingale*?"

Vic swallowed around the sudden lump in her throat. "Yeah. My dad had a liking for birds."

"Nice," Phee said softly.

"I always thought—"

Phee's radio crackled sharply and the dispatcher came through.

"All units, be advised: Boating accident reported near the lower islands. Two craft involved. Injuries confirmed. Dispatching coordinates now."

Phee straightened instantly and unclipped the radio from her vest.

"WPU One, copy that. En route to coordinates now."

Her eyes met Vic's, the earlier ease replaced by sharp focus. "Let's move."

Vic was already pushing back from the table, adrenaline flooding her veins. The boat launch was so close, they didn't bother moving the Jeep but jogged up the street. Two other crew members, Milt Weatherby and Juanita Hernandez, were already on deck, ready to cast off the tie lines.

Vic raced to the helm, heart pounding as she shrugged into her PFD, a bright orange Type III inflatable vest that automatically deployed in the water. She activated the twin Mercury outboard engines, their low growl building to a throaty roar as she eased the throttle forward. With a quick glance to confirm they were clear of the dock and everyone was secured, she opened up the engines, the Boston Whaler surging onto the open lake.

"Heading?" she called to Phee over the sound of wind and the steady thrum of the hull cutting through the waves.

Phee relayed the coordinates just as they appeared on the Raymarine navigation screen mounted next to the helm. Vic adjusted their course with a smooth turn, keeping an eye on the buoys flashing past on either side.

"What do we know?" Juanita called, her words choppy above the roar of the engines and the drumming spray against the windshield.

"Not much," Phee responded. "Injured likely in the water."

"ETA three minutes," Vic announced, gripping the wheel tightly as the boat surged over the swells. Her pulse quickened, every nerve on high alert. At sea, she'd thrived on the rush of spotting a school of tuna, heart racing as she maneuvered to cast the nets. But this—this was different. The stakes were higher. Each jump of the boat over the waves drove the truth deeper. She wasn't a fishing boat captain anymore. She was a first responder.

"There!" Phee pointed sharply to a speedboat floundering in the water. Nearby, half of a red kayak floated unevenly, bobbing with the waves.

Vic's stomach clenched at the sight. Two people on the speedboat stared into the water, their faces pale and stricken.

"Victim in the water off the bow, fifty yards," Juanita reported, scanning with binoculars.

"Get us closer," Phee said. "Be careful—there may be others in the water."

"Aye." Vic slowed when she spotted a woman floundering in the waves, coughing between panicked screams. Circling to approach the victim from the downwind side, she cut back on the throttle further to maintain a safe distance and avoid swamping her.

Milt quickly threw out a Type IV life ring attached to a thick towline, aiming it just past the woman. Meanwhile, Juanita and Phee began unstrapping the compact, inflatable rescue raft secured to the starboard side of the boat. With practiced efficiency, they deployed it into the water and climbed aboard.

Amidst the chaos, Vic could finally make out what the woman was screaming.

My daughter, my daughter!

Vic's gut twisted as she scanned the water near the victim, looking for any sign of a child. The fragmented half of the red kayak had already sunk beneath the surface, leaving no clue as to where the missing girl might be.

By the time Juanita and Phee had helped the woman into the dinghy and brought her aboard, another patrol boat arrived, pulling up alongside the disabled speedboat.

"We have a casualty. We need to get her back to shore," Phee radioed, as Juanita maneuvered the raft toward the second patrol boat. "We'll evacuate her. Milt, you and Vic start looking for a seven-year-old in a red T-shirt and blue bathing suit bottoms. Dive teams are on their way."

"Roger that," Milt replied, already retrieving a laminated chart from the storage locker to plot their search. He turned to Vic. "You know how to do a grid sweep?"

"Got it covered." Vic punched new coordinates into the navigation system to chart their search zone. She toggled the spotlight to scan the water as the Boston Whaler idled forward, its powerful hull slicing steadily through the small waves.

She clenched her jaw. If there was a child in the water, she wasn't leaving until they found her.

❖

The sun dipped below the horizon, painting the sky in shades of orange and pink as Nat stood on her porch, her concern growing. The shadows stretched long across the yard, every passing minute dragging the unease deeper into her chest. Vic's shift must have ended hours ago.

Logically, there were dozens of explanations why she hadn't returned—late paperwork, a debriefing, or maybe a drink with her crew.

Or with Phee.

Vic was young, new in town, and likely looking for a little fun after hours. None of her business. As the minutes ticked by, her worry slowly morphed into frustration with herself. The images of Vic and Phee together that she couldn't seem to avoid conjuring in her mind only heightened her annoyance.

She gripped the porch railing, the wood rough beneath her palms. Why did the thought of Vic laughing with someone else twist inside her like this?

"Enough of this," she muttered. The last thing she wanted was for Vic to pull in and find her pacing on the porch as if Vic was late for curfew. Spending another night tossing and turning was not high on her list of things she wanted to do either. But as she turned to head inside, the image of Vic's eyes—steady, unwavering—flashed into mind. And that quiet voice in her head whispered the truth—her discomfort wasn't about jealousy but about wanting Vic to be safe.

Another thing she couldn't do anything about.

What she needed was a distraction.

She called Meg, who answered instantly.

"Hey you."

"Does that invitation for a drink still stand?" Nat said.

"Um, sure. I just happen to be at the Dockside."

"Alone?"

Meg laughed. "Yes, alone. Are you joining me?"

"On my way."

When she walked into the local bar twenty minutes later, the low hum of conversation mixed with the clink of glasses and the occasional burst of laughter greeted her. The familiar scent of beer, fried food, and faint woodsmoke lingered in the air, a comforting reminder of countless evenings she'd spent there with Meg and other rangers. The bar's walls were paneled in dark-stained wood, lined with framed photographs of Lake George through the seasons—boats slicing through summer's blue waters, autumn leaves reflected on the lake, and the frozen stillness of winter.

A polished oak bar stretched along the left side, crowded with patrons perched on high-backed stools, their elbows leaning on the well-worn surface. Behind the bar, shelves stocked with bottles of liquor and rows of neatly stacked pint glasses gleamed under warm, golden light. Above it hung a pair of flat-screen TVs tuned to a hockey game.

The right side of the room held clusters of tables and chairs arranged haphazardly, each surrounded by small groups talking over the music playing faintly from the speakers. A dartboard in the back corner had drawn a handful of players, while a pool table stood unused for now, its green felt partially covered with a stray jacket and someone's forgotten scarf.

Meg had chosen a table tucked into the farthest corner of the room, away from the busiest sections. Nat appreciated the vantage point to observe without being easily noticed and wove her way through the throng of people, ducking past a man gesturing wildly with his beer and sidestepping a server balancing a tray of drinks. When she slid into the seat across from Meg, the relative calm of their corner was a welcome reprieve.

"I'm glad you changed your mind about getting together," Meg said, eyeing her intently despite her welcoming smile. She pushed one of the two drinks that sat before her over to Nat. "You look like someone just told you tomorrow's shift starts at dawn."

Nat let out a breathless laugh, more exhaustion than amusement. "Rough day."

"Want to talk?"

Nat shook her head, picked up her drink, and took a long sip. The alcohol burned its way down her throat, the sensation oddly comforting. "Just—long shift. Too much on my mind."

"I'm happy to provide a distraction, then."

"You're more than that," Nat said softly.

Meg stroked the top of Nat's hand. "I know that. So what's going on with you?"

"Nothing, really." Nat shook her head. She didn't and never would play mind games with Meg. "I just…I don't know. Things are complicated right now."

"Does this have anything to do with the new tenant?" Meg asked casually.

Nat stared, her heart racing. "What? No, why would it?"

"You're not usually this thrown, Nat. And she's the only thing that's new."

For a moment, Nat almost said it—how Vic made her feel seen

in a way that scared her, how every glance left her breathless. But the words caught in her throat.

Nat said with finality, "Believe me, there is nothing going on."

Meg studied her for a long beat, then nodded slowly. "Sure."

The unspoken truths hung in the air, lingering in the space that Nat wasn't ready to breach. She drew in a slow breath. What she didn't plan to do was spend the rest of the evening dissecting her tangled thoughts about Vic O'Brien. No lingering looks, no unresolved tension, and definitely no more wondering where Vic might be or who she was with.

She needed something simpler. Something she could count on.

And with Meg, there were no blurred lines—just trust, ease, and the promise of a connection that didn't ask for more than either of them could give.

Her voice was steady when she spoke. "Does the rest of the invitation still stand as well?"

Meg's smile returned, soft but sure. "You mean the part where we spend some personal time together?"

"If you're still interested."

Meg's gaze held hers, no teasing now—just quiet connection. "I'm ready anytime you are."

Nat finished her drink, the glass making a soft click as she set it down. The decision settled over her, heavier than she'd expected. "Then that would be now."

CHAPTER SIX

M y place is closer," Nat said as she and Meg left the Dockside. Early season tourists swelled the village streets that were usually quiet after midnight, hinting at the bustle yet to come during the summer. As they crossed toward the parking lot beside the bar, a pair of motorcycles roared to life. "Okay with you?"

"Sure, I'll follow you," Meg said. "That way you don't have to bring me back here in the middle of the night to retrieve my wheels."

Nat glanced at her. "You don't necessarily have to leave before morning."

Meg smiled, and for a second Nat thought she sensed sadness in her expression. "Well, you never know what might happen before morning. Either one of us could get a call. Better safe than sorry."

"You're right," Nat said.

Safe.

Maybe that should be her new mantra. *Better safe than sorry.* That's what she was doing right now, wasn't it? Being safe. Meg was safe, comfortable, known. And that was pretty much what she'd been doing her whole life. Keeping to her plan, never taking chances, being safe. She'd always been happy with that.

So why was she anything but comfortable right now? Why did her skin feel like it was a mass of nerve endings that the slightest breeze set afire? Why was she too aware of every brush of Meg's arm, not because it excited her but because it didn't? And why was she so damn eager to get Vi— She caught her breath. *Meg.*

Meg was the one she wanted in her bed.

Nat faltered, just enough for Meg to notice.

Meg stopped her with a hand on her arm. "Is everything alright?"

"Of course." Nat kept her tone light and managed a nod. The tension in her chest told her otherwise. Everything about this felt out of sync—her, the night, the steady pulse of longing she couldn't quite suppress. She glanced at Meg. Why did being safe suddenly feel so wrong? "Other than the fact that, you know, I haven't seen you for a while."

Meg laughed as they stopped in front of her personal vehicle. "Well, there is that. So I'll see you in a few minutes, and we'll take care of that posthaste."

Nat drove carefully along the twisting turns of Route 9 toward home. She'd only had one drink and that had been a while ago—but safety first. There was that word again.

When had safety become an adversary?

Meg pulled in behind her, and they walked inside together. Nat reached back for Meg's hand, needing the contact, needing to feel grounded in the familiar. Moonlight dappled the floorboards as Nat led Meg into the bedroom. The door clicked shut behind them, and she pulled Meg close, pressing their bodies together in a kiss that felt like drowning—a way to silence the voice in her head screaming another name.

She tugged Meg's shirt free and slid her hand beneath, caressing her middle.

"In a hurry?" Meg murmured against Nat's lips.

Nat's stomach clenched, the pulsing need pushing reason aside. "I've missed this."

Not quite a lie. She'd missed what this used to feel like—before everything changed.

"Mmm, I see."

Meg tumbled them onto the bed, and they shed clothes in a tangle of limbs, moving together in a well-practiced dance.

Nat rolled onto her side, sliding one leg over Meg's. Her body responded as it always had with Meg—familiar, practiced—but her mind drifted elsewhere. Every gasp Meg pulled from her echoed hollowly, every touch a reminder of how much she wasn't feeling. Needing to banish the distant shadow of someone else's presence, she kissed a path to Meg's breasts. She cupped Meg's breasts and brushed her thumb over a nipple while taking the other into her mouth. When she sucked, biting lightly, Meg gasped, her back arching.

When she stroked a trail down the center of Meg's abdomen, Meg grasped her wrist.

"You'd better slow down if you don't want me coming all over you any second," Meg murmured, her voice quivering with need.

"Just exactly what I want." Nat pressed her center to Meg's tense thigh and groaned, lost in the heady sensation of lust and the pounding pressure between her thighs. She was close already too. All she needed was to bury herself in Meg's pleasure. Urgency building, she cupped Meg and found her wet and ready.

"Oh my God," Meg cried, "you're going to make me come right away."

Nat entered her, brushing Meg's clit with every long, slow thrust. Meg tightened around her fingers, and Nat rocked against her leg, climbing higher. So close now. So close but she couldn't reach the peak. Sweat dripped down Nat's neck. Her muscles clenched. She needed to come so badly. If she could just—

Meg gripped her shoulders. "I'm coming. Fuck."

When Meg came with a shudder, an image flashed unbidden in Nat's mind. Stormy gray eyes, an angular jaw, raven hair.

Vic's face.

Nat's rhythm faltered. Confusion and guilt seared through the fog of lust. She squeezed her eyes shut, trying to will the image away. Carefully, she lifted her weight from Meg's body, rolled onto her back, and stared at the ceiling. Awash with frustration, confusion, and remorse. What was she doing?

Breathing hard, Meg turned on her side and kissed Nat's jaw. "So, that was fairly spectacular."

Nat laughed flatly. "Sorry if I rushed you."

"Oh, don't apologize. You can do me like that any time you want."

Nat's guilt eased. Meg was always Meg, and right now, Meg was happy. "So noted."

"You okay?" Meg asked gently.

"I'm good," Nat said quickly. The arousal that had clouded her mind, and apparently her judgment, had faded to a gnawing echo of itself. After the shock of fantasizing about some other woman while she was with Meg, she wasn't going there again.

"You sure?" Meg propped herself up on an elbow, brow furrowed. "We might be awesome in bed, but we're friends first, right?"

Nat kissed her lightly. "Absolutely. I'm just tired. Sorry."

"Okay." Meg's tone said she wasn't buying it, but she didn't push. She rested her head against Nat's shoulder. "I'm here whenever you want to talk."

"I know," Nat said as Meg yawned. "Go to sleep."

"Mmm," Meg murmured, already fading.

Nat stared at the ceiling, Meg's rhythmic breathing a soothing backdrop. She might have fallen asleep too if Vic's face hadn't still lingered in her mind. What the hell was happening to her? This thing with Meg had always been simple, uncomplicated. Now, with one unbidden thought, everything felt upended. Confusion roiled as sleep escaped her, scattered by racing thoughts and the phantom storm of Vic's eyes.

❖

The dawn sunlight slanted through the trees as Nat and Meg made their way down the path from Nat's front porch to the driveway, their boots crunching on gravel. Nat squinted against the onslaught of a bright, beautiful sunrise. Each step felt heavier than the last, exhaustion clinging to her like damp air. She'd showered after Meg had fallen asleep, hoping to blast the memory of the night away along with the weariness in her body. Hadn't worked. She'd barely slept, her mind churning with restless thoughts. The clarity of dawn did nothing to erase the memory of Vic's face—unbidden, persistent—searing into her consciousness when she'd least expected it. Nothing like that had ever happened before.

Meg paused at her car door, turning to face Nat. "Listen, about last night—"

The low rumble of an engine cut her off.

Nat's pulse spiked as Vic's dusty truck rounded the bend and pulled into view, gravel spraying beneath the tires.

Meg's eyes widened, darting between Nat and the truck. "I should go before this gets awkward."

"There's no need for you to run. We're all adults here."

"I'd just as soon not be in the middle of something."

Nat sighed. "You're not. I'd tell you—"

"Could've fooled me." Meg squeezed her arm and added softly, "Hey, I know. We're good."

"Meg—"

"Call me later? When you've sorted out some things." She yanked open her car door, tossing Nat a fleeting glance.

Nat managed a nod before Meg drove off, leaving nothing but dust and the echo of their unfinished conversation. What else could she have said? Meg knew her too well not to know something was off, and she cared about Meg too much to pretend otherwise. But she really didn't have anything to say that would make sense. She couldn't even decipher her own tangled feelings.

Nat waited as Vic's truck rolled to a stop, the engine cutting off with a final sputter. Vic climbed out, moving slowly, like every muscle ached. Her uniform was rumpled, stained with oil and dirt. Vic walked over, her usually forceful stride absent, her face pale and drawn. Dark circles shadowed her eyes.

Nat's chest tightened. "I'd say good morning, but I'm guessing it isn't."

"Hey," Vic said, her voice rough around the edges. "Not so much."

Nat shoved her hands into her pockets. "You look like hell."

A ghost of a smile flickered across Vic's face. "Feel like it too."

Silence stretched, charged with unspoken questions Nat couldn't very well ask. Vic might have spent the night with Phee for all Nat knew—or someone else. The thought left an unpleasant burn in her middle, but she'd just have to learn to live with that, at least until the end of the season when Vic moved on.

Vic studied her, as if trying to read her mind. Thankfully she couldn't, especially when her thoughts kept returning to the bigger question she couldn't ask.

Why can't I stop thinking about you?

"Long night?" Nat finally asked. A safe question.

"Boating accident." Vic's gaze met hers, steady but clouded. "Two craft involved. It was bad."

Nat frowned. Regional incident reports came across her desk, but unless her rangers were involved, she wasn't notified directly. Events completely confined to the lake were handled exclusively by the Water Patrol Unit rather than a joint response. "I haven't seen the reports. What happened?"

Vic shoved a hand into her hair, which she'd obviously done countless times as her usual wavy hair was disheveled. "A speedboat coming through one of the island channels at top speed. Took out a kayak."

"Casualties?"

"Mother and daughter," Vic said, her voice hollow. "The mother's stable at the medical center. We couldn't find her. The little girl. We tried. We looked. The divers are still out. I was so certain I could—" She looked away, swallowing hard.

"I'm glad you're okay." Reflexively, Nat reached for her hand and squeezed. "Damn it. That's so hard."

Vic nodded. "I…uh…this is the first time I've had to deal with a situation like this. Especially a kid."

"I'm so damn sorry, Vic."

Nat pulled her into a hug. She would've done it with anyone, but when her arms went around Vic's waist and their bodies touched, lightning streaked through her. Vic's body was warm, firm beneath her touch, molding to hers as if by design. Vic shuddered, her breath quick against the side of Nat's neck.

"Nat," Vic whispered hoarsely, "I—"

Nat turned her head, her lips brushing Vic's. Before Nat could even register what they were doing, Vic's arms tightened around her and she slanted her head, deepening the kiss. Nat's body surged into autopilot. She gripped Vic's shoulders. Vic's tongue teased hers. Her legs trembled. She heard a moan, thought it might have been her. Hunger pierced her like a dagger thrust.

Vic's thigh, lean and hard, slid between her legs. Her hands were everywhere, roaming over Nat's body as if she couldn't touch her everywhere fast enough. Every touch sent shivers down Nat's spine, igniting a desire she hadn't felt in a long time. Nat tangled her fingers in Vic's hair, pulling her closer. Without breaking the kiss, Vic gently turned Nat until her back was against the Jeep.

Nat gasped as pressure built deep inside. She was close to giving in, so close to losing control. So close to reaching the pinnacle she'd ached for a few hours before. She couldn't, she couldn't…not like this. Not with Vic. She pressed a hand to Vic's chest, put space between them.

Vic pulled away, gasping. "God, I'm sorry, I—"

Stunned, Nat searched Vic's face, expecting…she wasn't sure what, half dreading regret or, worse, condemnation. Instead Vic's tight jaw and dark, hazy eyes reflected what raged inside her. Hunger, need, desperate desire.

"No," Nat said, struggling to catch her breath. "No, that was on me. *I* should apologize."

Vic shook her head, finding Nat's hand and lacing their fingers together. "I'm pretty sure I'm the one who pressed the go button. I've been wanting to kiss you since the jump."

They stood mere inches apart, staring at one another. Vic's eyes were stormy, and Nat had a distant memory of the only time she'd seen the ocean on a gray day when the waves whipped wildly. Strength and power a hundred times that of the lake, even at its fiercest, roiled in Vic's gaze now.

Nat ached with every fiber to kiss her again, to taste the heat of her mouth and the faint salty tang of her lips. She wanted Vic's hands on her again.

She swallowed and took a step away.

Vic sighed, exhaustion etched into every line of her face.

Nat said, "Go inside. You should get some rest."

"I don't know if I can sleep now," Vic whispered.

Nat chose not to think about what she might mean, refused to think about the need she saw in Vic's eyes, or the gnawing desire that clawed at her insides. "Do you have any food in the cabin?"

Vic laughed, a short empty sound of surrender. "Haven't exactly stocked the kitchen yet. Keep meaning to do that."

"Let me make you something to eat," Nat said, the words tumbling out in a rush. "Go shower."

Vic hesitated, and for a moment, she looked like she might refuse. But, giving a small, grateful smile, she nodded. "You know, you're making a habit of feeding me."

"Small favors," Nat whispered.

"Not to me."

"I'll just be a few minutes." Nat squeezed her arm. Vic's skin beneath her shirt radiated heat.

Vic disappeared into her cabin, and Nat went inside as if she was sleepwalking. Caught in a dream. What was she doing? This thing between them, whatever it was, had her clinging to the edge of a precipice, exhilarated and terrified.

Even knowing she could fall, and if she did, the consequences might leave her broken, she couldn't seem to back away to somewhere safe.

❖

Vic leaned against the wall in the narrow shower stall, hot water sluicing into her hair and over her face. Her body, caught between exhaustion and raw need, vibrated like a live wire—every nerve exposed, every thought jagged and unrelenting.

The memory of Nat's touch haunted her: the heat of her kiss, the taste of her desire. Her stomach twisted, a surge of frustration spiraling in her core. Damn it. She hadn't been this restless since she was a teenager, adrenaline laced with desire and confusion, when the mere thought of touching another girl would send her into the stratosphere. Which was where she dangled now, on the screaming edge of desire, and the ground was a long, long way down.

She dragged her fingers through her hair, water cascading down her shoulders, trying to scrub the heat from her skin. Trying to make sense of what had just happened.

Had it all been a mistake?

Nat had backed away—had even apologized. For what, Vic wasn't sure. Did Nat think she didn't *want* to kiss her? Or did Nat not want to kiss *her*? Why did this have to be so complicated? If two adults wanted to get involved, why should there be a problem? Unless Nat was attached.

The answer had been right there in front of her. Meg leaving at dawn, which she'd so carefully pretended not to see. The uncertainty in Nat's eyes, the hesitation in her voice. Maybe Meg was the reason Nat regretted their kiss. If that was so, she'd back off too.

Even as she made the silent vow, the thought of letting go cut deeper than she expected.

The soft knock on the cabin door jolted Vic into hastily pulling on the pale green lobster T-shirt, worn holey at the shoulders from years of being drenched in salt spray and dried in the merciless sun, over her damp skin. The fabric clung to her as she padded barefoot across the cabin to open the door.

Nat stood on the threshold, a red crockery bowl cradled in her hands. Her eyes widened, and Vic flushed. Great—she was half-dressed with no underwear on. The threadbare shirt and sagging sweatpants probably left little to the imagination.

"I, uh, brought you some oatmeal," Nat said, her voice slightly breathless. "Thought you could use something warm and filling."

Vic stepped aside, gesturing for Nat to enter. "Thanks. I really appreciate it."

As Nat brushed past her, Vic caught a whiff of her scent—evergreen and mountain laurel, with a hint of something tangy—distinctly Nat. It made her head swim, desire coiling hot and tight in her belly again.

Nat set the bowl on the small table, her hands trembling slightly, and turned to face Vic. "About earlier…"

Vic held up a hand. "No harm, no foul, Nat. It was a kiss." She sucked in a breath. Screw it. When had she ever shied away from saying what she felt? "One I very much enjoyed and would like to do again."

Nat stiffened. "I don't think that's a good idea."

Vic felt the punch in her solar plexus. So there it was. A very definite no. She nodded. "I understand."

Nat tilted her head. "Do you?"

"Meg?" Vic said.

"Meg?" Nat echoed. "No. I mean, probably not what you're thinking, anyhow. We *are* good friends. We're not in a relationship, but sometimes we…" She trailed off, shrugging. "But it's never been anything more than that."

"Right," Vic said, increasingly uncomfortable talking about Nat and Meg, a picture she preferred not to have in her mind. "Like I said, I understand."

"Okay," Nat said quietly. "That's good, then." She paused. "You do realize that I'm far too old for you."

Vic laughed. "I'm sorry, what?"

"Our age difference," Nat said stiffly. "That's reason enough to avoid a repeat of…whatever that was just now."

"Right, sure." Vic shook her head. Really? Nat couldn't come up with a better excuse to brush her off? "You don't need to give me a reason. A simple no is enough."

Nat's breath hitched, and for a long moment, she simply stared at Vic, an array of emotions playing across her face—surprise, uncertainty, and finally, a flicker of something that looked a lot like longing. "Good. That's—that's good."

Vic reached out for the bowl. "I should take that and let you get on with your day."

Nat stared at the bowl as if she didn't recognize it. "Of course. You'll probably want to get some sleep. You're not on duty again today, are you?"

"Backup," Vic said.

"Well, hopefully it will be quiet." Nat retreated toward the cabin door, reached back, and opened it. "Take care today."

"You too," Vic called as Nat stepped outside. "Be careful out there."

As Nat left, closing the door softly behind her, Vic sank onto the bed, the bowl of oatmeal resting on her thighs. Nat was right, there were probably a million reasons why getting involved was a bad idea. Number one being that Nat wasn't interested. And where Vic came from, no meant no.

Now all she had to do was convince her body—and, she very much feared, her heart—of that.

CHAPTER SEVEN

A t a few minutes to seven, Nat crested the last rise to the Thunder Ridge DEC camp, her spirits lifting as she breathed in the crisp morning air through her open windows. The lake shimmered below, a mirror of silver light catching the early sun's rays. Campers—seventeen-year-olds on the brink of adulthood spending what they probably didn't realize would be their last idyllic summer in the mountains—hurried up and down the hard-packed earth trail from the cluster of cabins above the lodge. They would be her official charges for the day.

Vic had been one of them, once.

She shouldn't be thinking about Vic—not here, not now.

Her focus was the kids. On the job.

On anything but the softness in Vic's eyes or the kiss that shouldn't have been. Their schedules had kept them from bumping into each other—or maybe Vic had just been avoiding her. Not that she could blame her.

Scowling, she pushed the memories away and parked near the firepit in front of the lodge. Her boots crunched softly on the pine needle–strewn path as she strode toward Sarah and Marty, waiting with clipboards in hand. Both wore long pants, hiking boots, and flannel shirts layered over T-shirts. Sarah's honey-brown hair was caught back in a ponytail, a few wispy strands escaping to frame her face, which was alight with her usual warm smile. Nat hadn't seen Marty since the previous summer, when Marty had been one of the campers themself. Since then, Marty had cut their sandy brown hair into the current side-fade, floppy-on-top style, had added a few pounds of what appeared to be muscle, and had lost the cautious reserved expression they'd often worn before. What a difference a year's time and some of the friendships Marty had forged at camp had made.

"Morning," Sarah called. "Ready for another day of imparting mountain lore and an appreciation for nature?"

Nat chuckled, the sound feeling thinner than usual. "As ready as I'll ever be. Though let's be honest—we're mostly here to make sure they don't get lost in the woods or become bear snacks."

Marty grinned, their confidence more apparent than it had been last summer. "Same difference, Evans."

"Marty. Good to see you back," Nat said. "We need experienced counselors who can step up and take charge."

Marty ducked their head but couldn't hide the pleased grin. "Thanks, Nat. I've learned from the best."

"How are Ford and Suwallia—are you still in touch?"

"Oh, sure." Marty blushed faintly at the mention of two of their camp mates from the summer before. "Ford is a Coastie cadet and loving it. Suwallia is trying out for the US national archery team this year."

"That's terrific," Nat said. That blush was interesting. Every place she looked she seemed to be noticing people connecting. Maybe she was just imagining it—projecting, more like it. "When you talk to them again, tell them I said good luck."

"Will do," Marty said, their eyes shining.

"How many this morning?" Nat asked.

"Eighteen," Sarah said, glancing at the call sheet. "Three groups—six for each of us."

"I guess Lily is still on leave?" Nat asked, referring to Sarah's sister-in-law, Dr. Lily Davenport, who had been the camp medic the previous summer.

"Mmm," Sarah said. "She's got a few weeks left on her maternity leave, but she says she wants to do a little part-time volunteering here starting next week. Timara Jones is our PA for the season." Sarah tilted her chin toward the trail. "That's her now."

The woman striding toward them was taller than average and athletically built, with light-tan skin and dark-brown hair worn in short braids. She moved with easy grace and confidence, and as she drew nearer, her striking amber eyes radiated warmth and intelligence.

"Nat, meet Timara," Sarah said as Timara reached them. "Timara, this is Natalie Evans, one of our senior rangers."

"Nice to meet you," Timara said, extending a hand. Her grip was firm and sure.

"Likewise," Nat replied with a smile. "First time at camp?"

Timara laughed, a rich, melodious sound. "At camp, yes. But I've done my share of wilderness firefighting training—I'm on leave from the Saugerties FD for the summer. I'm looking forward to getting to know this part of the Adirondacks better."

"Well, you've come to the right place," Nat said. "Thunder Ridge is a great introduction to the region. The trails and lakes here are some of my favorites in the park."

"I can see why," Timara said. "It's breathtaking. I feel lucky to get to spend the summer here."

"We're lucky to have you," Sarah said warmly. "We'll keep you busy, but hopefully not with anything more serious than the usual rashes, bug bites, and GI upsets."

"Sounds like fun." Timara grinned as Nat and the others laughed. She glanced toward the campers clustering around the firepit, their excited chatter filling the crisp morning air. "Looks like the troops are rallying. I better go introduce myself and let them know where to find me if they need me."

While Sarah and Nat reviewed the weather forecasts and the hike itinerary, Marty divided the campers into three groups. Nat scanned the eager young faces, anticipation surging for the day ahead. The wilderness called to her, its wonders waiting to be shared. Like most rangers, she enjoyed sharing her love and knowledge of the flora and fauna with the campers and visitors.

"How long have you been doing this?" Timara asked Nat as Sarah finished the last of the equipment checks.

"Feels like all my life." Nat laughed. "I'm a local, so the mountains have always been part of my life."

She paused. She rarely disclosed personal information, even with her closest friends, and Timara was just being friendly. Still she held back, unlike that first night with Vic when she'd shared more than she ever did with a virtual stranger. "They had day programs here when I was younger, and my mom worked a couple of jobs, so this place was a haven for me." She looked around. "I guess it still is."

Timara nodded. "I envy you. I grew up in the city, steaming sidewalks in the summer and public swimming pools that were always too crowded."

Finally organized, Sarah's group took the lead, the campers

filled with energy and enthusiasm that Nat suspected would wane by the end of the day. Still, their youthful energy was contagious, and she welcomed it. She needed something to clear her mind from the continuous thoughts of Vic. Thinking about *not* thinking about her didn't help either, so she focused her attention on her group.

The morning passed swiftly as they climbed the meandering trail, fields of wildflowers stretching out on either side. Nat pointed out various plants and signs of animals, using examples to discuss conservation and wilderness survival techniques along the way.

As they climbed higher, the trail became rockier and the trees thinner, affording them a view of Lake George stretching southward, hemmed in by the rugged peaks of the Tongue Mountain Range and the distant profile of Buck Mountain to the east, its slopes catching the midday sunlight. Nat never tired of the sight or the sense of awe at nature's splendor. When they reached a lookout point, she handed her binoculars to one of the campers in her group to pass around. Soon she was fielding questions about birds, berries, and boat rides, and remembering all over again why she loved her job.

"Thanks," she said as Jose, the self-appointed leader of her group, handed her back the binocs. Tall for his age but still carrying the lanky frame of someone not quite done growing, Jose adjusted his baseball cap with practiced ease. Quiet confidence set him apart, though his focus stayed on keeping the group organized rather than seeking attention. His sharp, inquisitive gaze took in everything—the rustle of leaves in the wind, a yellow warbler darting between low branches, a small white trillium petal peeking out between the stones. A neatly tied cord bracelet, its vibrant colors contrasting with his practical, well-worn hiking gear, stood out against his brown skin.

She absently scanned the lake, watching a sailboat tack against the wind. A flicker of movement caught her eye—a green and white Water Patrol boat skimming across the lake's surface just past Shelving Rock Point. Maybe that was Vic out there, and as soon as she thought of her, memories of their shared kiss sent heat rushing to her middle. Damn it.

No matter how hard she tried, she couldn't stop replaying that electrifying moment. The softness of Vic's lips, the way their bodies melded together as if they were always meant to... She shook her head, dispelling the distracting thoughts. Enough already.

The crackle of the radio jolted Nat from her reverie, and she tapped the call button. "Evans here, go ahead."

"Nat," said Lucy Brant, the dispatcher, "we're seeing a rapidly forming storm system heading your way. Gonna get heavy rain in a few minutes."

"Acknowledged," Nat said, scanning the sky as she waved Sarah over. The morning had been cloudless and bright when they'd set out, and the radar forecast clear for the whole day. But late spring and summer storms were unpredictable, and now the horizon was awash with angry gray clouds moving in fast. "Weather coming—heavy rain forecast."

Sarah's gaze met Nat's with a look of silent understanding. Heavy rain could mean flooding, mudslides, or a dozen other problems in the high country, and they had a mostly inexperienced group to guide out.

"Marty, start rounding up the kids," Sarah instructed, her voice calm but firm. "We need to get off this mountain before the weather turns."

"Let's take the southern trail back," Nat suggested. "It'll curve around Huckleberry Mountain and through thicker forest. We'll have better cover and less chance of a mudslide."

Sarah nodded, already beginning to herd the campers together. "Good plan. I'll take the lead with my group, you bring up the rear with yours?"

"Fine." Nat shouldered her backpack and took a quick head count. Her group included a few of the repeat campers—kids she hoped would stay calm if things got tough. "Marty, your group will follow Sarah's."

"Roger that," Marty said, turning to their campers. "Come on, crew, let's get moving."

Nat smiled briefly. Marty's father was a military guy, and Marty had all the markings of a kid brought up to be self-confident and reliable. Solid in an emergency, quick to follow directions, and highly responsible.

"How about me?" Timara asked quietly as the campers started back down the trail behind Sarah and Marty like a string of ducklings.

"Stay back with me," Nat murmured. "You can move forward if anyone gets injured up ahead."

"Got it," Timara said brightly.

They set off down the mountain, the chatter of the campers gradually fading as the first rumbles of thunder rolled across the peaks. Nat kept a close eye on the sky, urging the stragglers to keep pace.

But the storm moved faster than any of them anticipated. Rain lashed sideways in icy torrents, immediately soaking them all and turning the trail into a slick, treacherous slope. Mud sucked at their boots with each step, the footing growing worse by the minute.

A yelp sounded from up ahead, followed by a chorus of worried voices.

"Wait here," Nat said to her kids. "Timara, follow me."

She pushed forward, heart pounding as she caught sight of Sarah kneeling beside a fallen camper.

"She twisted an ankle," Sarah explained, helping the teen to her feet.

Nat searched her memory for a name. "Caitlin, right?"

"Yes," the blonde said, her lips trembling but her chin up, a defiant look in her eyes. She leaned on Sarah but appeared to be able to put weight on her foot. "I'm okay. Stupid root."

"Let's have Timara take a quick look anyhow," Nat said gently.

While Timara squatted to check Caitlin's ankle, carefully testing for signs of serious injury, Nat turned to Sarah and Marty, the storm roaring around them. "We can't risk anyone else getting hurt. This trail is already a mudslide waiting to happen."

"This could go on for a while, and the trails will only get worse. We can't sit it out up here," Marty pointed out, their expression calm. "What's our best alternative?"

"If we head down to the inlet," Nat said, raising her voice to be heard over the howling wind, "we can reach the shore and evacuate by boat."

"Are you talking about the old trail to Blueberry Pond?" Sarah sounded skeptical. "That hasn't been maintained since we were kids."

"All the better—the undergrowth will stabilize the mud. And the trial is passable—I hiked it just a few weeks ago."

Sarah nodded briskly. "Let's do it."

Nat reached for her radio, her fingers trembling slightly. "DEC dispatch, this is Evans. We're detouring down the southern slope of Randall's Peak to the inlet north of the Rockland Bay boat launch. Requesting Water Patrol and additional DEC units for evacuation, over."

The radio crackled to life. "Calling for backup now. What's your ETA?"

Nat let out a relieved breath. "Forty-five minutes."

"Roger that," Lucy said.

Nat glanced at Sarah. "Let's get these kids home."

❖

The Whaler leapt from one swell to the next on the whitecap-covered lake, visibility dropping by the second. The wind howled, slamming sheets of rain sideways.

"Storm's getting worse fast," Phee yelled against the wind and the whine of the engines. "Head back to port."

"Aye," Vic shouted, tugging her cap lower as rain and spray drenched her in a cold, relentless wall of water. Every wave struck the hull like a fist, and every second they stayed out risked flipping the boat entirely. "Course?"

"Make another sweep through the channel and down to Buzzard's Bay. Make sure no one else is out here."

"Aye, Chief." Vic set the coordinates and brought the Whaler about, its powerful engines roaring. Shaking water from her eyes, she squinted through the downpour, scanning the churning waters for any signs of stranded craft.

The radio crackled to life, and the dispatcher's voice cut through the storm. "DEC Dispatch to all units. Rangers report campers stranded on Huckleberry Mountain. Requesting immediate evacuation at the inlet north of Rockland Bay."

Phee's jaw tightened as she grabbed the radio. "WPU One responding. Changing course for Rockland Bay."

Several DEC units acknowledged, their responses faint over the interference of the storm.

"Setting course for Rockland Bay," Vic said, swallowing against the metallic taste of nerves, the cold dread that washed over her sharper than the icy rain. "Campers? From Thunder Ridge?"

"Most likely. Storm probably caught them off guard. Hug the shoreline," Phee directed. "We'll make better time."

"Aye."

Phee gripped the handrail as the Whaler surged in the roiling chop. "Dispatch, how many individuals are involved?"

"DEC Ranger Evans reports eighteen campers and three staff members," came the reply. "Injuries reported."

Vic stiffened, her grip on the wheel so tight her hands ached.

"Severity?" Phee asked.

Static filled the silence, then, "Unknown. Ranger Evans maintaining communication."

"That's not good," Phee muttered, peering into the icy rain as if she could part the storm clouds by willing it. "If they were minor, Nat would've said so."

Vic struggled to quelch the rising fear. Nat, up on that mountain in with eighteen kids. Unprotected in the vicious storm. God. Her chest constricted as worst-case scenarios tumbled in a dizzying array through her mind.

Nat was in danger. Every second counted.

"Hold on!" Vic shouted and gunned the throttle. Her heart pounded in time with the slap of the hull against the water, a roiling mix of fear and determination squeezing her chest.

The Whaler slammed through the churning waves, engines screaming. The wind shrieked, ripping at her jacket and hurling pellets of icy rain into her face.

"Stay on course, O'Brien," Phee called.

Vic cut as close to the shore as she dared. The storm raged on, dark clouds swirling in the sky, shrouding them in a gray curtain of chaos. Time slowed. The lake churned with choppy, white foam, but she held the shallow-hulled Whaler steady in the rough waters. Rain pounded against her skin, the cold droplets like tiny needles piercing her flesh. The wind whipped her hair around her face, the strands sticking to her cheeks as she struggled to keep the craft on course.

Her thoughts churned with turbulence as wild as the storm: Images of Nat and the others in danger on the treacherous mountainside, injured or worse. The same Nat who had awakened unexpected feelings more intense than she'd ever known. Feelings she had to keep at bay now so she could do her job—when Nat and the others depended on her.

"They'll be okay. They'll be okay," she whispered, her words lost on the wind.

Phee radioed dispatch, the communication barely audible through the static. "DEC Dispatch, WPU One on approach to Rockland Bay. Status of Evans and the campers? Over."

"Evans reports they're descending now, over."

"ETA?"

"Unknown."

The shoreline appeared, a dark, jagged line against the storm-tossed lake. Vic scanned it for any sign of the stranded campers. Rain lashed her face, droplets clinging to her lashes. The small crescent of beach was empty, no sign of the bright orange rain ponchos or huddled forms she so desperately hoped to see.

"They're not here," she yelled, panic threatening to rise in her throat.

A second WPU boat arrived, its lights slicing through the rain as it slowed to idle nearby. A DEC craft followed moments later, the crew exchanging quick hand signals with Phee.

"I'm going to put in to shore," Vic said, angling the Whaler toward land. "They can't be too far away unless there's trouble."

"Hold position." Phee shot out a hand, gripping Vic's shoulder. "Nobody knows these mountains better than Nat. She'll get them here."

Vic clenched her jaw, the instinct to act clawing at her. "What if the trail's blocked? Or someone's hurt?" Her voice cracked despite her best efforts. "We've got rescue gear. We could send a team up—"

Phee's gaze softened. "Nat's a seasoned mountaineer, Vic. She'll bring them down when it's safe. We have to trust her."

Trust. The word hung heavy in the air, laden with unspoken meaning. Vic knew Phee was right, knew that charging blindly into the wilderness would only put more lives at risk. But the thought of leaving Nat out there, facing the storm alone…it twisted like a knife in her gut.

Vic drew in a shuddering breath. "Aye."

The word tasted like defeat on her tongue.

The minutes crawled by, each one feeling like an hour. The sky darkened to an ominous black. The lake swelled, whitecaps breaking against the hull with a deafening roar. Vic gritted her teeth, her chest tight with the effort to stay still. Every shadow on the shore, every flicker of light, sent her heart racing—only for it to plummet when the beach remained empty.

The radio buzzed again, faint but clear this time. "Evans to all units—approaching shore. Two staff injured, possible concussion. Requesting medics."

Vic's breath hitched, her hands locking around the wheel until her knuckles blanched. A concussion. *Could be anyone—but what if it's Nat?*

"She'll make it," Phee said beside her, voice low but steady, reading the fear etched across Vic's face without needing to ask.

Vic forced a nod, fighting the need to be doing something. "We need to be ready."

"Already are."

"Hold on, Nat," Vic whispered, throat raw with the effort to keep her voice steady. "I'm here. Just hold on."

She turned back to the shore, willing Nat to appear, Phee standing silent watch beside her.

And waited.

CHAPTER EIGHT

Nat shook her head, droplets flying from her soaked hair. The biting chill seeped into her waterlogged uniform, but she gritted her teeth and pushed onward through the driving rain. Each breath burned in her lungs, her legs heavy with exhaustion, but stopping wasn't an option.

One step at a time. One step closer to getting everyone home safe.

On a normal day, they'd make the shore in another twenty minutes. But today was anything but normal. Visibility was nonexistent, and the ominous gray sky pressed down like a suffocating blanket. Wind rattled the trees, sending branches crashing to the muddy ground.

Nat squinted against the stinging rain, trying to make out the trail ahead. Thunder cracked, reverberating along her ribs, jangling her nerves. She looked over her shoulder, doing a head count, relief warring with worry. All still accounted for. The campers followed like shadows—silent, soaked, scared. At least their rain ponchos provided some protection, but the storm was unrelenting, each gust slicing into their resolve.

Every one of them watched her. Waiting for reassurance.

Every one counting on her.

"You're doing great, everyone! Stick together. We're almost there," Nat called over the screaming wind. In the back of her mind, a different voice whispered. *Where is Vic? Did she make it to the inlet? Is she safe? Will she be there, waiting?*

"We're good," Jose shouted. He looked pale from cold and probably a good dose of fear, but his voice was strong and determined. Others in the group echoed his determination.

"Won't be long now, and you'll be riding home!" Nat scrubbed water from her face and checked for some sign that the clouds were lifting. Leading them on this trail had been her decision, and she didn't regret it, but the narrow path turned slicker and more treacherous with every passing second. She slipped on the muddy slope and threw out a hand to catch herself on a tree trunk. "Watch your step along here. Take it slow."

For a second, Nat wondered if the evac craft had made it through the rough waters to the inlet yet. Her team would be there, she trusted. And Vic and the sheriff's unit would be too. All she had to do was get everyone the rest of the way down. Her chest tightened as she pictured Vic waiting at the shoreline, her expression steady but ready. The swift flood of comfort surprised her.

The monotony of putting one foot in front of the other numbed her senses until a piercing cry cut through the relentless drumbeat of rain. Her heart lurched. Just ahead, a gangly teen lost his footing on the slick incline. Arms pinwheeling, he pitched forward, his yell of alarm swallowed by another crash of thunder.

"Denzel!" Nat shouted, rushing forward.

Ahead of her, Timara lunged and grabbed a fistful of his sweatshirt. She twisted, wrenching him back from the sharp drop-off, but the force of the motion dragged her down. They hit the ground hard, sliding through mud and jagged roots. The boy scrambled to his knees, but Timara lay still.

"Timara!" Nat hurried to reach them, her pulse pounding in her ears. Blood streaked through Timara's rain-soaked hair as she pressed her hand to her temple. "Lie still. Don't move."

Timara blinked up at her, her eyes glassy. "Ow. Damn it. Hit my head on something."

She struggled to sit up.

"Stop." Nat put a hand on her shoulder. "Let me get a look."

"I'm fine," Timara muttered, still struggling to rise.

"You're not fine. Stay down. Let me check."

Campers crowded around, and Marty, always the first to take charge in a crisis, said, "Everyone keep to the trail. Single file, remember?"

"I'm okay," Timara mumbled. "What about Denzel? Is he alright?"

Denzel hovered nearby, his eyes wide and guilty. "I…I'm so sorry! I didn't mean to—"

"It's alright. Not your fault." Nat kept a steadying hand on

Timara's shoulder. "You did good, Jones. Probably kept him from breaking something. Now…" She held up three fingers. "How many?"

"Three. Let me up."

"Not yet. Any pain anywhere besides your head? Any double vision?"

"No. Damn it. I'm okay. My ass is wet, though." Timara batted at Nat's hands halfheartedly. "I'm fine, Nat, really. We need to keep moving."

"The only place you're moving is over to that boulder so I can clean and dress this properly." Nat used her command voice, but it had no effect. She would have been as stubborn in Timara's place, but she wasn't giving in. "I don't have to tell you how much scalp wounds bleed. I need to make sure it's not too deep."

"Fine." Grumbling, Timara allowed Nat to help her up and guide her to a relatively sheltered spot beneath an overhanging ledge. "We can't keep them waiting in this, though."

Nat surveyed the pale faces as they huddled miserably nearby. She motioned to Sarah. "You and Marty divide up our group between you and keep going. We'll follow as soon as we can."

Sarah hesitated, then nodded. "Alright. When we reach the inlet, we'll send a rescue team back for you."

Nat shook her head. "Radio me when you have everyone secured, and I'll update you on our status. I don't want a team venturing back up the mountain if we can make it down on our own."

"Alright. Be careful."

Nat squeezed her arm. "You too. Go, we're good here."

Sarah led the campers off, and Nat pulled out a first aid kit and set to work cleaning the laceration with antiseptic wipes. Timara flinched, her jaw set, but she stayed still as Nat worked.

"Sorry about this," Timara muttered.

"You probably saved that kid's life," Nat said quietly, dabbing the blood away. The cut wasn't deep, but scalp wounds always looked worse than they were. "This isn't too bad."

"I told you that," Timara said testily. Her muscles tightened with tension, along with barely leashed frustration as she gritted her teeth.

Nat smiled. "Medics are the worst patients. Hold still."

Timara sighed but obediently tipped her head forward while Nat applied a gauze pad and bandage. Eventually, her breathing eased, and the tension in her rigid shoulders unwound.

"There," Nat said, squeezing Timara's shoulder gently. "All set. How's your vision? Still okay? No dizziness or nausea?"

"No, I'm good." Timara reached up to touch the bandage gingerly. "Bit of a headache, but that's to be expected."

Nat nodded, satisfied. "We'll keep an eye on it. The second you start feeling worse, you let me know, got it?"

"Yes, ma'am." Timara grinned. "Bossy."

Despite the circumstances, Nat couldn't help but smile. If Timara was well enough to snark at her, she'd be just fine. And she knew, with absolute certainty, that Vic was out there somewhere along with her rangers, waiting for her.

"I'm good to go," Timara said.

"Then we're going to take it slow." Nat gripped Timara's arm and stepped back out into the raging storm.

Every blast of wind threatened to unbalance them. Every step was a challenge. They'd make it—no choice. Vic would just have to hold on a little longer.

❖

"Water Patrol, this is DEC Command. Do you copy?"

The communication over the open channel startled Vic from her restless pacing, her boots leaving muddy circles in the tight confines of the Whaler's cockpit.

"WPU One responding, over," Phee said.

"The campers are descending the ridge trail. ETA to the trailhead approximately twenty minutes. Be advised, injured parties remain on the mountain at this time. Over."

Injured still on the mountain.

A cold hand squeezed Vic's throat. Was Nat one of them? She snatched up the radio handset.

"Dispatch, this is O'Brien. What's the status of the injured? Do we have details? Over."

"Negative, O'Brien. No further intel at this time. Stand by."

Stand by. The words grated against every nerve.

Vic slammed her palm against the rail, the metallic thud swallowed by the howl of the wind. Her thoughts spiraled—Nat hurt, Nat stranded, Nat bleeding out in the mud while they waited down here like they had all the time in the world.

"I can take a team to shore in the raft and head up the trail to meet them," she said abruptly, turning to Phee. "If they're bringing wounded down, they'll need help."

"Absolutely not." Phee's tone was sharp as steel. "We're the evac team. Fastest boat, most medical supplies. We're here to pull them out, not charge off and risk more injuries."

"But—"

"Look, I get it. I know you're worried about her. I am too. Nat knows what she's doing out there. The best thing we can do is be ready for them the second they reach us."

"Aye, Chief," Vic said, the sharp taste of bile rising in her throat.

Nat wouldn't want her to endanger any of the campers or staff by making a reckless decision either. The words scraped out like broken glass, but orders were orders. And Phee was right. Their duty was clear.

But as she resumed pacing, she whispered into the face of the storm, "We're here. We're waiting. I'm waiting."

❖

The wind howled over the lake like a wounded animal, its keening cry rattling through the hull of the Whaler. The minutes crawled by with agonizing slowness. Vic scanned the trailhead again, her gaze sweeping over the drenched shoreline. Every shadow looked like Nat. Every flicker of movement set her pulse skittering. The rain slid in cold streams down her neck, soaking her through the slicker, but she barely noticed. Her heartbeat thudded against her ribs—an endless, merciless reminder of time slipping away.

Beside her, Phee worked with calm precision, checking their gear and prepping the boat for a fast evac. Vic envied her focus, but she couldn't shake the hollow dread gnawing at her. She'd faced plenty of emergencies at sea, from sudden storms that tossed their boat like a toy to engine failures that left them drifting for hours. She'd seen fires break out on deck, threatening to engulf the whole vessel, and crewmen suffer grisly injuries that required makeshift first aid until they could reach port. All of it had taught her to stay levelheaded.

But this wasn't like a storm at sea with her father. Back then, she could act. Here, she was stuck—waiting, helpless. That was Nat out there, and here *she* was—stuck. Doing nothing.

"They'll be here soon," Phee said, her voice low but steady. "Nat's one of the best. She'll get them through this."

Vic nodded, not trusting herself to speak. Telling herself that over and over hadn't helped yet. She reached inward for the fortitude her father had taught her.

Rely on your skill, Victory. Trust your mates. You know how to handle anything the ocean can throw at you. Believe me.

She missed him in that moment, fiercely. But his words, his lessons, grounded her now. Nat, all of them, needed her focused. That was her job.

A flash of orange—

"There," Juanita shouted, pointing toward shore.

Vic's breath caught. A figure emerged from the tree line, and an instant later, another bedraggled figure stumbled out of the underbrush. Followed by another, and another.

More campers staggered out, led by a woman directing them toward the shore. A woman who wasn't Nat.

The ball of worry in Vic's middle mushroomed.

"Told you they'd make it," Phee said, relief flickering in her eyes. "Bring us in. Smooth and steady."

"Aye." Vic tightened her grip on the throttle, eased it forward. Every instinct screamed to rush, but now was the moment for precision. For control.

We're coming for you, Nat.

In the few minutes it took to steer the Whaler safely into the shallows, the group on shore grew. Vic anchored the craft and headed for the portable raft.

"I'm going," Vic said and jumped into the raft with Juanita.

Milt already had the outboard running and opened the throttle. Other craft made for shore from the DEC boats. Vic searched the growing crowd on the narrow spit of sand for Nat. Where was she?

As soon as they touched land, she jumped out into the knee-deep surf and waded ashore, heading straight for the woman in charge.

"I'm Deputy O'Brien," she said as the woman turned weary eyes to her. "We have reports of injuries."

"Yes," the woman said, wiping rain from her face. "I'm Sarah Fielder, the camp director. Our PA, Timara Jones, took a fall on the way down. Hit her head pretty hard. Nat Evans…DEC Evans stayed behind to make sure she was okay to continue."

Vic's stomach unclenched slightly. Nat wasn't hurt, but she was still out there. A mix of pride and fear warred within her. Of course Nat would put the campers and staff first, even at her own risk. That sense of duty was one of the many things Vic admired about her, but right now, it only fueled her anxiety.

"How far behind are they?"

Sarah shook her head. "Hard to say. If they left quickly, they should be right behind us. I've tried radioing them, but I can't get any reception."

Vic nodded, her mind racing. Minutes were like hours in this weather. She searched the trailhead. No activity now. She took a breath, motioned to the waiting rafts bobbing in the surf.

"Let's get these kids loaded up. The injured and anyone with signs of hypothermia get priority seating on the Whaler. We've got blankets and first aid supplies on board."

Sarah nodded. "Okay, you heard her. Marty, anyone needing immediate attention goes first."

While the rangers and deputies herded the shivering campers into the boats, Vic radioed Phee. "The main group has reached the shore, but DEC Evans and PA Jones are still on the ridge. Jones sustained a head injury. Requesting permission to head up the trail with the rescue team to assist. Over."

Static crackled for a moment before the response came through. "Negative, O'Brien. As soon as the Whaler is loaded, we make for port. Over."

Trust your mates, Victory, her dad would say.

Vic gritted her teeth, squeezing the radio until her fingers ached. Every instinct screamed at her to ignore the command, to charge up that trail and find Nat.

But she knew her duty.

A captain never abandoned their crew. She wouldn't abandon hers.

"Copy that. O'Brien out." She clipped the radio back to her belt and turned to help usher the remaining campers to the boats.

They worked quickly, the wind still whipping the waves into a foaming froth. When they had the campers secured on deck, supplied with water and protein bars, and wrapped in thermal blankets, Vic got behind the wheel. She looked once toward the shore as she powered up the Whaler and charted the course to port.

The search team had already headed up the mountain. The beach was empty.

CHAPTER NINE

Vic maneuvered the Whaler up to the pier where EMTs, moving briskly in the biting wind and relentless rain, readied stretchers and thermal blankets. Medics carrying supplies and shouting instructions hurried in and out of treatment tents set up along the shore, their canvas sides flapping in the gusts, slicing through the gloom like jagged blades. The chaotic pulse of color reflected off the slick wood, turning every surface into a frantic blur of motion and sound.

Vic's stomach clenched, the scene mirroring the storm still raging inside her. The sharp tang of diesel fumes burned her throat, mingling with the earthy scent of rain-soaked wood. The metallic whine of stretcher wheels against the slick planks reverberated in her head—a dissonant chorus sharp as knives. She cut the engine and leapt onto the dock, grabbed the mooring line, and secured the craft with quick, practiced movements, the icy wind biting through her jacket. Her hands shook as she tightened the knots, the chill cutting deeper than the cold could account for.

Once the boat was anchored, she helped the campers disembark one by one, murmuring reassurances as they stumbled onto the dock. A teenage girl leaned heavily on one of the EMTs as he helped her up the pier over the slick wood. Another boy, still soaked despite his rain poncho, clutched his phone tightly, the screen casting a faint glow on his shivering hands. The air buzzed with fragmented questions, the occasional sob, and the distant drone of another boat approaching.

Are we going back to camp now?

When will we get something to eat?

Why are there medics everywhere?

The questions were as relentless as the rain.

"We just want to check you all out," Vic told them. "Everything's going to be alright. You'll be back at camp by dinnertime."

While their anxiety evaporated like mist now that they were safe and the excitement of their adventure surfaced, her unease grew.

Where was Nat?

The radio crackled.

"Another DEC boat inbound with more campers," Phee reported.

Vic scanned the incoming boat for any sign of Nat. No Nat. Her heart thudded, heavy and relentless, a cold knot in her chest.

Vic strode down the pier to meet the new wave of campers stumbling onto the dock. She intercepted Sarah, who had just disembarked with the second group.

"Any sign of Nat and Timara?"

Sarah shook her head. "Nothing yet. The last transmission said they were close, but no updates since."

"Close." Vic bit down hard on the word. Close wasn't enough. Close didn't mean safe. Her nails bit into her palms. The knot in her chest tightened. Every passing second felt like a crack deepening across fragile glass—one more second and the whole world would shatter.

Sarah must have heard something in her voice. Her expression softened. "My sister is leading the rescue team. I expect to hear—"

She broke off as a transmission crackled over her radio.

"Sarah, it's Chase. We have them. ETA to inlet twenty minutes."

"Status?"

"Mild hypothermia. Closed head injury. ER transport standing by at Bolton."

"Acknowledged," Sarah said curtly. "See that they go."

"Do my best. Will advise."

"Be careful," Sarah murmured as the radio went silent. She turned to Vic. "You heard?"

Vic nodded, fisting her hands. Twenty more minutes of waiting. Of wondering. "How serious does it sound?"

"Hypothermia is to be expected after a few hours out in this—but I know Nat. She's not going to want to go to the ER."

Phee appeared at Vic's side, her brow furrowed with concern. "Any word?"

Sarah repeated Chase's update and asked, "How are the kids?"

"All fine and busy texting all their friends about their big day."

"Great," Sarah sighed. "I can't wait for the calls to start from all

the parents. I'd better go check on them and get them back to camp."
She glanced at Vic. "Sorry, I don't remember your name."

"Vic O'Brien," Vic said, her throat tight. Everyone was so calm.
Why were her nerves on fire? Why did she feel about to jump out of her
skin? Why the hell couldn't she do anything but stand around?

"Thanks for everything, Deputy O'Brien, Phee," Sarah said and
hurried away.

"I'm sure they're okay." Phee *sounded* sure, but her eyes still
looked worried. "Some warm fluids and dry clothes will take care of
things."

"Right, I know." Vic scanned the lake again for a sign of the white
boat emblazoned with the green and yellow DEC logo. "Where will
they take them?"

"Warrensburg is closest. Not far from headquarters on Route 9."

"Right." On impulse, she blurted, "The kids are all taken care of.
Can you cover for me? Nat will need a ride home—I thought I could
meet her at the ER."

Phee gave her a curious look, her eyebrows raised slightly. "I
didn't realize the two of you were…close."

Vic shrugged, trying to appear nonchalant. "We're friendly, and
we live at the same place. It just makes sense for me to take her home,
that's all."

Phee's expression remained skeptical, but she nodded slowly.
"We're good here, and your shift is long over. Go ahead. Take the Jeep.
I'll grab a ride back with Milt."

"Thanks," Vic said, flooded with relief. Finally she could do what
she'd been aching to do for hours. Go find Nat. "I owe you one."

"More than one," Phee said with a teasing smile as she tossed Vic
the keys to the department vehicle. "Do me a favor and let me know
how they are."

"Will do." With a quick wave, Vic jogged up the dock and hurried
toward the lot where they'd left the Jeep. Had that only been that
morning? The hours of anxious waiting broken by moments of frenzied
action made the day feel like a week.

The drive seemed to take forever, every winding turn on the rain-
slick roads conspiring to slow her progress. By the time she pulled into
the hospital parking lot, her nerves were strung so tight she was ready to
snap at the next person who told her she'd just have to wait. She hurried
through the automatic doors, the smell of antiseptic and the cacophony

of urgent voices hitting her like a caustic wave. The admitting area was filled with ER staff and first responders, all seeming to shout at once.

No Nat.

She stopped an ER tech who was passing by, a big, blond guy in scrubs adorned with colorful fish. His name tag read Sandy Tolliver, RN. "Can you tell me where the DEC rangers are being looked at?"

"Not here yet," he replied laconically and tilted his shaggy head toward a row of orange plastic chairs. "You can wait over there."

Wait.

Vic clenched her jaws. Not his fault. Don't take his head off. "Thanks."

She paced, trying to avoid the hive of activity as ambulances arrived with flashing lights and medical staff rushed to and fro. Her hands itched with the need to do something, to act—but there was nothing to do except wait.

Finally, the double doors whooshed open, and Nat appeared, a thermal blanket draped her shoulders. Exhausted but whole.

"Nat!" Vic hurried toward her, every step accelerating until she was running.

❖

Nat's pulse skipped a beat when she saw Vic, standing out in the chaos of the ER like a beacon. Despite the glaring lights, the people rushing everywhere, and the cacophony of shouts and beeping, blaring equipment, for a heartbeat, everything else disappeared. Leaving only Vic.

Nat hurried toward her, her exhaustion dropping away. Vic was here, safe and sound—and looking at her as if she was the only one in the room. Vic grabbed her shoulders and pulled her into a fierce embrace, and the tension of the last hours melted away. Vic's solid warmth was a welcome anchor in the chaos. Giving in to the rare pleasure of just being held, she leaned in, letting the contact soothe her frayed nerves.

An ER tech called out Timara's name, and reality erased Nat's brief escape. She gently pulled back, resting her hands on Vic's forearms.

"Why are you here?" Nat asked. "What about everyone else? Sarah and Marty and the kids?"

"All safe," Vic said.

The weight in Nat's chest lifted, just enough to let her breathe fully for the first time since the storm began. Timara was being cared for, and the others were out of danger. "Thank goodness."

"What about you? Are you hurt?" Vic's sharp gaze scanned her face, her voice low and tight. "Nat? Are you hurt?"

"I'm okay. Really." Nat tried to summon her usual easy smile, but the concern etched in Vic's expression shook her deeper than she wanted to admit. "Just some minor wear and tear."

"You need to get checked out too." Vic grasped Nat's arm. "Come on—we'll find someone to look at you."

"I don't need—"

A sandy-haired ranger appeared, still wearing a headlamp and with climbing gear dangling from her chest harness. She clamped a hand on Nat's shoulder. "Yes, you do. No way am I facing my sister if I let you skip out on the medical clearance."

"She's right," Vic said.

The ranger held out a hand to Vic. "Chase Fielder. You one of the new deputies?"

"Yep. Vic O'Brien. Water Patrol."

"Oh yeah—I watched you bring the Whaler into shore," Chase said. "Pretty piloting in that chop." She glanced at Nat, her brow raised.

"Thanks—so, uh, Nat?" Vic said, her focus never leaving Nat. "You want to go on back? I think you're expected."

"Outnumbered here," Nat muttered, secretly touched that Vic had been waiting for her. Of course, that was just Vic doing her job, right? Checking on everyone. Of course. Just the same, she didn't argue, letting Vic guide her toward the nearest exam room—surprised by how much she wanted to lean on her. "I might as well. I want to get out of here so I can check on the campers."

"I'll drive you up to Thunder Ridge when you're ready," Chase said.

"Oh," Nat said, "you shouldn't hang around here. Go home, get a warm shower, and play with your baby."

Chase's face ignited with a blazing smile. "The kid is four months old. He doesn't do much except eat and…well, you know."

Nat squeezed Chase's arm. "You and the crew need to eat and take a break. I'll find a ride."

"I'll take you to the camp," Vic said.

Nat shook her head. "No, you won't. How long were you out on that boat waiting for us?"

"A little lake run in the rain is nothing compared to a nor'easter in the mid-Atlantic. I'm staying," Vic said flatly, looking from Nat to Chase as if expecting someone to argue.

"I'm out of here, then," Chase said, retreating hastily.

Nat sighed. "Well, the sooner someone tells me I'm fine, which I already know, the sooner we can all get warm, dry, and fed."

"Sandy?" Vic called to the tech as he passed by. "DEC Evans needs to be checked out."

"Right. Follow me." He led them down a hallway and pulled back a curtain on an exam room. "Someone will be down to check you out in a few minutes."

"Thanks," Nat said. "Can you tell me if Timara Jones has been seen yet? I'm the one who treated her in the field—scalp laceration, possible exposure?"

"I think so. I'll see if I can get an update."

"Appreciate it." He left, pulling the curtain closed behind him. Vic's drawn features made Nat's exhaustion a distant worry. "You look beat."

Vic grimaced and tugged her already tousled hair. "Seriously, I've been through a lot worse. Of course, I didn't have twenty people wandering around a mountainside in a flood to worry about."

Nat couldn't stop staring. How could anyone obviously exhausted, cold, and definitely in need of clean, dry clothes look so damn sexy? Why had she never seen a woman who captured her interest like Vic before now—when the timing was terrible, and she'd long decided against risking her safe, secure life for, what, excitement? Hardly. Sex? She stifled that thought. Looking was allowed. Touching? That was a no. "We weren't really in serious trouble. I'm sorry we put all of you in a miserable situation."

"That's what we're all here for, right? I was pretty worried there for a while," Vic said softly. "When they said you were still out there, and then the radio call about hypothermia and head injuries…" She coughed and looked away, as if the admission cost her something. "I just needed to see for myself that you were okay."

Nat swallowed around the lump in her throat, ignoring the warmth flooding her face. Vic was just doing her job, but the way Vic looked at her—raw and unguarded—made it hard to believe that was all it was. The fierceness in Vic's gaze stirred her as no one ever had, not even Megan.

"I'm okay, Vic." She touched Vic's hand. "Cold and tired, but okay. You didn't need to come all the way out here."

Vic's fingers tightened around hers, and she took a step closer until the heat radiating off Vic's body somehow warmed hers.

"Yes, I did," Vic said, quietly but firmly. "I needed to be here."

Nat's breath caught, the tenderness in Vic's tone urging her to sink into Vic's arms again for a few more minutes of comfort. A lifetime of caution and self-reliance held her back, such intensity too foreign, too unfamiliar—and more than a little unsettling.

Gently, Nat withdrew her hand from Vic's grasp, trying to ignore the flash of hurt that darkened Vic's eyes.

"Thank you for being here," she said softly, her voice not quite steady. "It means a lot to me, truly. But you don't have to stay. I'm sure you're exhausted too, and—"

"I'm not going anywhere," Vic interrupted, her jaw set in that stubborn line that Nat was coming to recognize—and, secretly, like. "Not until I know for sure that you're alright."

Nat started to protest, but the words died on her tongue when Vic brushed a stray lock of damp hair from her forehead. Her fingertips lingered, the unexpected gesture warming her in places she hadn't realized she was cold. She leaned into the touch without meaning to, craving more. Vic always seemed to have her craving more of exactly the things she'd determined not to want.

"Vic…" Nat whispered.

Vic's gaze dropped to Nat's lips, and for a breathless moment, Nat was certain Vic was going to kiss her right there in the middle of the ER. She wanted to pull away, to put some distance between them before she said or did something foolish, like giving in to another kiss that shouldn't be. But she couldn't move. Time hung suspended, the world narrowing to the desire in Vic's eyes and the tenderness of her touch.

Nat struggled to escape the mesmerizing pull. "I don't—"

The curtain rustled, and they sprang apart. A middle-aged, brown-skinned man with deeply lined cheeks and tired, puffy eyes entered wearing a pristine white coat and carrying a tablet. He surveyed them with a mix of friendliness and concern. One glance at the tablet, then from Nat to Vic.

"DEC Evans? I'm Dr. Patel."

"That's me." Nat held out her hand, trying to vanquish the ghost of Vic's touch that lingered on her skin.

The doctor's grip was warm and firm. "I understand you were part of the rescue team today?"

"Yes, that's right."

"Out in the weather awhile, were you?"

Nat laughed shortly. "Felt like forever out there. But we got everyone back safely, so that's what matters. Have you examined Timara Jones yet? Is she okay?"

"I believe one of the other staff is with her now." Dr. Patel gestured to the stretcher covered with a sheet and a folded blanket at the foot. "Now, let's have a look at you and make sure *you* didn't suffer any ill effects from your adventure, shall we?"

Nat sighed but nodded. No point in arguing. She sat on the edge of the stretcher as the doctor reviewed her vitals and asked the usual barrage of questions. She couldn't help but sneak glances at Vic, who hovered nearby, her expression a mix of concern and something else Nat couldn't quite decipher. Protectiveness? Possessiveness? No, now she *was* just projecting.

Wishful thinking or not, she liked it—liked Vic's stubborn attentiveness.

Having Vic here, knowing she'd rushed to the hospital just to check on her, sent a warm flutter through her chest. Being cared for in quite this way was strange and unfamiliar. She'd grown so used to being the one to take care of everyone else, always putting her own needs last, that Vic's singular attention left her feeling off-balance. She couldn't fault the people in her life, though. She had developed the walls that kept everyone, including Meg, at arm's length. Until now, she hadn't let herself feel the loneliness.

Dr. Patel finished his exam and stepped back, looking relaxed for the first time. "Everything looks good. Your temp is a little low, but that's to be expected given the conditions you were in. I'd like you to go home, take a hot shower, and get some rest. If you develop any new symptoms—headache, dizziness, confusion—come back."

"Of course," Nat said, hopping down from the stretcher. "Thank you."

As the doctor left, Nat smiled at Vic. "Satisfied? Now, can we find Timara and hopefully get the hell out of here? I want to get back to Thunder Ridge."

"What part of *go home, get a hot shower, and rest* didn't you hear?" Vic's tone held just a touch of teasing, though her gaze was serious.

Nat raised a brow. "You're pretty stubborn, Deputy O'Brien. A bit on the bossy side too."

Vic grinned. "You have no idea."

"I'm beginning to get the picture." Nat laughed softly and shook her head. The pictures she was getting at the moment weren't any she wanted to entertain in the middle of the ER. Or possibly anywhere. Every time she caught Vic studying her when Vic thought she wasn't looking, her heart raced and tension coiled deep inside. This *thing* she had for Vic, this magnetic pull she couldn't explain or escape, as if some invisible force was drawing her in, eroding her defenses bit by bit, was exhilarating. And unnerving. All she could think about was kissing her again.

And…no.

"Come on." Nat pushed curtains aside. "Let's find Timara."

As if conjured, Timara, a series of Steri-strips covering a long line on her left temple, stepped out of a cubicle across the hall. When she saw Nat, she said hastily, "Please get me out of here."

"We're on it." Grabbing her hand, Nat headed toward the exit. "Timara Jones, Deputy Vic O'Brien. Vic's going to give us a ride back to the lodge."

"Thanks," Timara said.

"No problem," Vic said, triggering the automatic doors so they could all step out into the chilly evening.

The rain had finally stopped, leaving behind a damp, earthy scent that Nat found infinitely preferable to the antiseptic odor of the ER. She took a deep breath, and the last of the day's stress trickled away.

"How are you feeling?" Nat asked Timara as Vic hurried ahead to open the rear door of the Jeep.

"Headachy." Timara climbed into the back seat with a murmured thanks. "And hungry."

"That's a good sign." Nat squeezed her arm. "Stretch out and rest. I'll sit up front."

The drive back to Thunder Ridge was quiet, the silence broken only by the steady thrum of the engine and the occasional swish of the wipers clearing away the last traces of rain. Nat leaned her head back against the seat, exhausted but acutely aware of Vic beside her. The next thing she knew, Vic was gently shaking her awake.

"Nat? We're here."

Nat blinked, momentarily disoriented before the familiar lodge came into view. "Oh. Sorry." She turned to check on Timara, who yawned as she straightened up in the back seat. "I guess we both went to sleep on you."

Vic laughed. "Can't imagine why you're tired."

Vic was already out of the Jeep and coming around to Nat's side, offering a steadying hand as Nat clambered down. The warmth of Vic's hand could easily become addicting. Nat abruptly withdrew her hand and turned to help Timara out of the rear seat.

"Where's your cabin?" Nat asked Timara.

"Up that big-ass hill behind the lodge," Timara said with a sigh.

Nat laughed. "I bet we can find you a room in the lodge tonight. Besides, you shouldn't sleep way up there alone."

Timara gave a surprisingly spirited laugh. "You offering?"

Vic coughed lightly. "I don't think—"

"I'm flattered," Nat said, "but I'm afraid the only thing you should be doing tonight is sleeping."

"Story of my life," Timara muttered.

Vic laughed, and Nat smiled at her. "If you want to go—"

"Nope," Vic said, calmly cutting her off with a small shake of her head. "I'm not leaving until you are."

Strangely, Nat didn't mind Vic taking charge at all. If she hadn't been so damn tired, she might have been more worried by that. Instead, just this once, she embraced the simple comfort of letting someone care for her.

CHAPTER TEN

"You'll be more comfortable here tonight than trekking back up that hill," Nat said when she settled Timara into one of the spare rooms upstairs in the lodge. She retrieved an extra blanket from the chest at the foot of the bed and draped it over the bottom of the bed. "It's chilly up here at night."

"Tell me about it. You should try sleeping in the cabins. Thermal underwear recommended."

Nat laughed. "I'll take your word for it."

Timara leaned back against the headboard, her gaze tired but a glimmer of her usual good humor breaking through. "Thanks for insisting I bunk here tonight. I really do feel fine, other than a headache, but I'm not sorry to skip that climb."

"You're welcome," Nat said softly. "If anything feels off— worsening headache, nausea, dizziness—you need to let Sarah know immediately."

Timara rolled her eyes. "Yes, ma'am." Then, tilting her head, she added, "So, about Deputy O'Brien. She's...interesting."

Nat stiffened, focusing a little too hard on adjusting the blanket. "Interesting?"

"Come on." Timara grinned. "She's hot. And she seemed pretty into you. I wouldn't have pegged you for the whole *tall, dark, and broody* type, but I can see the appeal."

"Timara," Nat warned, feeling the blush blooming.

"I'm just saying. First Sarah's sister looking like sex on legs, now this one. It's like all the gorgeous women suddenly decided to show up here."

"Chase, you may have noticed, is happily married—"

"Yep, off-limits. How about O'Brien, though?"

"I really couldn't say."

Timara made a humming sound. "So there's hope."

Nat shook her head, though her stomach twisted. "I think you need rest more than planning a campaign on available women."

Timara's lids fluttered, and she muttered, "Always tomorrow."

Closing the door gently, Nat paused in the hallway, her pulse racing. Timara was right. Vic was attractive and beyond sexy. Quiet strength and steadfastness made her all the more appealing. And the way Vic had looked at her earlier—like she was the only thing that mattered in the world? She'd never experienced that kind of intensity.

Nat shook her head and hurried downstairs. She didn't need this. Not now. She had the rest of the season ahead, time she'd be working with Vic, and that should be all she was thinking about. What she needed was to get home—to the quiet and safety and sanity she'd built there.

Campers gathered in groups throughout the lodge, excitedly recalling the events of the day for their friends who had missed the "fun."

"Have you seen Vic?" she asked Sarah, who came out of the kitchen with a tray of muffins.

"I think she's in the common room," Sarah said. "Is Timara okay?"

"She's alright, but I gave her strict orders to call you if she feels unwell."

"How about you? That was a rough patch up there today."

"Tired is all. I'm heading home."

"Go. Vic has been waiting, and you shouldn't drive down the mountain tonight." Sarah brushed her arm. "I'll take care of getting your vehicle down to you in the morning."

"Thanks."

Nat found Vic in the common room, holding a ceramic mug and leaning against the huge stone fireplace. Nat paused in the entryway, watching her as she chatted with Marty and one of the campers. As if feeling her attention, Vic looked her way.

Her slow smile struck a blaze in Nat's depths.

After a word to the others, Vic made her way over to Nat. "Timara okay?"

"All settled." Nat tilted her chin toward the gaggle of campers.

"They don't seem to have suffered any ill effects." She shook her head and laughed. "The resilience of youth."

Vic shrugged. "I think it's more because they never realized the danger, and if they did, they trusted you and the staff to take care of them."

Nat studied her. "That's the job. You'd have done the same."

"I know," Vic said, rubbing a hand over her face as if to erase an image she didn't want to see.

"So," Nat asked carefully, "were you so worried because you didn't think I could handle things out there?"

"What?" Vic stared. "No. Of course not. I just…" She grimaced. "I don't do so well waiting when I want to be doing. If I'd been up there on the mountain with you, I'd have been happier."

Nat laughed. "Don't be too upset when I tell you there was nothing you could have done up there with us—you were exactly where you needed to be."

Vic scowled. "I can't argue. I'll feel better when I take you home, like I've done something."

"Oh," Nat said softly. "You've been invaluable all day long."

"I'll drive you home, then," Vic said tightly.

"Vic," Nat said, sensing Vic struggling with more than just the stress of the evacuation operation. "Are you okay?"

For a moment she thought Vic wouldn't answer. Then, on a long exhale, Vic said, "I don't want to lose anyone else I care about."

Stunned, Nat gripped her hand. "That means more than I can say."

Vic squeezed her fingers. "Come on. Let's go home."

❖

The moon rose just as Vic started down the mountain. The sky through a break in the trees was a velvet backdrop studded with stars, a reminder of nights spent on the open ocean, far from any shore. Out there, the stars had seemed close enough to touch, the black expanse of the sea melding seamlessly with the endless sky. She'd felt small then, insignificant against the vastness of the universe. But she'd also felt free, knowing she could follow the fish or turn back to try again another day. She and her father decided their own fate.

"Sailor's moon, we used to call it," Vic murmured, the memory brushing over her like a familiar tide.

"Mmm," Nat said, tilting her head to the side as she gazed out the window. "Gorgeous."

"Yes." Vic stole a glance at Nat in the silvery light—her profile strong and elegant, captivating. The kind of beauty that lingered in the heart.

"Do you miss it very much?" Nat turned to look at her. "The sea?"

"Every day." The admission tumbled out, surprising her. "Feels like part of who I am. It was always there…" She shrugged, a little embarrassed. "Still calls to me, I guess."

"I'm sorry. It must be so hard for you."

Vic shook her head. "Everything changes, and I got lucky, ending up here. A new job, a fresh start, a great place to stay."

She'd almost said *a reason* to stay, but held back. Resisted saying anything to disrupt the delicate connection.

Nat laughed. "I think you might be easy to please."

"Not always." Vic smiled. "But I *am* particular."

"Particular." Nat said the word as if she was trying to figure out what it meant. "That sounds…intriguing."

Vic's breath caught. Were they flirting? God, she hoped so. "*That* sounds encouraging."

Nat turned in the seat to face her. "Does it?"

"Sure," Vic said, as lightly as she could manage. "Twenty questions was my favorite game."

"I hated that game," Nat muttered.

"Yeah, me too."

"Good." Nat leaned back in the passenger seat with a sigh, her face limned in silver in the moonlight. "We'll find some other way to communicate, then."

"Sounds good to me." Any kind of connection sounded good. Right then, she itched to trace the elegant line of Nat's jaw, to tangle her hand in the silken strands of her hair. Not a good idea. She kept her hands firmly on the wheel.

As they descended into the valley, the trees pressed close on either side. The charged silence vibrated with all they hadn't said. For an instant, Vic longed for the open sky, for the freedom of the endless horizon, but then Nat's hand brushed against hers. The fleeting touch sent electricity skittering along her skin, and like a sea change, there was nowhere else she'd rather be.

Nat's driveway was dark when Vic pulled in, the cabin a shadowy silhouette against the star-flecked sky. She cut the engine and angled toward Nat.

"It's becoming our thing, isn't it?" Vic mused. "Spending time together when one of us is practically dead on their feet."

Nat laughed, a sound that always sent a shiver down Vic's spine. "I'm not as tired as you think. Seeing the campers safe and sound, reveling in reliving their adventure at the lodge—it energized me."

Vic let out a long breath. "I'm thankful everyone is okay. It's kind of my worst nightmare—a rescue mission where people you...care about...are at risk."

"Believe me, I know." Nat's fingers grazed Vic's arm. The featherlight touch sent another shock wave rippling along her nerves. "You can stop worrying about me now."

"I'm not sure I can do that." Vic tensed.

Nat's thumb traced small circles against Vic's palm, each gentle stroke sending tiny sparks racing over her skin.

"I'm not even sure I'd want you to," Nat said with a deprecating laugh. "And that makes no sense at all."

"Doesn't it?" Vic's arm tingled where Nat's fingers lingered, the warmth of her touch seeping through the fabric of her shirt. "Is it so hard to believe I might care about you?"

"Actually, yes." Nat's eyes were wary. "Even more so than discovering I don't mind."

"Why should you?" Vic asked.

Nat hesitated, the silence heavy. "Just independent, I guess."

"Used to going it alone?" Vic realized she'd told Nat all about her dad, but she knew almost nothing about Nat's family.

"Not exactly," Nat said. "My mother was a single mom and worked two, sometimes three jobs. She loved me, I never doubted. But I learned to look after myself pretty early on."

"Sometimes our strengths get in our way," Vic mused.

"That's very Zen of you," Nat said mildly.

Vic laughed. "Sorry, I'm not usually prone to deep thoughts."

"Oh, I don't know. I have a feeling there's a lot going on in there all the time."

Vic's heart stumbled as arousal unfurled low in her belly. This was an unfamiliar dance, this push and pull of longing and restraint. She'd never been so mesmerized and uncertain at the same time. She wanted more—more of Nat's touch, her voice, her everything—and feared moving too fast. Feared she'd ruin whatever this was, and Nat would pull away again.

"Like now," Nat said. "Very deep thoughts going on."

Vic sensed Nat waiting, and Vic knew with bone-deep certainty that she didn't want to stop. She wanted more.

"Definitely not now," Vic said softly.

"Oh?" Nat searched Vic's gaze. "What were you thinking, then?"

Vic swallowed. *Never be afraid of who you are, Victory. And never be afraid to go after what you want.* Her father's voice again.

"I was thinking about kissing you. I have been, ever since…" She shook her head. "I know you said no, but I can't help it."

Nat's expression softened, a hint of vulnerability replacing her usual confidence. "I've been thinking about it too."

Vic tensed, a surge of desire pulsing between her thighs. "I should go. If I stay…"

"I don't want you to go," Nat said softly, her voice barely more than a whisper. "Not yet."

Vic's heart pounded a staccato rhythm against her ribs. "I don't want to go either."

Nat took her hand, their fingers intertwining as naturally as breathing. "Then stay."

Vic didn't think, didn't question. The air thundered with possibility. She leaned in, slowly, hesitantly, giving Nat every chance to pull away, to change her mind. But Nat didn't. Her gaze locked with Vic's, her lips parted in anticipation, and that was all the permission Vic needed. Vic kissed her, softly at first, a whisper of skin against skin. Nat gripped her shoulders, pulling her closer, and Vic's hesitation gave way to a wave of heat and desire. She cradled Nat's cheek and deepened the kiss, her tongue teasing Nat's. She moaned, fire raging into every cell. The kiss was everything Vic had longed for and more—soft and electric, demanding and tender.

When they finally broke apart, both breathing heavily, Vic rested her forehead against Nat's, savoring the closeness.

"Nat," she whispered, her voice trembling from the primal need thrumming deep inside. "I've wanted this, wanted you, every single day."

"I know," Nat murmured, her breath warm against Vic's cheek. "I've been fighting it, trying to convince myself that we couldn't, shouldn't. I don't want to fight it—fight you—tonight."

"Are you sure?" Vic struggled to hold back. As much as she

wanted her, she wanted Nat to be certain. "I don't want you to be sorry in the morning."

"Will you be happy with just tonight?"

"I'll be happy with one *day* at a time."

Nat sighed. "You *are* particular. Let me be clear, then—no promises, no regrets. Just...this. Just us."

Vic unbuckled her seat belt. "I'm clear."

Nat did the same and pushed open her door. Cool night air rushed in. "Come inside."

Vic followed without hesitation. She didn't know where the night would lead, but she knew one thing with absolute certainty—one night would never be enough.

❖

Nat took Vic's hand and led her toward the house, expectation thrumming a pulsing beat urging her to act, not think. To follow her instincts. She'd never felt so alive, so filled with desire. Each step ignited a fresh surge of adrenaline. She tightened her grip around Vic's fingers. Every brush of skin on skin, every shared breath, burned.

In the dim light of the porch, Nat hesitated—just for a heartbeat. With Megan, there'd often been a nagging doubt that whispered she wasn't being totally fair to either of them. Would she feel that way about Vic in the morning?

Her heart raced, uncertainty swirling beneath the longing. She turned to Vic. "Are you sure about this?"

"If you are." Vic cupped her cheek, thumb brushing over her skin with reverence that made Nat's heart ache. "I've never been more sure of anything in my life."

The tenderness and desire in Vic's eyes stole Nat's breath. She pushed aside thoughts of Megan, of tomorrow, of every reason why this was a mistake. Vic's touch heated her skin despite the chill, her body warmed where their shoulders touched. Vic's desire radiated in every glance, and that was all that mattered. For this night—for the hours until dawn, Vic was hers.

"Then let's not waste another minute." Nat held open the door.

Vic entered without hesitation, her steps sure and steady. The quiet click of the latch resounded like a shot in the stillness, the charged silence stretching taut as a bowstring. Nat gripped Vic's wrist and led her down the hall. The house, so familiar, seemed as changed as she felt. The whitewashed walls glowed with the silvery light streaming through the windows. Shadows danced across the thick woven rugs and her worn but cozy furnishings. The faint scent of woodsmoke from the fire she'd started the night before still lingered.

"Do you want something to drink?" Nat asked, hesitating midway to the stairs.

"Thanks, but I don't think I could drink anything right now." Vic's voice was rough, her stormy eyes weighted with meaning that needed no explanation.

Nodding, her throat dry, Nat took a small step closer. "So..." Her breath hitched as Vic's gaze dipped to her lips, the tension palpable, almost suffocating. "We could just—"

"I don't want to overthink this," Vic interrupted softly, her voice trembling with barely restrained emotion. She lightly rested her fingers on Nat's hip, their bodies separated by mere inches now. "I've been hoping for this moment since..." She faltered, a hint of vulnerability breaking through her usual confidence. "I don't even know when it started. Just that I've been thinking of you, wanting you, so much."

Nat's doubts crumbled under the raw honesty in Vic's voice. "I don't want to overthink it either."

Vic cupped Nat's cheek, her thumb tracing the curve of her jaw. The warmth of her touch was grounding, anchoring Nat in a moment both surreal and utterly real.

"You're so beautiful," Vic murmured, her voice fierce with awe. "I don't even think you know how much."

Nat's heart pounded so loudly she imagined Vic could hear it. "I don't..."

She faltered as Vic leaned in, their lips a whisper apart. The words she'd meant to say dissolved into nothing. Vic kissed her, softly at first, as though testing the waters. But the tentative press of her lips quickly gave way to something deeper, more urgent. Nat responded instinctively, threading her fingers into Vic's hair to pull her closer. The kiss was everything she hadn't known she needed—explosive, consuming, and impossibly tender.

Vic broke away just long enough to murmur against her lips, "I've dreamed about kissing you, having your hands on me...but this—this is so much better."

Nat laughed softly, the sound breathless and tinged with wonder. "I didn't expect this...you." Her words tumbled out, unguarded and raw.

"Disappointed?" Vic murmured, her lips brushing the corner of Nat's mouth.

Nat gasped. Such a simple touch. Destroying all her shields. "More like amazed."

Vic groaned, the sound low and full of need. Pressing kisses along the curve of Nat's jaw and down the column of her neck, she gripped Nat's hips and pulled their bodies flush.

Nat arched into her, surrendering to the dizzying heat. "Bedroom."

"Yes," Vic said breathlessly. "Another second and I won't be able to think. Or stop."

"You won't need to." Nat silenced her with another kiss, pouring all the unspoken words and simmering desire into the connection. She gripped Vic's shoulders, steadying herself against the rush of heat pooling low in her belly. The tidal wave of need threatened to destroy all her carefully constructed arguments, but she didn't care. She would deal with the aftermath tomorrow. Tonight there was only Victory. "I want you."

Nat took her hand and led her upstairs by the light of the moon. She didn't want to turn on the lights. If this was a dream, she wanted to savor it. Pausing in the hall outside the bedroom, she stroked the edge of Vic's jaw. Her fingers trembled, but she couldn't stop herself, couldn't pull away. Still hungry for the taste of her, Nat clasped Vic's nape and plunged her tongue into her mouth. Vic circled her waist with both arms and pressed against her so hard Nat's back hit the half-open bedroom door. She groaned, need so fierce she couldn't think.

"Sorry," Vic gasped, starting to lean away.

"No." The sound of their uneven breathing filled the quiet space. "I need to feel all of you—God, everywhere."

And Vic's hands *were* everywhere. Racing over Nat's back, over her hips, and streaking up to cup her breasts. Nat's thighs shook and she broke the kiss, resting her forehead on Vic's. "Bed."

"Yes."

Before Nat could move, Vic bent slightly and picked her up with an arm behind her knees. Cradling Nat to her chest, she strode to the bed in three quick strides. The effortless strength in Vic's embrace made Nat's pulse stutter.

When Nat landed gently on the bed, she laughed. "Alright. That's a first."

Vic kicked off her boots and lay beside her. "Good."

Nat pressed against her and kissed her, toeing off her boots and kicking them somewhere into the room. She caressed Vic's back, mapping the contours of her body through the thin fabric of her shirt. The tension enveloping them crackled like a live wire, and Nat reveled in it. Not enough. She craved the feel of Vic's bare skin and pulled Vic's shirt from her pants. "I need you."

"Can I undress you?" Vic asked.

"You can do anything you want."

Vic rolled away just enough to pull her shirt over her head and push the rest of her clothes away. She rose, naked, onto her knees, moonlight spilling across her shoulders and breasts. Sleek and muscular, every line and curve powerful and graceful. So quintessentially female.

"Oh, God." Nat caressed the smooth expanse of Vic's back, tracing the dips and curves, memorizing every inch of her. "You are incredible."

"I am about to explode," Vic gasped. "I'm so fucking turned on, it's killing me."

"I'd say go slow," Nat said, pressing her palm to the center of Vic's chest, thrilling to the way Vic's body strained against her, "but I can't seem to help myself when it comes to you."

"Well, in that case…" Vic hooked a finger beneath the hem of Nat's shirt and tugged it up. She trailed hot, open-mouthed kisses along Nat's jaw and down the column of her throat. When she paused to suck at her pulse point, Nat moaned and threaded her fingers through Vic's hair, holding her close. Vic kissed her neck, her collarbones, and the hollow at the base of her throat. Opening her shirt, Vic skimmed soft kisses trailing lower on Nat's abdomen. She laughed when Nat hissed. "*I'll* just take my time."

"You *are* bad," Nat gasped, her breath hitching.

"I think that's your fault," Vic murmured, her voice low and rough. She unzipped Nat's pants with excruciating slowness, a delicious rasp that ignited a fresh wave of heat. She eased the zipper down completely, her fingertips brushing Nat's hip as she worked her pants down her legs. "You make me a little brainless."

"Mmm," Nat said, her mind hazy with desire. She wanted to relish every moment, but her body screamed for Vic's touch, for the heat of her mouth, for the press of her fingers. For fast, more, *now*.

Vic removed the rest of Nat's clothing, inch by torturous inch. She traced each new expanse of exposed skin, setting Nat aflame with every stroke. Nat couldn't remember ever being this desperate, this wanton. Her heart pounded and her breath came in shallow gasps. Vic finally tossed the last of her garments aside. For a moment, Vic simply knelt there, her gaze roving over Nat's body like she was committing every detail to memory.

"You're stunning," Vic murmured reverently, her eyes dark with desire. "Absolutely breathtaking."

Cool air washed over Nat's skin. Desperate to feel Vic on top of her, she pulled Vic down into a searing kiss. Vic covered her, molding to her. Skin against skin, racing heart to racing heart, as if always meant to be. Through the kiss, Vic continued to explore every curve and plane, stoking the inferno building inside her.

"Please," Nat panted against Vic's mouth. "I won't last."

"Then we'll start again. I want to enjoy every moment of this." Vic traced the contours of Nat's face. Her tenderness made Nat's heart ache. "I want to memorize every inch of you, to make this last forever."

"We have all night." Nat gripped Vic's wrist and pushed her hand down to the delta between her thighs. "But right now, I need you to touch me. Please."

"As you wish." Vic smiled, a slow, sexy curve of her lips that nearly sent Nat to the edge.

"Oh my God," Nat whimpered. "Vic, please…"

Vic brushed over her center, ever so lightly. "What, Nat? Tell me."

"Make me come," Nat breathed into Vic's ear.

"I will." Vic caressed the sensitive skin of Nat's inner thighs, her touch deliberate and still maddeningly slow.

"Oh fuck." Nat's hips canted upward. "I'm so close."

When Vic's fingers finally pressed her clit, Nat cried out. Vic circled and squeezed, building her higher with each deliberate stroke. Nat clutched at Vic's shoulders, digging into taut muscle as the pleasure coiled tighter and tighter.

"Inside me," Nat demanded. "I'm coming…fuck."

Vic pressed her forehead to Nat's breast as she filled her, her strokes deep and rhythmic. Nat raked her nails down Vic's back, and the world shattered. Her climax crested, fierce and consuming, as she muffled her cries against Vic's shoulder. Time ceased to exist. There was only Vic, the slide of skin on skin, and the wild storm unleashed inside her. When Vic brought her to the brink again, and then again, Nat feared she would never be the same.

Finally feeling strength return to her trembling limbs, Nat eased Vic onto her back and leaned above her on an elbow. "I hope you're not tired."

Vic huffed, although her breathing was uneven. "Not a bit."

"Good." When Vic reached for her, Nat pressed her down with a hand between her breasts and quickly slipped between her legs. "I want you in my mouth. May I?"

"Hell yes," Vic said. "I'll only last a minute, though."

"We'll see," Nat murmured, and kissed her way down Vic's body, worshipping every inch with her mouth, savoring the way Vic trembled. She paused to nip at the curve of her hip.

"Fuck," Vic shouted, her legs straining.

"Possibly. We'll see."

"You're going to wreck me," Vic whimpered.

"Mm. Not yet. Soon." Smiling, reveling in the power, she alternated between soft, languid strokes and firmer, more insistent movements, finding a rhythm that had Vic writhing beneath her.

"God, Nat," Vic groaned, her voice breaking. "I can't take any more. I'm so close."

Nat gripped Vic's hips to keep her grounded, exulting in every sound Vic made, every shiver and moan. The sense of control, of being the one to unravel Vic so completely, was intoxicating.

"Please," Vic choked out, her voice breaking with desperation. "I need—"

Nat pressed her tongue harder, flicking in a way that sent Vic spiraling. With a strangled cry, Vic came undone, her body bowing off the bed as her climax exploded. Nat didn't stop, drawing out every wave of pleasure until Vic lay gasping beneath her, her breaths ragged and her skin slick with sweat.

Vic tugged at Nat's shoulders, pulling her up until their bodies touched. "That was…" Her voice trailed off. "You're incredible. I'm destroyed."

"I hope not." Nat nestled her cheek on Vic's chest, listening to the rapid thrum of her heartbeat. Vic's arms came around her, holding her close, as if she was something precious.

"Are you okay?" Vic asked quietly.

Nat's breath hitched at the raw vulnerability in Vic's voice, the tenderness in her touch.

"I don't know what I am right now," she admitted, her voice barely above a whisper. "But I know I don't want this night to end."

"It doesn't have to," Vic said, her voice steady despite the vulnerability.

"No. Not tonight." Nat leaned into Vic's warmth, content not to think about what the morning would bring. In that moment, she wanted nothing more than to lose herself in Vic's arms.

CHAPTER ELEVEN

Nat stirred, a warm arm draped over her middle, sunlight filtering through the open shutters, leaving golden ribbons on the patchwork quilt. The pine-tinged air, one of her new favorite scents, drew her fully awake. She opened her eyes in her familiar room, yet everything felt different—as if something fundamental inside her had shifted. Because it had.

The woman lying next to her, naked and heartbreakingly beautiful, was the reason. Memories of the night with Vic crashed into awareness, a sensual flood that stole her breath. The way Vic had touched her, kissed her—tasted her—every vivid detail seared into her skin like an indelible mark she doubted she'd ever forget.

Vic murmured something in her sleep, the sound low and comforting. Her arm tightened around Nat's waist, pulling her closer, as if afraid to let her go.

"Morning," Vic murmured, her voice thick with sleep.

That single word, soft yet weighted, unraveled something deep in Nat's heart. The tenderness in Vic's touch made her heart constrict. She wanted to melt into the embrace, to savor the closeness. And that was dangerous—letting Vic in, a mistake waiting to happen. The moment she did, she'd want things she had no business wanting. More time with Vic, more chances to touch and be touched. Doubt crept in like a cold fog, reminding her of the decision she'd made, and already had trouble keeping. No emotional entanglements, no risk of loss. Count on herself, stay safe. The rules had always been so simple. So easy. Why did they suddenly feel like chains?

Nat closed her eyes. She'd never been this reckless, never let herself fall into something that had the power to shatter her. This desire for Vic, the longing for something real and lasting, was foreign and frightening.

Vic nuzzled Nat's neck, her breath warm on Nat's skin. "You okay?"

Nat forced a smile. The moment their eyes met, a quiet kind of knowing flickered in Vic's expression, the resignation sending a pang through Nat's chest. "Yeah, just…thinking."

Vic propped herself up on one elbow, studying Nat with those perceptive gray eyes, sharp despite the lingering vestiges of sleep. She brushed her thumb lightly across Nat's cheek. A simple gesture, patient and tender. "About last night?"

"That. And…us." Nat sighed, tucking a strand of hair behind Vic's ear. "It was wonderful, Vic. Really. I just…I need you to know that I'm not looking for anything serious right now."

Vic's jaw tightened just a fraction. A flicker of hurt shadowed her eyes before she masked it with a nod. "Right. Of course. I get it."

"I hope this won't make things uncomfortable between us." The distance in Vic's tone made Nat's chest ache. God, why did this feel like discarding something precious before it had a chance to bloom? Words lodged in her throat. She'd never been good at baring her vulnerabilities, even to herself. Instead, she leaned in and kissed Vic softly. "Last night was wonderful."

There was nothing soft about the way Vic kissed her back, fiercely, as if making one final claim before letting go. When Nat pulled away, Vic held her gaze, a bittersweet smile on her lips.

"I know you're not ready for more, Nat. I heard you. But I'm here, if you ever change your mind."

With that, Vic slipped out of bed and gathered her clothes, each movement careful, controlled. As if reining herself in.

Vic disappeared into the bathroom, the click of the door a gentle echo in the silence that descended. Nat sat up and wrapped her arms around her middle, trying to ignore the thought of Vic walking away.

As she intended her to.

The ache in her chest deepened.

The rustle of the sheets as Nat swung her legs over the side of the bed seemed unnaturally loud in the quiet room. She stood, the cool floorboards a bittersweet reminder of the warmth of Vic's body that ghosted over her skin. Moving to the window, she gazed out at the morning. The towering pines swayed in the breeze, morning mist curling between their trunks like smoke. Birds chirped somewhere out of sight. The ethereal beauty of the Adirondack wilderness failed to soothe her as it always had.

She turned at the sound of the bathroom door opening, and Vic emerged, fully dressed. Something about seeing her like this, back in uniform, made the last few hours feel even more fragile—like something Nat had only imagined. Their eyes met, unspoken emotions heavy in the charged air.

"I should go," Vic said softly, her voice sure but tinged with regret.

Nat nodded, swallowing past the lump in her throat. Her voice barely worked. "I know."

"Don't apologize for how you feel, Nat. I understand." Vic crossed the room and stopped close enough that Nat registered the heat of her body again. She leaned into the familiar magnetic pull, allowing herself that small comfort for just another moment.

Vic leaned in, her lips brushing against Nat's in a soft, lingering kiss that sent a shiver down Nat's spine.

"But I want you to know," Vic said, her voice rough, "that last night meant something to me. *You* mean something to me."

Nat's heart stumbled, the look in Vic's eyes, dark and intense, nearly crushing her defenses. "You're special. I hope you know that."

Vic pulled away, her fingers trailing along Nat's jaw in a tender caress. "If you ever change your mind, if you ever decide what we shared last night is enough, or at least a beginning, I'll be waiting."

"Don't," Nat said. "Don't wait for me. I'm not the one."

"So you say." Vic didn't argue. Didn't press. "Take care of yourself out there."

And then she was gone.

Heart aching, legs unsteady, Nat hurried to the window for one last glimpse as Vic strode down the path to her cabin. Couldn't Vic see they were worlds apart—in age, in experience, in courage? Or lack of it. A coward she might be, but she wouldn't let *her* need trap Vic in a relationship that was less than she deserved.

She watched, her cheek resting on the window frame, until Vic disappeared inside. With a sigh, she turned away from the window, forcing herself to believe she'd done the right thing. Even as everything inside her screamed otherwise.

❖

Nat performed her morning routine in a daze, scarcely aware of her body operating without her. She shrugged on her uniform, the fabric crisp and utilitarian—a familiar armor against feelings she couldn't afford to entertain. But no shield could protect her from the sensation of Vic's lingering touch on her skin—the heat of her hands, the slow, reverent way she had traced every line of her body.

A single night. That was all it had been. But somehow, that night had unraveled the careful order she had spent years constructing.

Her hands trembled as she fastened her duty belt, checking her gear with mechanical precision, carefully tightening each buckle, each strap, as if securing them could hold her together.

Driving to Thunder Ridge Lodge, she focused on the familiar landmarks blurring past the window, a distraction from the memory of Vic's breath against her neck. The lush beauty of the forest beneath a pristine June sky reminded her of what mattered. What had always sustained her.

She pulled into the parking lot and took a deep, steadying breath. She had a job to do. A responsibility. The certainty of that had always been enough. She'd been happy. Hadn't she?

She climbed out of her truck and drew deeply of the crisp morning air. The scent of pure lake water and rich, damp earth should have soothed her. It always had before. But beneath the familiar, Vic's warm, intimate scent lingered.

One night shouldn't turn her world upside down. She couldn't let that happen again.

Intending to turn up the trail to Timara's cabin, she paused when Sarah exited the lodge, coffee cup in hand, and leaned on the porch railing. She waved, the warm welcome on her face soothing Nat's heart just a little.

"Hey," Nat called, detouring to join her.

"You're up early," Sarah said. "Did I miss a lesson on the schedule?"

"Nope." Nat climbed the steps and joined Sarah at the railing. "We've got a prescribed burn scheduled up at Little Lake today. I just wanted to check on Timara and the kids before I headed out. Is she still here?"

"She just went up to her cabin. I woke her a time or two last night to make sure she was doing okay." Sarah took a slow sip of coffee. Too slow. "Got a minute?"

"Sure, what's up?" Nat steeled herself. She knew that tone. Sarah was about to dig at something Nat wasn't sure she was ready to unearth.

Sarah studied her, her gaze steady and searching. Nat recognized the look—quiet scrutiny, the kind that saw straight through her. That was the problem with old friends. They saw too much. "I was going to ask you the same thing. Everything okay? Yesterday was a hell of a first hike."

"One I'm happy to put behind me." Nat forced a smile. "I'm fine. Just a little tired. Long night."

Sarah's eyebrow lifted. "Long night, huh? Wouldn't have anything to do with a certain dark-haired newcomer who stayed glued to you all night?"

Nat froze, felt her cheeks flush. "What? No—of course not." She brushed past Sarah and headed for the door. "I could use some of what you're drinking."

Sarah followed her inside, undeterred. "Oh, come on, Nat. I saw the way O'Brien was looking at you yesterday. She was hell-bent on driving you home—*making sure you were okay*—and now you're sneaking in here at the crack of dawn looking like you haven't slept a wink. It doesn't take a genius to put two and two together."

"I'm hardly *sneaking*." Nat sighed, pouring herself a mug of coffee and taking a long sip before turning to face Sarah. "Could we just let this go?"

"Sure. That means yes, though."

Nat wanted to snarl, but that would just prove Sarah's point. *She'd* let this happen. "Fine, you're right. Vic and I...we spent the night together. But it was just a one-time thing, nothing serious."

There. Said. Over.

"A one-time thing, huh?" Sarah leaned against the counter, her expression softer. "That's not like you, Nat. I thought you didn't do casual."

Nat shrugged, forcing herself to take another sip of coffee, as if delaying would erase the conversation. Sarah watched her like a hawk in a tree eyed a sparrow. Right. "I don't, usually. But with Vic...I don't know, it just sort of happened. And it was amazing, don't get me wrong. But that's the end of it."

"Since we've been friends forever, I know you're good on your own." Sarah squeezed Nat's shoulder. "But if O'Brien got to you that much in such a short time, maybe that means something."

"What it means," Nat said, struggling to hold on to her conviction, "is I had a moment's insanity."

Sarah snorted and sipped some coffee, looking far too satisfied with herself. "Sounds like more than a moment."

Nat scowled. Why did Sarah have to be so damn perceptive?

"Can we let this go, please?" Nat exhaled, rubbing the tension headache forming behind her eyes. "It doesn't matter. She's here for the summer. That's it. And she's too young for me. And"—she threw up a hand, exasperated—"she makes me reckless."

Sarah put down her coffee cup, her expression suddenly serious. "That doesn't sound like a casual thing. And screw the age thing. She's way past being a kid."

"Twenty years is a lot of time that I've lived and she hasn't." Nat shook her head, frustrated at trying to explain something she didn't understand herself. Such as how she'd gotten into the mess to begin with. "She has a lot of living yet to do."

"Well, so do you."

"When I'm seventy, she'd be fifty."

Sarah shrugged. "Mmm, yes. And if my math is correct, you'll have shared twenty-five years by then with another two or three decades to go."

Nat exhaled sharply, gripping the edge of the counter. She couldn't do this right now. Not with Sarah. Not with anyone. "Can we *please* let this go?"

Sarah shrugged. "Can you?"

Nat gritted her teeth. "I already have."

Sarah sighed and shook her head. "I love you, but God, you have a hard head."

"Must be why we're friends. And I love you too, even when you're a pain in the ass." Nat paused at the door, already halfway out. "Call me when Timara gets up? Let me know how she is?"

"Of course. And Nat—maybe take things one day at a time?"

"Sure." Nat hurried out before Sarah could challenge her in the lie. She'd made the right decision—for Vic and herself.

Hadn't she?

CHAPTER TWELVE

Vic stepped into the steamy shower, tension coiling in her body like a heavy weight. The heat seeped into her muscles, but the ache inside her chest refused to dissolve. She leaned her forehead against the cool tile, closing her eyes as flashes of the night before played out in her memory like a bittersweet movie. Nat's touch, her kisses, the way their bodies had moved together in perfect harmony—every moment had felt so effortless, so natural, as if they had been made to fit together in that way. The slow burn of desire, the whispered words between kisses, the raw intensity of how they unraveled each other had been everything she hadn't known she'd needed.

It had felt so real. So damn real.

And then morning had come. Morning, with its sharp edges and cold light, had stripped everything down to what it really was: an ending disguised as a beginning, framed by Nat's excuses and hasty retreat.

Nat's words slicing through Vic's hopes with precision.

I don't want anything serious. I hope this won't make things uncomfortable between us.

The words had stung—no, more than that, they had cut deep, sharp as a gutting knife, leaving her raw. She'd tried to play it off, to act like it didn't matter, but the disappointment burned. She had thought, had hoped, that their connection had been real, had been something that might turn into more than a night shared after a tumultuous day.

But apparently not. Vic clenched her fists, the water that pounded against her shoulders doing little to wash away the sting.

Nat had lowered her shields for a brief few hours, probably because she was weary and still reeling from the anxiety of leading all the campers to safety. Maybe what Vic had considered intimacy was nothing more than convenience. She'd been there when Nat needed a release. She'd pushed Nat for what *she'd* been wanting for weeks, and Nat had given in to the moment. *For* the moment, and no more.

She twisted off the water, muscles tight with exhaustion that ran deeper than a sleepless night. The slightly rough towel dragged against her sensitive skin. When she passed the towel down over her abdomen, soreness mingled with the phantom touch of Nat's lips. She imagined Nat kissing her there, making her torturous way lower as she'd slid down between her thighs, her mouth a teasing agony.

Her clit twitched a warning sign.

"Fuck." She tossed the towel aside.

Not what she needed, not when the distance felt like a chasm she couldn't cross.

Not what she needed at all.

"What part of *no* didn't you get," she muttered. Nat had already made it clear, more than once, that she wasn't looking for anything to happen. That made sense, right? After all, Vic wasn't staying around. Was she?

What the hell *was* she doing? Besides falling for someone who didn't want her.

She shook her head, throwing that thought overboard. That was not happening. She'd already let herself think last night meant more than it had. She wasn't chasing after someone who didn't want her. One night would have to be enough. She didn't have much experience with casual. Past time she learned.

A chime from her phone cut through the silence, pulling her from the spiral of memories. A text from Phee flashed across the screen.

Hey, you up? Breakfast?

Vic hesitated, thumb hovering over the reply button. She didn't feel fit for company right then. Mostly she wanted to snarl and brood.

Which was probably a good reason to say yes.

Sure, she typed, hitting send before she could change her mind. *Meet you on the wharf?*

In ten. See you.

Vic set her phone down. Part of her wanted to check if Nat had messaged. If she'd changed her mind. But the screen remained empty, and the weight in her chest grew heavier.

She exhaled, wondering what the hell she'd unleashed. "I think I'm in trouble here."

❖

Vic pulled into the lot adjacent to WPU's designated dock in the center of Lake George Village where Phee waited by the entrance, leaning against the fence, her signature aviator sunglasses perched on her nose. She'd gathered her dark hair into a loose ponytail and pulled it through the back of her WPU cap. She looked effortlessly relaxed—pretty much the opposite of the storm still brewing inside Vic.

Vic hurried to meet her. "Sorry, waiting long?"

"Nope, just got here." Phee pushed off the fence with easy confidence, eyeing her more closely now. "You look like hell, O'Brien."

Vic forced a grin. "Good morning to you too, Chief."

"Didn't get much sleep?"

"Rough night." Vic shrugged, trying to mask the exhaustion dragging at her limbs. Rough morning too. Nat's absence had carved out a hollow ache she couldn't quite shake.

"Uh-huh."

Vic shouldered her gear bag and pretended not to hear the amusement in Phee's tone.

Phee led the way across the street with her usual brisk stride. "We need to fuel up. We have a long run today."

"We do?" Vic kept pace as Phee headed toward the restaurants on the main street.

"Yep—checking camping permits on the islands ahead of the holiday."

Vic slowed. "I can't believe I forgot it's the Fourth next weekend."

Phee laughed. "It's been a hectic month, rookie."

"How long will I be the rookie?"

Phee chuckled, pointing the way to the front door of a diner. "Until we get another new guy on the crew."

Vic laughed, holding the door open for Phee, who brushed against her as she entered. The scent of fresh coffee and butter filled the air, the low murmur of morning patrons mingling with the clatter of silverware.

"Phee, darlin'," a robust thirtysomething with flaming red hair and a warm, booming voice called. "Usual table?"

"Yep."

"You know the way, honey. Be right there."

Vic shot Phee a raised brow. "Come here often?"

Phee patted her midsection. "Too often."

Vic settled into the booth across from Phee and grabbed one of the laminated menus propped behind the salt and pepper shakers. "Thanks for the invite. This looks great."

"My pleasure." Phee slid her sunglasses off, her gaze traveling over Vic's face. "Good food, good company."

Vic caught the gleam in Phee's eyes and was saved from conjuring a reply as the redhead arrived, pencil and pad at the ready.

"What'll you officers have?" she asked.

"I'll have the veggie omelet with a side of fruit," Phee said, setting her menu back.

Vic hesitated, her eyes lingering on the pancakes. Comfort food. Her father used to make them for her on the mornings they weren't at sea. Something to look forward to when they had to be on land.

"I'll have the pancakes." Her voice caught, and she coughed to hide it. "With a side of bacon."

The server jotted down their orders. "Coffee coming up."

Phee studied Vic, her gaze penetrating. "So how's it going?"

"The job, you mean?" Vic asked.

"That and...whatever. New place, all that." Phee smiled. "You know I'm not just here to bust your chops, right? You can talk to me if you need to."

For a heartbeat, Vic considered it—letting Phee in, admitting how tangled everything felt when it came to Nat. But the words stuck in her throat.

"I'm fine." *Fine* was always a good default setting. "The crew is great. And if I can get out on the water, do some decent work, I'm happy."

"Yesterday was more than decent," Phee said carefully, apparently not satisfied with *fine*. "You handled a tough day really well."

"Thanks. I know my way around a boat," Vic said, mildly embarrassed but still pleased.

"Mmm." Phee leaned back as the server delivered their food, the scent of warm syrup and crispy bacon rising from the plates. "I bet you know your way around quite a few things."

Vic paused. She didn't have a ton of experience, but she was pretty sure Phee was flirting. She didn't have a clue where to go with that. Her mind just wouldn't. Not when her skin still burned from the memory of Nat's touch.

"Sorry," Phee said after a second. "Just so you know, I'm the unit commander, but Charlie is the boss."

"Okay," Vic said, starting in on the pancakes to divert the conversation.

"So if we were to *fraternize*, we wouldn't be breaking any rules." Phee apparently wasn't ready to change the topic.

"Okay," Vic said again. She liked Phee, and Phee was hot. But she wasn't Nat. Nat, who didn't want her. "I'm not quite sure I'm ready to fraternize."

"I hear you." Phee smiled, an easy relaxed smile. "The crew and I were thinking of grabbing a drink after work on Friday. You should join us."

Vic hesitated, her fork hovering over her plate. Part of her wanted to say yes, to enjoy being part of the team. But another part, the part that was still raw and bruised from Nat's rejection, whispered that maybe it was too soon, too risky.

"I don't know," she said, pushing a piece of bacon around her plate. "It's already been a long morning."

"It's barely eight, O'Brien."

Vic exhaled. "Exactly."

Phee forked up a portion of omelet and paused, meeting Vic's gaze. "To be clear, there's no agenda here, Vic. Not with me. Friday's just a chance to unwind and get to know everyone a little better. After that…well, who knows."

Vic didn't have a real reason to say no. All that waited for her at the end of a day was a small, empty cabin less than a two-minute walk from Nat's house. Not where she wanted to be.

"Yes," she said firmly. "Count me in."

Phee grinned. "Let's get out there, then. Nothing like a day on the water to clear your head."

"Or drown it," Vic muttered under her breath.

As they approached the dock, Phee adjusted her sunglasses. "Ready for a full shift of dealing with entitled tourists and reckless boaters?"

Vic snorted. "Living the dream, Chief."

Phee grinned. "Excellent. This is going to be fun."

CHAPTER THIRTEEN

Vic smiled at the hand-crafted sign swaying above the door on a wrought iron pole in front of the taproom in the center of Lake George Village. O'Brien's. Funny. Seemed like every small town she'd passed through on the long drive down from Maine had one.

Damn—had that only been six weeks ago? A heartbeat. A lifetime.

So much had happened since she'd arrived—a new job, new friends. And Nat. Always Nat.

Since that night together, she'd rarely seen Nat except to wave as they passed in their separate orbits—one coming, the other leaving. One night she'd even stood in her darkened cabin, staring at the lights from Nat's windows, wishing she had the courage to walk up, knock on her back door, and confess she couldn't stop thinking about her. Couldn't stop wanting her.

Pride—and respect for Nat—stopped her. Nat had been clear. No entanglements, no regrets. And as much as it pained her, she would honor that boundary. She had to.

She'd thrown herself into work—long hours on the water, answering distress calls, keeping busy enough that she didn't have to think about warm skin, tangled sheets, or Nat whispering her name into the dark. But late at night, when the silence closed in, the ache returned—deep, persistent, and entirely unwelcome.

She squared her shoulders, exhaling a slow breath. If friendship was all Nat could offer, she'd take it. Even if every part of her wanted more.

Starting now.

She pushed open the heavy wooden door and walked into a wall of sound—clinking glasses, a cacophony of voices, and blaring commentary from the TV sports announcer. The taproom's exposed ductwork snaked across a matte black ceiling, Edison bulbs casting muted pools of light that barely reached the corners of the cavernous space. A long wooden bar stretched along one wall, most of the seats occupied. Round tables dotted with half-empty glasses filled the center of the room. She squinted through the dim lighting, scanning for Phee in the crowd.

Phee's distinctive laugh carried over the din. There, in the corner. Looking relaxed as she chatted with Juanita, Phee sat at a big round table crowded with pitchers of beer, drink glasses, and bottles. Vic wove her way through the crowd, resolutely shoving aside the gnawing emptiness that sometimes crept in when she let her guard slip. Tonight was about new beginnings.

"Am I late to the party?" she asked, sliding into the open seat between Phee and Milt.

"Just getting started." Phee scooted closer to Juanita on her far side to make room. "You almost missed first round, though, rookie."

Milt poured a beer and pushed it her way.

"Glad you made it," he said, his deep voice rumbling over the background noise.

She took a swallow—cold and tangy. "Thanks."

Phee leaned close. "I was starting to think you'd bailed on me."

Vic managed a weak smile. "Not a chance."

Phee studied her for a beat, her playful demeanor softening. "You good?"

Vic hesitated, then shrugged. "Yeah. Just…tired."

"That's becoming a bad habit." Phee didn't press further, but she briefly squeezed Vic's shoulder—a silent offer of support Vic hadn't realized she needed.

Across the table from her, Charlie was mid-story about his oldest daughter's double-double performance in the summer basketball league, and for a moment her heart ached in that way she hadn't yet grown used to. Damn it, she really missed her dad.

Phee slowly sipped her beer, watching Vic. "I was starting to think you'd stood me up, O'Brien."

Vic grinned, Phee's easy tone a welcome reminder that she'd decided to let go of the past, for a few hours at least. "And miss out on your charming company? Never."

In the dim glow of the taproom, the usual humor in Phee's eyes was tempered by something quieter, something assessing. "Flattery will get you everywhere, babe."

Vic liked Phee—a lot. Liked her confidence, her sharp humor, and the way she carried herself with the effortless ease of someone who always knew where she stood. And yeah, as her heart was beating and brain functioning, she appreciated Phee's easy sensuality and killer smile.

But.

Liking someone and wanting to take it to the next level were two different things. She'd followed her instincts with Nat—hadn't been able not to. Their connection had been undeniable—from the first night when Nat had anchored her without even trying, to their quiet moments sharing an impromptu beer and the details of their day. Nat's compassion had been a lifeline in the storm of grief and loss that had swamped Vic for months. When passion flared, she'd experienced intimacy that branded her deepest reaches.

And then Nat had let her go.

Vic took a long swig of her beer, hoping to drown the memories before they pulled her under. "Not flattery when it's true."

Phee's brows lifted. "Smooth. I'm impressed."

"Don't be." Vic shook her head. "It wasn't a line."

"Oh, I know," Phee said softly. In the muted light of the taproom, her usual bravado receded, tempered by a hint of vulnerability. "That's what's so damn charming about you, Victory. You don't know how ridiculously hot you are."

Vic hesitated, at a crossroads. She couldn't have Nat, but she could have this. The laughter of friends, the warm buzz of good company, the uncomplicated thrill of attention from a woman who wanted her.

If she wanted.

Did she?

"You could just say yes and stop thinking so hard," Phee said too quietly for anyone else to hear. "Unless I'm way off base here, and then you can just tell me so. I won't break."

"You being crushed never crossed my mind." Vic exhaled sharply. "All I've got to offer is casual, and I already like you too much for that."

"That's an answer I can respect," Phee said. "I'm a one day at a time woman myself, and I had a feeling you might not be. Plus…" She lifted her beer, took a sip, then glanced past Vic, tilting her head toward the entrance on the far side of the room. "Plus, I had an idea you might have another reason to say no."

Vic turned in her seat.

And her breath hitched.

Nat.

Threading her way through the crowd with Meg Oloff, their arms brushing in a way that looked too familiar, too easy.

A dull, unwelcome heat curled in Vic's gut, and she jolted, jealousy twisting inside her.

Nat had been open about her casual history with Meg, but seeing them together was a punch in the ribs.

Vic turned away. Looked back at Phee. Forced a smile.

"No," she said, ignoring the lie scraping her throat. "No reason at all."

"Well," Phee said, raising her glass, "things can change, can't they, given time."

"Everything does," Vic murmured.

And maybe it was time she finally accepted that.

Nat stepped into the bustling taproom, not entirely sure why she'd come. The press of bodies, the low hum of conversation and bursts of laughter, and the clink of glasses contrasted starkly to the quiet of her cabin. Meg had stopped by divisional headquarters a little after six p.m. and strong-armed her into coming out, challenging her to declare what better she had to do. When she couldn't find an answer, she'd relented.

Spending time with Meg was easy, after all. Uncomplicated. And it beat sitting at home, struggling to read a book or clean the house when it didn't need cleaning, or any of the other dozen things she'd been doing to keep her mind off Vic. Not very successfully.

"Now aren't you glad you came?" Meg said as Skipper, the owner and bartender, pushed frothy mugs across the gleaming bar top toward them. She took a sip of her beer. "Really, a good IPA cures all ills."

Nat laughed "I don't really have any ills needing to be cured at the moment."

"Don't you? You've been hiding," Meg said solemnly. "Anything going on?"

Nat took a long sip before responding. "You mean besides the lost hikers, a bear sighting in the public campgrounds, or the debris fire up in Schroon Lake?"

"I meant with you." Meg gently poked Nat in the arm.

Nat swiveled on the barstool, uncertain how much she wanted to say. Meg hadn't suggested they spend any intimate time together recently, and she'd been grateful that she hadn't had to think of a way to say no. She couldn't be intimate with Meg when her thoughts were filled with another woman. But more than that, she hadn't wanted to. Now that she'd been with Vic... She sighed.

"Hectic schedule, that's all," she finally said, turning to scan the room.

Her breath hitched when she spotted Vic with Phee at a table across the room. A pang of jealousy, sharp and unbidden, pierced her carefully constructed veneer of indifference. Vic looked up as if sensing her, and Nat's stomach twisted with an all too familiar surge of longing and desire. Even in the noisy, crowded bar, the world narrowed to just the two of them, the space around them electric.

Her heart clenched, a sharp, unexpected ache tightening in her chest. Vic looked...tired. Tired, but still beautiful in that way that never failed to undo her. Vic straightened, the easy confidence she wore with everyone else slipping away. No teasing grin this time, no playful invitation to come join her—just raw, open vulnerability in her eyes.

Nat's pulse roared in her ears. The weight of Vic's gaze, of everything they hadn't said, pulled at her. The temptation to cross the room, to close the chasm separating them, bore down on her like a tidal wave.

She took a half step forward and caught herself, halting abruptly. What was she doing? She'd just spent days convincing herself that distance was the right choice.

Her hands trembled. She shoved them into her pockets and turned sharply away, ignoring the regret lodged in her throat.

Meg, ever observant, followed Nat's gaze. "Something—or some*one*—catch your eye?"

"What? No." Nat tore her attention away from Vic, hating how obvious she must have looked. "No. Sorry. You know what it's like this time of year. I'm a little sleep deprived, that's all."

"Well, it's not me making you lose sleep." Meg's tone was playful but her gaze was serious.

"I know." Nat sighed and squeezed Meg's arm. "It's just...I don't feel like I can be present. All the way present, I mean, and that doesn't feel fair."

"I've never asked for promises or even for a next time." Meg turned her hand over and linked her fingers with Nat. "I love you, you know." She laughed when Nat stiffened. "Not that kind of love, Nat— I'm not *in* love with you."

"Damn it, Meg." Nat extracted her hand after a gentle squeeze. "Don't you think I wish sometimes that things were different between us?"

Meg shrugged. "I don't think about it. I've never looked for more."

"I'm just in a weird place right now," Nat said, looking away. "Don't pay any attention to me."

"I'm not going to disappear or fall apart if you tell me you have feelings for someone else," Meg said. "We're friends. That's what matters most to me."

"I have feelings that I don't want to have," Nat said, sounding bitter and not liking it. "I don't even know how I've gotten myself into this."

Meg nodded. "I won't ask for the details, but is she not respecting your limits?"

"No, she is. I'm the one who can't seem to stop myself from acting like a fool around her."

"We'd be talking about a certain charming newcomer, I assume?"

"It's obvious?"

"Only to anyone who isn't blind or dead." Meg leaned forward, her expression softening. "Nat, I've known you a long time. I can tell when something's on your mind. And right now, that something seems to be a whole lot of Vic O'Brien."

Nat groaned. "Wonderful."

"I take you've, ah, been with her? And there's a problem?"

Nat sighed, tracing the condensation on her glass. How could she begin to explain the tangled mess of longing inside her and the undeniable pull that defied all logic and reason?

"It's complicated," she said at last, the words feeling woefully inadequate.

"Isn't it always?" Meg lifted a brow. "Look, I get it. Sometimes getting close to people is the scariest thing we can do."

"You've got that right," Nat murmured.

"So what are you afraid of?"

Nat glared. "You're relentless, you know that?"

Meg smiled. "You were saying?"

Before Nat had to answer—and face truths she wasn't ready for—her phone buzzed with a 911 text. Her stomach tightened as she scanned the message. "Ah, damn it. We've got a small plane down in the high peaks."

All around the room, officers and first responders were checking their phones, conversations dying away. Chairs scraped as people rose, tossing money on the tables.

"I got it too." Meg rose, catching Nat's arm. "Don't let fear keep you from something that could be amazing. You deserve happiness, and if Vic is the one who brings you that? Don't let her slip away."

"No time to worry about that now." Nat left a twenty on the bar. "I want to check with Charlie."

"Go—I'm heading into the station." Meg kissed her cheek. "Be careful—it's going be rough going up there after all the rain we've had."

"I will. You too."

Nat caught up with Charlie, Phee, and Vic on the street just as another call came through. She signaled for them to hold up as she answered. "This is Evans."

"Nat, it's Paulie Antonelli. Single-engine plane down somewhere up on Bear Mountain. No exact coordinates yet, but we're looking at a probable crash site along the ridgeline. We'll need fire control and a med team ASAP. If we can't land a chopper, we'll have to insert teams on foot."

"I'm with the Warrensburg sheriffs now—they're mobilizing. We'll stage a camp at the foot of Snow Cap Trail and start the ascent. What do you have on board?"

"Two pilots and a dozen dogs."

Nat frowned. "Say again?"

"A pilot flying a mercy mission—transporting dogs from a kill shelter to an adoption center up in Hazelton. Looks like we're dealing with an animal rescue situation on top of everything else."

Nat's resolve hardened. "Understood. We'll get there as fast as we can."

She disconnected and turned to Charlie. "We'll need every available deputy."

"You'll have 'em," he said briskly.

"We'll assemble at Bolton," Nat said.

Charlie signaled to his officers. "Let's go...time to do some hiking."

Phee and Charlie hurried toward their vehicles, but Vic hung back. When she started to speak, Nat shook her head.

"We have to go," Nat said, her heart aching.

"I know." Vic stepped closer, her voice low, urgent. "You know we're not done, right?"

Nat swallowed hard, the burn of words she wanted to say searing her throat. She hesitated, afraid of opening a door she'd never be able to close.

The fear won.

"I can't. Not now."

Before either of them could say anything else, Nat ran, the shadows in Vic's eyes haunting every step.

CHAPTER FOURTEEN

The DEC convoy rumbled to a stop at the base of Snow Cap Trail, kicking up gravel and dead pine needles in its wake. The rain had started as they'd left Bolton and now fell in a steady downpour.

Nat swung out of the passenger seat before her truck had fully stopped, her boots hitting the packed earth with a sharp crunch. Around her, the hum of engines and clipped commands filled the air as rangers, fire crews, sheriff's deputies, and medics moved with swift, practiced efficiency. Work crews scurried to off-load everything needed for a wilderness base camp—tents, medical supplies, generators, portable lights, communication equipment, and emergency rations. Every ranger carried their own climbing gear, field tools, single-person tents, first aid kits, and enough supplies to sustain them in the mountains for days if necessary. They had no way of knowing how long the extraction would take and prepared for the worst.

Nat surveyed the bustling scene, searching for Vic. She couldn't find her in the milling crowd and swallowed her uneasiness. Vic had her job to do, and so did she. Vic would be fine.

She held on to that thought as she strode toward the medical tent to meet Chase, who'd just arrived with her wife, Timara, and Marty.

"Lily was with me at the lodge when the call came in," Chase said. "Sounded like you'd need as many hands as you could get, and these two volunteered."

"You got that right." Nat mentally calculated where everyone would be best deployed. "Lily, can you oversee getting the triage center set up down here?"

"Sure," Lily said. "Just leave me another medic, and we can handle things."

"Good. Timara, you're with Lily." Nat turned to the rangers gathered around and gestured to Grant McHenry, the leader of the team responsible for setting a fire line and securing the crash site. "Get your team started up the mountain. The extraction team will move in behind you as soon as the perimeter is set."

"Got it. Once we have containment, I'll radio a status report." McHenry signaled his team. "Let's go, boys and girls."

The rain started as the first team set off at a jog, disappearing into the tree line. The Bolton Fire Department's rescue units arrived, red strobes slicing through the late-night sky. A Warrensburg sheriff's SAR unit rolled in right behind them. Megan hopped out of the BFD command unit, her expression all business as she wended her way to Nat.

"Where do you want us?"

"I need another medic with us," Nat said, "and your SAR unit needs to start the ascent as soon as they're geared up."

Megan nodded, reaching for her radio, but before she could relay the orders, Nat's radio crackled.

The state police dispatcher came through, voice clipped and professional. "Evans, be advised—high winds at altitude, unsafe for air insertion. Chopper is grounded. Unable to deploy team. Visual confirms debris field at approximately three thousand feet, quarter mile northwest of Snow Cap Trail. No movement detected."

Nat grimaced. A visual was good, but no air drop meant a significant delay in reaching the survivors. Hypothermia was a very real threat. The nighttime temps at that elevation could be lethal.

"Roger that." Nat exhaled sharply, shoving down frustration. Nothing new—air support wasn't always a given in mountain rescues. They'd get there on foot. They had no choice.

As Nat continued directing newly arriving personnel, Phee and Vic strode into base camp with the sheriff's SAR unit. Of course Vic would be with them. She was always in the thick of the action. Nat squelched her worry. No time.

Their eyes met briefly, no words possible in the rush to deploy the rest of the teams.

Vic gave a small nod.

Nat smiled back, but unease coiled low in her gut. The situation was unpredictable—forest fires, fuel explosions, unstable wreckage. Vic was trained, capable—but this terrain didn't care about training. The mountain swallowed people whole.

Nat tamped down the worry. Again.

"Alright. Listen up." Nat raised her voice as the dozens of rangers, deputies, and other first responders gathered around her. "You all know what's at stake. A plane's down in rough country. We have survivors who won't last the night without help, and a pack of terrified dogs lost in the wreckage. We move fast, we move smart, and we bring them all home."

A ripple of nods and *copy that's*. Then everyone shouldered packs, tightened harnesses, and synchronized radios. Nat locked eyes with Vic one more time across the buzzing base camp, and for just a breath, everything else fell away. The awkwardness, the tension, the unanswered questions evaporated, and she sent a silent message.

Be careful. You matter.

Then the moment was gone.

Chase appeared at her side. "We're ready. You?"

Nat nodded. "Let's move."

Chase touched her arm briefly. "We'll get them out, Nat. All of them."

The reassurance, simple but firm, helped Nat push down the gnawing anxiety. "I know."

With a sharp exhale, Nat hoisted her pack, turned toward the darkened trail, and led her team into the mountain. Vic was somewhere behind her, maybe watching, maybe not. With Phee. The thought twisted inside her like a live wire.

No time for that now.

Until the mission was over and every last soul accounted for, she needed to maintain control—navigating chaos, making decisions, securing the safety of her teams and the survivors.

Failure was not an option.

In her personal life? She was lost.

But here? She was at home.

❖

The ascent was hell. The rain lashed sideways, icy needles piercing through the layers of Nat's waterproof gear. She adjusted the straps on her pack, the weight digging into her shoulders.

McHenry's team had cut downed trees and strung rope lines where the trail had washed out, but the climb was still brutal, even for seasoned rangers like Nat and her team. The relentless rain had transformed the narrow trail into a churning mess of mud and debris, making each step a fight against the sucking earth beneath her boots. Loose shale and slick boulders shifted treacherously underfoot. Thick, clawing branches lashed at her face, undergrowth snagging her pack. The howling wind funneled through the ravine in ghostly wails. Every breath burned, her lungs fighting the climb, but she didn't stop—couldn't.

Nat clenched her jaw so tightly her face ached. Ahead, the path twisted sharply upward, narrowing to little more than a crumbling ledge. The team's headlamps bobbed in the darkness like fireflies, illuminating the wet gleam of jagged stone and the skeletal limbs of downed trees. Mud clung like dead weight to her boots, but she powered through, one foot in front of the other. Every muscle in her body burned, but she didn't slow.

She couldn't. No time to waste.

No one complained. They all knew what was at stake.

"Alpha team, this is McHenry. You copy?"

Nat had kept her radio open and answered, "This is Alpha One, go ahead."

"Be advised: Ground fire sighted. Cutting lines…headed off trail."

"Copy that. ETA your location twenty minutes." She adjusted the straps on her pack and motioned for her team to keep moving. Wiping rain from her eyes, she glanced at Chase, whose worried look echoed her concern. Fire on this terrain meant danger on multiple levels— unstable ground, potential explosions from the wreckage, and a threat to the downed occupants' chances of survival.

When they reached the point where damaged treetops and a miasma of smoke hung in the air, Nat signaled a halt. "We'll have to cut our way through to the crash site. It's a quarter of a mile from here. Brady, Dee—you're up."

The two rangers slung chain saws off their backs and took the lead, others following with axes and shovels. No one spoke. The roar of the saws split the night as wood chips and splintered bark flew in all directions. Nat turned her face to avoid the sting and pulled her neck gator up to filter out the acrid scent of burning wood.

"Move fast, but stay alert," she called over the noise. "If the wind shifts, that fire could turn."

When they broke through the final wall of tangled underbrush, the debris field yawned before them. The scent of fuel hit her first—sharp, acrid, wrong. Smoke curled through the darkness, thick and cloying.

Fire crackled weakly at the edge of the debris, spitting sparks into the rain.

The wreck lay crumpled against the ridge, its metal skin torn open, the rotor blades a twisted ruin. One wing had sheared clean off, its battered frame lying in the brush like a discarded relic. The nose cone was a collapsed accordion of warped metal, the fuselage ripped open along one side, spilling its contents across the damp forest floor. A half-burned seat, crushed metal containers—probably emergency supplies—lay strewn about. The tail section remained largely intact, tilted at an unnatural angle. The smoke from the engine curled into the rain-laden air, ghostly tendrils weaving between the branches.

All was eerily silent.

Nat swallowed back the sharp tang of adrenaline and focused. They had one priority: securing any survivors.

She scanned the wreckage for signs of movement. Nothing.

Her stomach knotted as she keyed her radio. "SAR team, set a sector search."

Her radio crackled, and Phee's voice came through. "Copy, Alpha One."

Nat motioned to Chase, who waited nearby with Marty and Meg. "Secure the wreckage. Report any structural hazards."

Chase nodded. "On it."

"Let me get the fire team in here first," Meg said. "We need to foam it down before something sparks."

Nat took a breath, forcing herself to ignore the devastation. No sign of the pilot, and that had to be their first priority. Megan wasn't wrong about the fire hazard. Climbing through the wreckage of a downed aircraft was a calculated risk—one wrong step and a section could collapse, pinning a rescuer beneath unstable metal. The risk of explosion, even with the fire crew suppressing hot spots, was real. Engines caught fire unexpectedly, fuel exploded, and toxic fumes plumed into suffocating clouds.

Which was why Nat intended to take the lead. And every second that passed was one less second they had to save whoever might be still alive.

"Fine, get them started." Nat adjusted her gloves, already mapping her path through the debris. "But I'm going in. Now."

Megan frowned but nodded. "If I say get out of there, you move."

"Right." Nat didn't plan on waiting for disaster to strike.

She checked the mangled cockpit first. The windshield had shattered, glass glittering wetly in the light of her headlamp. One door had been ripped off, probably on impact. Inside, both seats were missing, either torn from their bolts or thrown clear in the crash. A mess of tangled wires, exposed electronics, and fractured instrumentation spilled across the control panel. The stench of burned plastic stung her eyes.

A crimson pool spattered the ground beneath the missing door.

Blood. Trailing into the brush.

Nat's pulse kicked. A survivor had moved—or been dragged.

She pushed into the undergrowth, ignoring the sharp snap of twigs beneath her boots. The crash site faded into shadows behind her, the shouts of the rescuers fading into the wind hissing through the trees.

"Hello? Can you hear me?"

Nothing.

"Hello? Anyone?"

Then—movement.

A faint disturbance, just beyond the beam of her headlamp.

She moved in that direction, heart pounding.

"Come on, where are you?" she muttered, sweeping the light across the twisted foliage.

Then—there.

A man. Face down in the mud, his body crumpled, his clothes torn and charred. The shattered windshield had done its damage: Glass glistened in the deep gash above his temple, rain turning the wound into a river of red. Blood slicked his face, pooling near his mouth. One arm lay at an impossible angle, bone threatening to puncture skin.

Nat dropped to her knees, sliding through the wet earth as she reached for him. She tore off her glove and pressed her fingers gently against his throat. Pulse—weak, erratic. But there.

Relief hit fast—then vanished.

She grabbed her radio. "I've got the pilot! Medic, now!"

❖

Vic flipped the hood of her rain jacket up over her helmet, bracing against the mist that seeped through every gap in her gear and settled against the back of her neck like ice. Cold, insidious, inescapable.

The storm steadily worsened. Thunder rumbled in the distance. The wind cut through the trees, rattling the branches with restless urgency. Rain pounded the canopy, drumming against leaves and sending rivulets streaming down the sloped terrain. The mud sucked at her boots with every step as she pushed deeper into the undergrowth.

The plane had torn a ragged path through the forest, gouging a deep trench in the sodden earth. Broken saplings jutted out at odd angles, their splintered edges stark against the darkness. On either side of her, the glare of headlamps cut jagged beams through the downpour. As she reached the wreckage, the sudden quiet felt wrong. Hollow. Her stomach churned with the acid burn of adrenaline. No cries for help. No rustling movement. No survivors struggling to be found.

Was no one alive?

The plane's crushed cabin had been empty—no sign of the dogs. They were out there somewhere, probably injured, definitely frightened.

"Come on," she whispered, pushing soaked hair out of her eyes. "Where are you?"

Then—a faint whimper.

Her pulse jumped, and she froze, holding her breath. Blocked out the wind, the radio chatter, the pounding of her own heart.

A muffled bark.

Small. Weak. Close.

She surged into the thicket, clambering over a fallen tree. Bits of wreckage crunched beneath her boots.

"Over here!" She turned her head, listening—*there*. "Got a live one—dog trapped!"

Ahead, a battered metal crate had slammed into a tree and lay half-buried in mud. Its mesh door was partially crushed, barely hanging off the hinges. Inside, a black Lab puppy huddled in the farthest corner, its ribs pressing starkly against damp fur, wide brown eyes glassy with fear.

Vic dropped to her knees beside the crate, scarcely registering the cold seeping into her legs.

"It's okay, buddy. I got you."

Gritting her teeth, she fought with the door. The damn thing refused to budge, the slick metal slipping between her fingers.

Somewhere, someone called for a backboard. A medic rattled off vitals. The tension in the air hummed, electric, but her whole world narrowed to the desperate pup inside.

"Easy, baby," she whispered. "Just another minute…"

The door gave with a sharp snap and scraped open.

The puppy cowered, too frightened even to run.

Vic extended her hand, slow and steady.

"It's okay," she crooned. "You're safe now."

The puppy, its fur matted with mud, finally crawled forward and tentatively nuzzled into her palm. Dizzy with relief, she scooped the dog into her arms, his small body quivering. She unzipped her jacket and tucked him inside. His heartbeat thrummed against hers, a frantic stutter.

Behind her, Phee called out, voice sharp with urgency. "Two more—one's out, the other's stuck."

"Got a couple sprung crates here," Charlie called.

Vic turned in his direction. "Let's spread a search line. There must be more."

Charlie was already radioing the others. "Eyes up. Watch for movement. Loose debris, shifting ground—stay sharp."

Vic carried the rescued pup to the makeshift triage area. Marty stood waiting, hands outstretched.

"Take care of him," Vic said, her voice cracking. Poor little guy.

Marty cuddled the puppy. "I got him. Go."

Vic wheeled, muscles still tense. The wreckage loomed ahead, a skeletal husk against the sky. No sparks. No fire. But that didn't mean it was stable.

Then—

"Might have a victim trapped under the fuselage," Nat yelled.

Vic raced toward the plane, Chase right behind.

Nat crouched beside the twisted wreckage, peering into the mangled remains of the fuselage. Vic dropped beside her, scanning the collapsed frame. Rain slicked off the metal, pooling in the crevices.

"There's someone," Vic said urgently. "We need to get them out. The whole thing could shift any second."

"Hold," Nat snapped, gripping Vic's shoulder. "No one goes under there until we stabilize it." She signaled Chase. "Get the hydraulics in here, ASAP."

"Roger," Chase said, already on the run.

"Let's clear some of this rubble," Nat said.

Muscles quivering with impatience, Vic grunted, "Aye, aye."

Together, they heaved at the debris. The metal groaned—a slow, ominous sound. The rain hammered harder, turning the ground into an oily swamp. Chase's team rushed in, setting stabilizers against the shifting wreckage. The hydraulic lift hissed as it took the strain.

"Nat," Chase said urgently. "The pilot's critical. Likely spleen rupture, multiple fractures. They need rapid evac or he's not making it."

Nat's spine went rigid. She pressed her radio. "Medics—get the pilot down to base. Now."

Her voice was all command. No hesitation.

A minute that felt like hours later, Chase said, "We're clear here."

Nat leaned in toward the victim. "Can you hear me? We're going to get you out."

A low moan.

Nat turned to Vic. "Cervical collar and backboard. Pass them in to me."

Vic hesitated.

Tight space. Unstable wreckage. Bad call.

"That's too tight, Nat," Vic said, voice low. The beams had already twisted. The slightest bump, and the whole thing could collapse. "Let me go in."

Nat met her gaze. The wreckage loomed over them, a mass of mangled steel. The acrid scent of jet fuel thickened the air.

Nat didn't look away. Didn't blink.

"Do not be a hero." Her voice was firm, clipped. "If this shifts, you're out. No debate."

Nat squeezed her arm—just for a second. Just enough.

A beat passed as Vic held Nat's gaze. "Aye, aye, Lieutenant."

A fresh gust of wind howled through the trees, rattling the branches overhead. The fuselage shifted. Not much—but enough. Enough to make her stomach knot.

Go. Now.

She dropped to her knees and slipped beneath the wreckage's twisted shell. The scent of oil and blood thickened, damp earth mixing with the sharp tang of metal. The limited light from her headlamp barely cut through the wreck's depths.

Vic crawled further under the crumpled fuselage, and the world went dark.

CHAPTER FIFTEEN

Lily Davenport jerked around as the triage tent's flaps snapped open, rain whipping through the entrance in a cold, lashing gust. The floodlights outside cast harsh, shifting shadows across the soaked ground, turning the medics and first responders into blurred silhouettes against the storm. Juanita ducked inside, her rain gear dripping.

"Got the pilot here. Middle-aged male. Unconscious, hypotensive, and hypothermic. Abdomen is tense—we're thinking it's the spleen."

"Bring him over here." Lily pointed to the makeshift surgical station—a steel field table draped with sterile sheets beneath the portable halogen lights.

The field medics hustled in, boots squelching in the thick tarp flooring as they maneuvered the stretcher through the crowded tent. The pilot lay strapped in, barely moving, his face bloodless, lips pale and slack, dark curls matted to his forehead with sweat and rain. An air splint encased his right arm and MAST trousers compressed his lower extremities.

Juanita fell in beside them, connecting the lines and leads snaking across the patient's chest to the monitors set up by the table. "We've got another one incoming—bad shape." Her voice was taut, sharp with urgency. "Blunt force trauma, probable internal bleeding."

Lily's stomach clenched. The pilot was already critical. How many more? "Understood. Let's get him stabilized and out of here ASAP."

Lily shifted focus to the pilot. Weak, thready carotid pulse. Shallow breath sounds. No significant fluid in the lungs—yet. "BP's 80 over 50. His core temp is too low. We need to get some warm fluids into him."

"Right here," Timara said, inserting the tubing into the saline bags and hanging them on the portable IV pole. She opened the lines wide. "Pulse ox is dropping."

Frowning, Lily scanned the monitors, the faint bluish tint of his fingertips igniting a ripple of concern. She listened to his chest again. "He's moving air. I'd rather not intubate him out here."

Timara adjusted the flow on the saline. "Pressure's coming up— 87 over 56. PO2 ninety-three."

"Good." Lily turned to the FD paramedics waiting with a gurney. "He's all yours. Advise the ER they'll need blood and an OR standing by. Probable intra-abdominal bleeding. Multiple extremity fractures. Closed head injury."

"Roger," the Bolton paramedic said. "Thanks, Doc."

As the medics lifted the pilot onto the stretcher, his eyelids fluttered. His left hand twitched. "Dogs," he muttered, voice faint behind the O2 mask. "Brenda. Where…"

Lily grabbed his hand before he could rip at his mask. "Brenda— she was on the plane? We've located the other person. And we're rounding up the dogs."

His gaze flickered, hazy but desperate. "Please…"

"We'll get them. We're taking you to the ER now." Lily squeezed his hand and signaled to the medics. "Go."

The paramedics wheeled the stretcher out into the storm. Lily watched them disappear into the rain, her chest tightening. The pilot had held on long enough to beg for them—his copilot, his dogs.

Lily braced herself.

They'd find them all.

But could they save them?

❖

Water dripped steadily from the twisted wreckage, pinging off Nat's rain slicker as she shined her Maglite beneath the plane's crushed frame. The wind picked up, rattling the wreckage. Loose branches skittered off the fuselage, tumbling down the slope. Rainwater pooled in the deep gouges carved by the crash, sloshing beneath Nat's boots. Rain streaked down her face as she crouched, angling the beam into the wreck's hollow. The light trembled in her grip, casting shifting shadows over crumpled steel and jagged edges that threatened to give way at any second.

Vic was under there.

Nat's stomach knotted. Too much weight. Too much damage. Too damn unstable.

She could just make out Vic's movements, slow and deliberate in the confined space.

Nat clenched her jaw. *Careful. Be careful.*

The wreckage groaned, metal shifting with a sickening creak. Too unstable. Nat sucked in a breath.

"Vic!" she called, her voice sharper than she intended. "Talk to me."

A beat.

"I'm fine. All's good."

Bullshit.

Another shift of metal. The fuselage sagged another inch.

Nat's pulse hammered.

"You need to get out of there—now."

Vic kept inching forward. "I see them."

Lightning flickered in the distance, illuminating the wreck in a split-second flash. Vic's silhouette was clearer now—one knee in the mud, bracing against a twisted support beam, reaching beneath the collapsed panels.

"Another minute, Vic, and you're out. The ground's like porridge, and that plane wants to slide off this slope." Nat's stomach lurched. She could see it happening—the whole wreck careening down the mountainside, Vic pinned beneath it, buried in a twisted heap of metal and mud. "That's an order."

"A minute." Vic didn't look up. Didn't hesitate.

Another beat.

Then Vic's muffled voice. "Almost there."

Goddamn it.

Nat clenched her jaw, fighting the urge to crawl in after her. Vic was doing exactly what she would have done—what any of them would do. Nat hated watching helplessly while Vic risked her life. Vic wasn't just a teammate. She'd become someone more, someone vital. Someone Nat couldn't bear to lose.

The realization hit like a blow, stealing the breath from her lungs. Not now—she couldn't go there now.

"Vic?"

Vic's voice came back, strained but triumphant. "Got her!"

Nat exhaled her first full breath in what felt like forever. "Easy—go easy."

Marty and Chase trudged through the mud with a stretcher.

"Storm's getting worse," Chase said. "We need to get her and the dogs down the mountain soon or we might not be able to."

"Vic has her," Nat said.

Vic finally appeared, dragging the backboard through the wreckage, her shoulders taut with strain. Nat crawled in a few feet and grabbed the end of the backboard. Once clear of the wreckage, she helped Marty and Chase lift the injured woman into the Stokes litter basket for transport. Two other firefighters grabbed on.

"Go," Nat said. "We'll round up the dogs and follow."

"Better be quick," a bearded firefighter warned, gripping the litter's side. "Juanita just radioed—the trail down is already washed out in places."

Nat glanced at Vic. "Head down with them. I'll stay with SAR and finish getting the dogs out."

Vic wiped mud from her face. Her hands were streaked with blood. "No way. We need every person to carry the animals."

"I'm staying too," Marty said.

Chase waved a hand. "Let's move, people."

Nat bit back a sigh. No time to argue. Vic was right. Again. They had a dozen dogs left to transport. "Fine. We need to figure out how to get them down."

Vic gestured toward the empty supply bags stacked near the triage area. "We can rig makeshift carriers from them. Most of them are puppies—small enough to fit."

Nat considered the logistics. "It's going to be slow going, especially on the steeper sections."

"We can do it," Marty said. "No way are we leaving any of them."

"No, we're not." Nat squared her shoulders. "Let's make sure we've got them all. Everyone carries two."

By the time they started down, the trail was little more than a flooded ribbon winding through the skeletal trees and jagged rocks. Nat took the lead, scanning the ground for unstable footing—exposed roots, loose shale, sinkholes. Every step was a calculated risk. Vic, Marty, and the last of the SAR team followed, loaded down with equipment and dogs in makeshift slings.

Nat glanced back, checking on the others, and met Vic's gaze. "Doing okay?"

Vic nodded, voice steady. "Yep. Slow and easy. I think the pups are liking the ride."

Nat almost laughed, surprised to find anything to enjoy in the middle of such a mess. Vic somehow always managed to show her another side of things. "Right, that's because we're the ones who are wet and muddy."

"Good to be a dog today," Vic said.

"Just be careful—I don't want you…" She caught her slip. "Anyone…getting hurt."

Vic's expression softened. "I'm good, Nat."

Nat swallowed and pressed on. Distance. That was the smart choice. But just now, she couldn't refuse the comfort of Vic's steady strength.

"Almost there," Nat called back. "Hot coffee and sandwiches await."

The tree line broke, and base camp came into view. A collective sigh of relief rippled through the group. Deputies and firefighters moved in, off-loading the dogs into waiting vehicles.

One clapped Vic on the back. "Hell of a job up there."

Vic flashed Nat a grin. "Nice navigating."

Warmth bloomed in Nat's chest, along with a sudden, fierce surge of connection that caught her off guard. She didn't resist, too damn tired to fight the feeling. "I mostly tried not to fall on my ass or lead us all over a cliff."

"I never worried for a minute," Vic said, her eyes burning with intensity. "Nat, I—"

"Nat," Charlie boomed, "the pilot and passenger have been transported. Local animal shelters are expecting a lot of wet guests."

"Right," Nat said briskly, turning away from Vic, the moment of connection lost. The exhaustion settled in then—deep, bone-wearying. Nat scanned the camp, teams breaking down tents, others loading trucks, NTSB already en route. What she wanted most was something hot to drink and a shower so long she'd forget she was ever cold.

As if reading her mind, Vic pressed a steaming coffee cup and an MRE into her hands. "Eat."

"Thanks." Nat studied Vic, whose eyes were bright despite being shadowed with fatigue. "Why do I think you're having fun?"

Vic grinned and looked even younger for a moment. "I feel great, don't you? We saved the plane's crew *and* rescued the dogs."

"You did a stellar job out there today," Nat said.

"I just did my part," Vic said, shrugging. "You get the flowers for running the whole show and keeping us all on point."

"Just doing my part," Nat echoed.

Vic gestured toward the ambulance, where a tech strapped a dog to a gurney. "That's my pup—the one with the burns. I want to go with him. He's pretty scared."

Nat's heart did that annoying stutter thing again. Of course Vic would want to be sure the puppy was secure. She cleared her throat. "Right. We're done here except cleanup. Go."

"Thanks," Vic said, already moving.

"Text me an update," Nat called after her.

"Aye, aye." Vic sketched a salute.

Aye, aye. I hear and I obey.

Nat watched Vic jog to the vehicle, wishing her damn heart would do the same.

CHAPTER SIXTEEN

C an I do anything to help?" Vic shouted above the wail of the siren as the fire rescue truck barreled toward the Northway, lights flashing. She ignored the pain from kneeling on the hard metal floor by the side of the stretcher, her heart aching for the three small patients lined up side by side with IVs running into their legs: a gangly gray pit bull pup with a broken rear leg, a pretty tricolor beagle with a puncture wound in her side, and a way-too-thin black Lab mix with burns on his face and forelegs. Their small bodies were covered in soot and burns, their fur matted with blood and ash.

Too much blood. Too damn much.

Her pulse hammered in time with the flashing lights outside. Trees blurred past. The highway stretched ahead, slick and black beneath the storm. The scent of antiseptic mixed with the sharper bite of copper, the memory of another night—another loss—threatening to claw its way up her throat. She shoved it down. They were alive. They had a chance.

"Just talk to them. Keep them calm." Kareem, the burly middle-aged paramedic with a full black beard and soft dark brown eyes, busy rewrapping a bandage, barely spared her a glance. "And keep an eye on the IVs. If a line stops running, let me know. These little guys are wiggly despite being sick."

"Scared." Vic gently stroked the top of one head after the other. "It's okay, guys. We're going to get you patched up, don't you worry. We're taking you to the best hospital ever. I heard they take care of the sickest animals there and make them all better."

The little black Lab puppy's dark eyes met hers, and he tried to lick her finger. Fierce protectiveness washed over her. "Can we give them anything for pain?"

"Already gave them each a little meloxicam—vet ordered it."

"Oh, good."

"I wouldn't get too attached if I were you," the paramedic warned from the driver's seat. "Pups in that condition...well, the kindest thing might be to put 'em down."

Vic held back a harsh retort. Like hell she would let that happen. These little fighters were special. They'd survived the crash—and they deserved a fighting chance now.

She petted the puppy's head and looked back into his trusting brown eyes. "Don't listen to him. You're gonna make it through this, you hear me? I'll be right by your side the whole way. Promise."

The puppy woofed softly, as if he understood, and pressed his muzzle into her palm. She was done for. Any notion of remaining detached flew right out the window. She was in this for the long haul now.

The vet ER came into view—a red-bricked beacon in the dark. The truck lurched to a stop. Before the sirens stilled, the back doors flew open. A team already waiting. Vic jumped out into a flurry of motion—people calling orders, techs reaching for the puppies, a gurney squeaking to a halt on the rain-soaked pavement.

"What have we got?" A tall, dark-haired woman in scrubs scanned the trio of puppies intently.

"Burns on this one"—Vic indicated the Lab—"and assorted trauma on the other two."

"We'll take it from here," the woman said, her tone softening. "I'm Dr. Graham Furness, one of the trauma vets. I'll be in charge of these little ones."

As she spoke, the techs wheeled the puppies away.

"Deputy Vic O'Brien." Vic watched them go, heart sinking. "Could you let me know as soon as there's any news? I'll be waiting right here."

"It could be a few hours, if you want to leave a number," Furness said, already heading for the hospital.

"No. I'm staying." Vic kept pace with the vet, who gave her a small smile.

"Of course. I'll keep you updated," Furness said.

When Furness disappeared into the treatment area, Vic sank into one of the hard plastic chairs in the waiting area, pushing rain-damp hair off her face.

Nothing else she could do.

All she could do now was wait. And hope.

❖

As the minutes ticked by, Vic replayed the aftermath of the plane crash—the harrowing climb up and down the mountain, the treacherous rescue of the pilot and passenger, the frantic search for the lost and injured dogs. Every detail clung to her like the dampness still seeping through her clothes. The feel of slick rocks beneath her boots. The bite of the wind howling through the trees. The wreckage groaning, threatening to collapse. The pained whimpers in the dark, the flash of fur as they pulled the dogs from the underbrush.

In every recollection, Nat. Taking charge: calm and steady, determined and sure, leading them all out of that hell. And in the rare quiet when the chaos stilled for an instant, Nat's eyes meeting hers across the wreckage, a silent check-in asking how she was holding up. A quick touch, a brush of shoulders, that silently said, "I'm here. We've got this."

No one had made her feel that way before—as if she was someone worth worrying about, worth protecting. A flurry of butterflies swirled in her stomach, and she chided herself for reading too much into it.

Nat was just…incredible. And doing her duty. And, more importantly, off-limits.

"Deputy O'Brien?" a deep male voice inquired.

Vic shot upright. "Yes?"

"I'm Malcolm, one of the techs." A tall, broad-shouldered man in green scrubs extended his hand. "I understand you came in with the puppies from the fire? Graham…Dr. Furness…asked me to come out with an update."

Vic stood and shook his hand. "Yes. How are they doing?"

"They're all stable right now. The burned puppy is in critical condition." His voice was solemn but his eyes kind. "With burns the care is often protracted, and sometimes euthanasia is the most humane decision."

"I understand." Vic thought frantically. No way was she giving up unless he couldn't be saved. "Can you keep him out of pain while you treat him?"

"Yes, but even if he doesn't develop any complications, he'll need several trips back to the OR to clean up the burns. Plus a long course of wound care." He hesitated. "It's a costly course of treatment."

And the puppy was a shelter dog with no home.

Vic didn't stop to consider any alternative. "Euthanasia is not an option, not until there's no other choice. I'll pay for his care, whatever it takes. He's a fighter, I know it. He just needs a chance."

Surprise crossed Malcolm's face. "Deputy, I appreciate your compassion, but it's a significant commitment."

"You can tell Dr. Furness he's mine now." Vic set her jaw. "Just do whatever it takes to give him the best chance at life."

"I'll tell her—I don't think she'll be surprised." He offered his hand again. "Thank you."

Vic nodded, swallowing hard. "I'll be out here."

"It will be a few more hours."

"I'll be here."

Vic sank into her chair, filled with worry and hope in equal measure.

Please. Please let him make it through this.

She drifted, exhaustion pulling at her, until her phone vibrated.

She fumbled it from her pocket.

It was 7:01 a.m.

Her heart stuttered when she saw Nat's text.

Everything okay? Didn't see your pickup at the cabin

Vic's hands shook as she typed out a response.

At the animal hospital. Waiting on surgery for the pups

She hit send and rubbed her face. The faint scent of smoke clung to her clothes. Fighting the weariness seeping into her bones, she walked outside for some air. Back inside, she paced around the spacious waiting area until she spied a glassed-in enclosure where a massive Great Dane in a body sling floated in a hydrotherapy tank. Her guy might need that. She imagined how she would handle his needs, lost in the motions of dog and caretakers.

Footsteps behind her, and she turned, expecting the vet.

"Vic!" Nat said. "What's the status? Is the puppy alright?"

Vic's legs went weak, the relief of seeing Nat breaking her tight grip on her emotions. She coughed to clear the lump in her throat. "He's in surgery. The vet said it's touch and go, but I couldn't just leave him."

Nat rested a hand on Vic's arm, her smile tender. "Of course you couldn't. You're a hero."

Vic huffed. Terrified was what she was. "I don't know about that. I just…I couldn't bear the thought of him being alone. He needs someone to fight for him."

"Don't we all," Nat murmured, her thumb tracing soothing circles on Vic's sleeve. "And he's got you. That's no small thing, Vic."

Vic's heart swelled, gratitude and something deeper filling her chest. She leaned into Nat's touch and whispered, "Thank you for being here. For understanding."

"You shouldn't have to go through this alone." Nat smiled. "Now, what do you say we grab some pizza while we wait? MREs were a long time ago."

Vic laughed, the sound surprising her. "Pizza sounds perfect. Only, it's, like, eight in the morning."

"Your point being?" Nat grinned, sliding her hand down to take Vic's. "C'mon, then. I know a place nearby that makes breakfast versions."

As they walked out of the hospital, Vic kept a grip on Nat's hand. The uncertainty in her chest eased. Whatever happened with the puppy, she wouldn't face it alone.

❖

The tiny place in a strip mall a quick five-minute walk away offered coffee and pizza with toppings appropriate for breakfast. Vic spied a tray with half a pepperoni pizza that looked fresh and ordered that. Her stomach was still on evening time.

She slid into a red vinyl-backed booth across from Nat, their knees brushing beneath the table. The accidental touch sent a flicker of heat up her spine, and for just a minute, she let herself dream, imagining the two of them together: Lazy mornings, tangled sheets, and soft kisses that turned into something more. Nat's head resting on her shoulder as dawn broke, setting the sky afire.

So real she could almost reach out and touch it.

For a fleeting second.

She knew better. Nat wanted something different. Something uncomplicated.

Nat studied her. "You know, I still can't believe you just up and decided to adopt that puppy. I mean, don't get me wrong, it's amazing, but not many people would take on a badly injured puppy—and foot all his bills—just like that."

Vic shrugged, tracing patterns on the tabletop. "I know it seems wild, but…I just couldn't walk away from him. He needs me."

"And that was all it took?" Nat's expression softened. "Of course it was. He needed you. Story over."

Vic frowned. She hadn't exactly considered all the details. "Hell. I should have checked with you. I didn't think about having a puppy in the cabin. If you need me to move out, I can—"

Nat covered Vic's hand. "Of course not. As long as you want to stay, the place is yours."

Forever. I want to stay forever.

Light-headed with relief and worry all mixed together, Vic let out a breath. "Thank you. I just…I don't want to have to leave. I feel like I'm finally starting to find my place here, you know?"

"I know. And you are. You belong here, Vic. Dog or no dog." Nat kept hold of her hand. "Are you okay? You're going on a day and a half with no sleep."

"I can't go home until I know he's stable." Vic swallowed. "I feel this connection to him, you know? Like we're meant to find each other. Is that weird?"

Nat shook her head. "No, it's beautiful. You've got such a big heart. The way you care about others, the way you're willing to put everything on the line for this little guy. It's wonderful."

"I don't know about that." Heat rushed to Vic's cheeks. "I'm just trying to do the right thing."

Nat brushed her thumb over Vic's knuckles, setting off a slow, shudder up Vic's arm. "And that's exactly what makes you so special. You don't even realize how amazing you are."

Vic's heart leapt, Nat's words wrapping around her like a warm embrace. She looked up, met Nat's gaze, and the rest of the world fell away.

Just the two of them.

For a heartbeat, even dreams seemed possible.

The spell broke as the person at the counter called out that their orders were ready.

Nat grinned, her hand lingering a second longer before slipping away. "Time for fuel. We've got a long day ahead of us."

"Us?"

Nat tilted her head, that smile—the one Vic was learning to love— playing across her very sexy mouth. "You didn't think I was leaving here without you, did you? I'm here as long as you are."

Vic's heart tripped over itself. She'd spent so long convincing herself not to want more, but then Nat would do something like this—just stay. Because Vic needed her.

"You've got to be as tired as I am," Vic said. "I can't—"

"Sure, you can," Nat said, voice soft, teasing—dangerous in a way that had nothing to do with risk. "I want to stay. You need a ride home. Simple."

Stay. Belong. Home.

Nat made her want all those things.

"Thank you."

"Mmm. Thank me by eating."

Laughing, Vic pulled a slice off the paper plate, the cheese stretching and finally landing on her chin.

"Here." Nat leaned over and swiped a napkin over the edge of Vic's jaw.

The act was simple. Casual. But the touch sent a sharp, hot flare through Vic's core.

Nat's face hovered inches away, her gaze locked with Vic's.

Vic's pulse hammered. It would take almost nothing—just a breath, just a shift—for her to close the space. "I have a very strong need to kiss you right now."

"I'm not sure the other diners could handle it." Nat leaned back, breaking the spell, and sighed. "Or me either."

"I'm sorry," Vic said. "That just…you just…damn it."

Nat smiled, but her eyes were guarded. "Hey, I'm not complaining about a hot younger woman taking an interest."

"I've got more than an interest," Vic said, holding Nat's gaze.

"I know," Nat said quietly.

But not a no. Not this time.

Vic blew out a slow breath. "Good."

❖

Walking back, Nat glanced at Vic, unable to look away. Strands of Vic's hair curled against her jaw, catching in the soft morning light, and for a fleeting second, Nat basked in the way the world seemed to soften when Vic was around. The sharp edges of exhaustion still clung to her, but in this moment—drenched, aching, running on fumes—Vic was breathtaking.

Nat tore her gaze away. Time to get a grip. Wrong time, wrong place—but that quiet, insistent pull toward Vic didn't fade. Just the opposite.

She'd hesitated driving to the ER, worried Vic wouldn't want her to come. After all, she'd been the one to set the boundaries. The one to push Vic away. More than once.

But Vic had welcomed her. And every minute they'd spent together had felt...precious.

Inside the fluorescent-lit waiting area, they settled into the plastic chairs, surrounded by a handful of weary-looking pet owners. The bright, antiseptic lighting made everything feel sharper. Harsher. This wasn't just any vet clinic. The animals here were fighting for their lives.

Beside her, Vic stretched out, shifting to get comfortable, her movements slower now, weighted by exhaustion.

"I'm awake," Vic muttered, eyes barely open.

"Go to sleep, then," Nat said gently. "I'll wake you when someone comes out."

"Yeah, okay."

Nat watched the tension in Vic's face fade as sleep took hold. The worry lines smoothed, the weight of the day momentarily lifting.

She looked younger. Softer.

She'd already lost so much. What if this puppy didn't make it?

The sudden, irrational urge to shield her struck hard. To protect that fragile, too-big heart from taking another hit.

A foolish wish. Vic wasn't fragile. She was strong—strong enough to take chances, strong enough to take on the suffering of others and still keep going.

Nat was the coward. *She* was the one afraid to take risks.

The doors to the treatment area swung open, and a tall, dark-haired woman in pale blue scrubs stepped out. She scanned the waiting room before heading their way.

Nat brushed her fingers over Vic's hand. "Hey, I think the vet's coming."

Vic snapped upright instantly, looking ridiculously alert for someone who'd just been dead asleep.

The vet's gaze landed on Vic. "I understand you're claiming the burned puppy?"

"Yes. Memphis is mine."

The vet arched a brow. "You named him?"

"Yes." Vic straightened. "This is DEC Lieutenant Nat Evans. She led the mission today."

The vet held out her hand to Nat. "Graham Furness. From what I hear, things were rough up there."

"The weather didn't help us much," Nat said easily, "but we got everyone out. That's a win."

"Yes, well, we all need those." Furness turned back to Vic. "Your puppy is stable, but he's not out of the woods yet—ours, at any rate. The main worry is infection. I'd like to keep him here on IV antibiotics for at least five days."

"Fine," Vic said. "Can I see him?"

Furness held up a hand. "You need to be aware that the cost—"

"I don't care about that," Vic said. "I'll cover it. I can leave a deposit."

Furness nodded briskly. "Alright then. Just a peek. Things are pretty hectic in the back right now."

Vic jumped up. "Thanks."

"I'm sorry, only one of you can come back," Furness added.

"That's fine," Nat said. "I'll wait."

She watched Vic disappear through the double doors, rubbing her thumb absently against the side of her palm. A few minutes later, Vic came out, her face tight.

Nat rose to meet her. "How does he look?"

"Small. Helpless. I hate that I can't tell him not to be scared." Vic bit off the words.

Nat's chest ached. She rested a hand on Vic's shoulder as they stepped out into a humid afternoon. "You were there for him. That will help him feel safe."

Vic sighed. "I never had a dog. Always wanted one, but being at sea all the time—just didn't work."

"Well, now you have one. Some things are just meant to be, when the time is right."

Vic gave her a long look. "You're right."

Nat heard what Vic wasn't saying. Felt it in the charged air. And struggled with the attraction that grew stronger every time they were together. It wasn't just physical. And that was the problem.

Now, though, Vic, exhausted and worried, just needed a friend. And if her hand lingered a moment too long on Vic's arm, or her gaze drifted to the curve of her lips, well, that was a secret she would keep to herself, locked away in the depths of her heart where it couldn't hurt anyone but her.

"I won't be offended if you sleep on the drive home," Nat said, trying for casual as she pulled out of the lot.

Vic smiled. "I'm okay. The pizza and that little nap took care of me for a while. And you. Thanks for being here."

Nat swallowed. "I'm glad I could be."

She should leave it at that.

But she ached to brush a strand of hair from Vic's cheek, to do something, anything, to ease the worry in her eyes.

She kept both hands on the wheel. Focused on the road.

When she pulled into the drive, she shifted into park but didn't move. She needed to say something. But everything felt tangled, unsteady. She needed to get out of the Jeep before she did something she'd regret. Before she did what she wanted to do and pulled Vic into her arms. She hurriedly climbed out of the Jeep and waited for Vic on the path.

"Listen, Vic…" She hesitated. "Try to get some sleep. You need it."

Vic laughed, a pale shadow of her usual energy. "You too."

Neither of them moved. Vic's eyes searched her face. Nat's breath caught. If Vic kissed her now…

Nat eased away a step. "I just want you to know that I'm here for you, okay? Whatever you need, with Memphis or…whatever, just come to me."

"I'll remember," Vic said softly. "Thank you."

"No thanks needed."

"Right," Vic said when Nat remained silent. "Have a good night, Nat."

Nat stood there longer than she meant to, as if some invisible tether still held her in place. She should be exhausted. She should be relieved the worst of the last thirty-six hours was behind them. Instead, her thoughts looped back to the way their shoulders had nearly touched in the waiting room, the way Vic had looked at her just now—like she saw something in her that Nat wasn't ready to face.

She exhaled, long and slow, shoving her hands into her jacket pockets as she finally turned toward her own cabin.

"Sweet dreams," Nat whispered as Vic disappeared down the path.

She already knew hers would be restless.

Chapter Seventeen

V ic closed her eyes as hot water cascaded over her aching muscles, washing away the grime and tension of another twelve-hour shift. She tipped her head back, letting the water pound against the knots in her shoulders, heat sinking into bone-deep fatigue. A week had passed since the crash, but the bruises remained—dull shadows that matched the ones under her eyes. The past few nights had been relentless. Call after call, one crisis bleeding into the next.

With a sigh, she shut the water off, bracing her palm against the tile for an extra beat before stepping out into the cool air. She towel-dried quickly, tugged on a clean uniform, and raked her fingers through damp hair. The station was quiet—a rare lull, though she knew better than to trust it would last.

Time to grab a coffee and make the familiar drive to the vet hospital. She'd spent every free moment—of which there never seemed to be enough—visiting Memphis. After the first day, the techs had let her sit with him, and as he improved, they'd instructed her in his burn care and dressing changes.

Today, he was finally coming home.

That was what mattered.

That, and the fact that no one else had died on that mountain.

Everything was falling into place.

Almost everything.

Everything except Nat.

Almost a week.

A week that felt like a month.

Somehow, her life had become divided into before and after the night Nat drove her home—as if something had shifted beneath her feet without permission.

Was Nat avoiding her?

Or spending time with Megan instead?

Vic bit her lip, frustrated with the constant questions that had no answers.

She wanted Nat to be happy—even if it wasn't with her.

But, God. The way Nat had looked at her that night in the Jeep.

The charged silence. The shift in the air.

Vic had wanted to kiss her. And for a second, Nat had looked like she might have let her.

She couldn't just forget that.

When she stepped into the kitchen, the scent of fresh coffee greeted her. Phee stood at the counter, a brief flicker of appreciation in her eyes as she held out a steaming mug of coffee.

"Thanks," Vic said, taking a sip. Strong, cream, no sugar. Exactly the way she liked it.

"Had a feeling you might need it. Long week."

"Feels like a month," Vic muttered.

"Any plans tonight?" Phee asked casually. "I was thinking dinner at my place. I could rustle up some pasta and chicken." She regarded Vic steadily, the teasing lilt in her voice undercut by something else. "I've got a nice bottle of pinot noir. Sound tempting?"

The invitation was clear. A little more than just a dinner between friends.

Vic hesitated. Maybe, if she wasn't bone-tired, half in love with a woman who kept pushing her away, and smart enough not to mess up a good friendship, she might have been tempted.

"Thanks, but I can't." Vic kept her tone equally casual as she pulled on her boots. "Gotta pick up Memphis."

"Ah, right. Your new roommate." Phee smiled a little wryly. "How's the little guy doing?"

"Better, I hope." Vic shook the tension from her shoulders. "It's been rough, but he's a brave little guy."

"I'm really glad he's coming home." Phee's expression softened and the flirtation faded, replaced by something gentler. "Another time, then."

Vic nodded, grateful she didn't press.

The time might come—but that time wasn't now.

❖

At the hospital, the familiar scent of antiseptic blended with the murmurs of anxious pet owners, barking dogs, and the quiet drone of the television tuned to a weather station. The receptionist on duty smiled as Vic approached the front desk.

"Hi, Deputy. Here to pick up your boy?"

"Yeah." Vic pulled out her credit card and handed it over.

The receptionist picked up a chart. "I'll let them know you're here. Just have a seat, and someone will be out with his discharge instructions."

Nearly weak with relief, Vic settled into the stiff plastic chair, still half expecting some last-minute complication to keep Memphis from coming home.

The waiting gave her too much time to think, and her thoughts drifted to Nat as they often did when work or worries over Memphis relented.

Every memory warmed her. Nat's steady presence during the crash. The gentleness in her touch as she'd handled the injured puppies. The way she'd insisted on staying at the hospital with Vic through Memphis's surgery.

And yet, the longing only grew.

Twenty minutes later, Dr. Furness emerged carrying Memphis, his small frame wrapped in bandages, his tail wagging weakly. A vet tech followed, carrying a plastic bag filled with medications, bandages, and wound care solutions.

Vic's heart clenched, but when his eyes lit up at the sight of her, the knot in her chest unraveled just a little.

"Hey, buddy," she murmured, reaching for him as the vet gently passed him over. "Ready to go home?"

"He's definitely ready," Dr. Furness said. "Call us if you have any concerns. We'll see you both in two weeks."

"We'll be here."

Driving back to the cabin, Vic glanced at Memphis, curled up in the puppy seat she'd installed on the passenger side.

He was hers now.

Her life would never be the same—and she didn't mind.

No matter what he needed, she'd be there. No hesitation.

Her life already looked so different than it had less than a year ago. The future she'd imagined was gone, and in its place, a different path—one she hadn't planned for but that somehow felt right.

If only...

She sighed. Memphis cocked his head, as if reading her thoughts.

Vic laughed, reaching over to scratch behind his floppy ear. "There's this woman," she mused aloud. "You met her. Nat? Amazing in every way? Gorgeous, sexy, super competent? Yeah, I have a thing for her."

She paused. A thing.

A weak word for what she really felt.

She could think of a million better ones.

Excitement. Tenderness. Desire. Curiosity. Longing. Belonging.

"Yeah," she muttered, staring at the road. "All those things. More than that."

She glanced at Memphis, whose eyes were already fluttering closed. "I'm in deep. And in deep trouble. Maybe."

Then she rounded the bend to Nat's cabin, and her breath caught.

Nat's Jeep.

Parked in the driveway.

Vic checked the porch—and her pulse skipped.

There she was.

Nat sat in a rocking chair, a glass of wine in hand, the golden hues of the setting sun casting a soft glow over her elegant profile.

Vic let out a slow breath. "Well, my day just got a lot better."

She pulled into the driveway, unhooked Memphis, and cradled him gently as she walked up to the porch.

"Hey there." Nat raised her glass as Vic approached, her expression a mix of warmth and uncertainty. "Caught me red-handed drinking alone on my porch. My deepest, darkest secret revealed."

"Not exactly a sinful secret." Vic chuckled, tension easing slightly. "I'm sure it's a rare occurrence." She stopped at the foot of the steps in a patch of sunlight flickering through the trees. "Though I have to say, you've picked a pretty good spot for it."

"Looks even better now." Nat slowly looked from Vic to Memphis. "How's our little fighter doing?"

Vic swallowed. Just that small glance, and she was revved. She wanted to say something else—something to bridge the gap that had formed since the crash, but the words stuck in her throat. "He's tough, aren't you, buddy? The vet says he's healing well."

The silence stretched, thick with everything unsaid since the crash.

Nat exhaled slowly. "I confess I've been hanging out here—hoping I'd catch you." Her voice carried that quiet honesty Vic admired. "I wanted to check on both of you."

Vic's pulse jumped, but she kept her voice steady. "I'm glad you did. It's…it's good to see you, Nat."

Nat set her wine glass down and stood. "Need a hand getting him settled inside?"

Vic nodded, ridiculously happy that Nat wasn't about to disappear. "That'd be great, actually. He's supposed to be quiet—no running and jumping."

Nat raised a brow as Memphis wiggled in Vic's arms. "Challenge number one."

Vic laughed, Nat's presence already lifting the exhaustion pressing on her shoulders. "Yeah, right?" She hesitated, then added, "I don't suppose you have any more of that wine?"

A faint blush crept over Nat's cheekbones. "Wow, sorry. Of course. I was so taken with…Memphis…I didn't even think to offer you a drink. Hold on—I'll grab the bottle."

When they reached the cabin, Nat, the bottle tucked under her arm, held the door open so Vic could carry the pup inside. Inside, Nat moved easily in Vic's space, as if she belonged there. Intimate. Maybe a little *too* intimate. The thought sent a flutter through Vic's stomach, and her skin heated.

"Where should we set him up?" Nat asked softly.

"By the propane heater." Vic led the way. "I put a bed for him there. Figured he could use the extra warmth."

She knelt, gently lowering Memphis. Nat crouched beside her, adjusting one of the stuffed toys so it nestled against him. Their hands brushed.

Electricity zipped up Vic's spine.

She glanced up, catching Nat's gaze, and everything went still.

"You're good with him," Vic said, her voice barely above a whisper.

Nat smiled. "He's a special little guy. Reminds me of why I became a ranger in the first place."

The tenderness in Nat's voice made Vic's heart clench. "To save puppies from wildfires?"

Nat chuckled. "To protect puppies and all lost creatures. To make a difference."

"You do," Vic said. "Speaking as one of those lost creatures."

Nat's gaze burned into Vic's. "You were never lost. You're far too strong for that. You were hurt, and you bore it. Your life was upended, and you're making a new path. You're the least lost person I know."

Vic stepped closer. "Is that what you think? That I'm strong?" She cupped Nat's jaw. "I'm not strong enough to ignore what I feel about you."

Nat's breath hitched, her pupils widening. "God, you're..."

Vic kissed her.

Nat gripped her shoulders, as if she'd been waiting for that, and kissed her back. Vic shuddered, heat and sweetness flooding over her, the world narrowing to the slow, deliberate slide of lips and the intoxicating taste of Nat's breath mingling with hers. She kept the kiss gentle, tasting and teasing, their bodies barely touching.

She didn't push, didn't rush.

She just let herself have this.

Nat brushed a soft kiss over Vic's mouth and eased back. "I seem to remember there are a couple of wineglasses in the cabinets somewhere. Let me pour you a glass while you make sure he's settled."

"As long as you don't go anywhere," Vic said, her breath still uneven.

Nat's smile was quiet but certain. "No, I won't." A minute later, she handed Vic a glass of wine, their fingers briefly grazing as she passed it over. She lifted hers in a silent toast. "To a speedy recovery for the little hero."

"Hear, hear." Vic took a sip, the air charged. Nat's gaze flickered to her lips, a question in her eyes. Vic leaned in to ki—

A sharp knock at the door shattered the moment. Vic jumped, heat rushing to her face as she jerked back.

"I'll get it," she muttered, throat tight.

She opened the door—and froze.

Phee stood there, pizza box in hand, grinning. "Surprise! Thought you could use some food since I couldn't convince you to let me cook for you."

Not now.

Not now.

Not now.

She forced a smile. "Phee, I...thanks. That's really thoughtful." She stepped back, holding the door open. "Come on in."

As Phee entered, Vic risked a glance at Nat. The warmth in her eyes was gone, replaced by something cool and guarded.

Vic wanted to explain—God, she wanted to explain—but the moment had already slipped away. The atmosphere shifted, the connection they'd shared evaporating like morning dew burned away by the harsh summer sun.

"Oh, hey, sorry," Phee said, her tone light but eyes sharp. "I didn't realize you had company."

Nat didn't miss a beat. "Hardly company—I was just helping Vic get the puppy settled."

Vic flinched at the flatness in her voice.

"There's plenty of pizza for three," Phee offered.

Nat shook her head, already stepping toward the door. "Thanks, but I should probably get going. Early start tomorrow."

Vic clenched her fists. *Do something.*

Say something.

But she didn't.

Nat made it easy for her, pulling open the door with a measured smile. "Text me if you need a hand with him. I'm right next door."

Vic swallowed hard. "Thanks. I—"

Nat hesitated. Then offered a small, polite smile. "Have a good night. Enjoy your dinner."

And then she was gone.

Vic caught the door before it slammed shut, the urge to chase after Nat warring with the fear she'd only make things worse.

"Sorry, Vic," Phee said quietly. "I should've called first, huh?"

"Not a problem." None of this was Phee's fault. "And that pizza smells great. I'll grab some plates."

"Forget plates. No dishes that way."

Vic nodded, but as she reached for a slice, all she could see was Nat—sitting across from her in the little pizza place, slipping Memphis his new toy, the kiss they'd just shared that still burned on her lips.

Memphis whimpered, and she tried to hide her relief. "I better take him out."

Phee grabbed her jacket, the pizza barely touched. "I should go too."

Vic exhaled. "I'm sorry—distracted."

"Looks like you've got your hands full," Phee said. "Go take care of the little guy."

Vic walked her to the door, grateful for the easy out—until Phee turned, hesitated, and then leaned in.

The kiss was soft, testing. Vic froze.

For a heartbeat, her body reacted on instinct before clarity struck like a lightning bolt. This wasn't what she wanted.

She pulled back gently. "Phee, I...I'm sorry. I can't."

Phee stepped away immediately. "Hey, no apologies. I hope you're not offended."

"No! It's not that." Vic grimaced. "I should've been clearer earlier. I...I have complicated feelings for someone else, and it's... complicated."

Phee smiled wryly. "Nat, right?"

Vic blinked.

Phee shrugged. "I've seen the way you look at her. And she's looking back."

Relief loosened Vic's shoulders. "You're not mad?"

"Of course not. We can't help who we fall for." Phee squeezed her arm. "Don't let it mess with your head, rookie. Try giving her space. Nat's a good one."

"I know." Vic closed the door after Phee and turned to Memphis, who watched her expectantly. "Give her space? Haven't I been doing that?"

Since Memphis didn't answer, she walked him, changed his bandages, and gave him a pain pill before finally crawling into bed.

But sleep wouldn't come.

Instead, she saw Nat's face as she'd left—the flicker of hurt, the regret.

Vic swung her legs over the side of the bed, the floorboards creaking softly as she padded to the window. Beyond the trees, the lake shimmered in the moonlight, quiet and knowing.

"I can't keep doing this," she whispered. "Dancing around... whatever this is with Nat."

She wasn't ready to walk away. Not yet.

After all, Nat had kissed her back.

CHAPTER EIGHTEEN

Vic stared at the blinking cursor on her phone, the empty text field mocking her. The crisp dawn air nipped at her cheeks as she stood on the cabin's porch, Memphis sniffing the dew-covered grass at her feet.

"What do you think, buddy?" she murmured.

The vet hospital had tried to retrieve records on the puppies Lester Nunyan had been transporting, but all they found was a number—seven females, five males. Memphis, skinny with oversized paws, was likely around three or four months old. Despite the trauma of the crash, being separated from his littermates, and waking up injured in a strange place, he explored every corner of the cabin fearlessly. When she opened the door, he'd ventured outside, checking once that she was still there before trotting down into the yard.

In a way, he reminded her of herself—adrift, alone. But Memphis faced the challenges better than she had. While she'd found solace from grief in work and the gradual sense of belonging, she remained paralyzed with indecision over Nat.

Memphis embraced his new circumstances without hesitation. She had to admire that. He wasn't letting uncertainty hold her back from building a new life.

Hell. A ten-pound abandoned pup had bigger balls than she did. What was she waiting for?

She glanced toward Nat's house. Was Nat thinking about their kiss? The one neither of them had wanted to stop? The one Vic couldn't stop replaying?

"How do I tell Nat I want more without scaring her off?"

Memphis tilted his head, watching her. His ears twitched.

Vic took a deep breath. "Right. I hear you. I won't know until I try."

She texted: *Hey. Can we talk later?*

Heart racing, she hesitated with her thumb on the send button. This was it—the moment that could change everything.

"What's the worst that could happen?" she asked Memphis.

He wagged his tail, completely unconcerned with her dilemma.

"She could say no. I'd be embarrassed. But at least I'd know."

And if she says yes...

She hit send before she could talk herself out of it.

"Well, it's done now," she told Memphis, pocketing her phone. "Let's get you taken care of."

Inside, she lifted him onto the kitchen counter. He whimpered as she unwrapped his bandages.

"I know, buddy. I'm sorry." She kept her touch light, cleansing the wounds with sterile saline before applying fresh dressings. "A few more days, and we'll have you feeling better."

Her phone sounded. Her pulse skyrocketed.

She grabbed it—Phee.

Not Nat. Maybe Nat hadn't seen the text yet. Or maybe the answer was no.

"Hi," Vic said.

"Morning. How's the boy?" Phee sounded chipper, and for a second, Vic hated her. In a friendly way, of course.

"Better than me. I hardly slept, worrying about his first night."

"Aw, that's sweet." Phee laughed. "Bring him to the station. Veronica is on desk duty—she'll watch him."

Vic groaned. "Why didn't I think of that? He's too small to leave alone all day."

"That's why I'm calling you." Phee sounded like she was rolling her eyes.

"You know, you're going to make some lucky woman a great girlfriend."

"Oh no—not in my game plan." Phee laughed harder. "Good times, good sex. That's it for me."

Good times, good sex. Would that be enough—if that was all Nat wanted?

"I'm lucky you're my friend," Vic said.

"You are. Now, we're due on patrol in thirty."

"I'm just finishing his dressing changes. I'll make it."

"See you soon, Deputy," Phee said.

Vic taped Memphis's bandages, her thoughts spinning. If Nat wanted to talk, what would she say? Could she even explain what Nat meant to her, how her presence made this place feel like home, the way Nat had brought peace to the chaos in her heart?

"There we go," she murmured, securing the last wrap. She scratched behind Memphis's ears, earning a warm lick on the hand. "You're a good, brave boy."

Her phone chimed again. She held her breath.

Nat.

She exhaled. Reread the message.

I'm free after seven. O'Brien's? Everything okay?

Vic typed: *Yeah. See you then.*

"Everything's perfect," she whispered, slinging her pack over her shoulder and grabbing Memphis's travel bag.

Or at least, it might be soon.

❖

The sun glinted off the unusually calm lake as Vic piloted the Whaler north from the harbor, the powerful engine humming. Phee, Milt, and Juanita scanned the shoreline and passing boats, checking for proper PFD use and verifying fishing licenses.

Just the kind of day she loved—clear water, a solid crew, and work that mattered.

The radio crackled to life, shattering the morning calm.

"All units, DEC requests assistance. Fire at the old Sinclair boathouse. Repeat, fire at the Sinclair boathouse—two miles north of Stillwater Harbor, east shore. Tanker support and possible evac needed."

Vic's pulse jumped. She locked eyes with Phee.

"Copy, dispatch," Phee responded, voice steady. "WPU One responding. ETA ten minutes."

Vic slammed the throttle forward. The bow lifted as the boat surged ahead.

"You know the place?" she shouted over the roar of the engine.

Phee nodded. "Bad news. It's been abandoned for years. Total tinderbox, and it's right on the preserve's edge."

Vic tightened her grip on the wheel. Most forest fires started from human carelessness—a tossed cigarette, an unattended campfire.

A burning building this close to the preserve? A disaster waiting to happen.

"Dispatch, this is WPU One," Phee radioed. "Are tankers en route?"

"Affirmative, Water Patrol. Two tankers launching now."

Vic adjusted course. If she knew Nat, she was already on scene, working the fire, leading from the front. "Let's do this."

Phee grinned. "Hell yeah."

Milt and Juanita stacked extra PFDs, anticipating a water rescue.

Rounding a bend, Vic eyed the smoke billowing from the remains of a boathouse, darkening the crystalline sky. Onshore, DEC rangers and firefighters from several districts, their engines and tankers surrounding the structure, fought the blaze.

Vic slowed to let the tanker boats set up their offshore perimeter. DEC patrol boats anchored farther out, diverting lake traffic.

"Water Patrol to DEC, status update?" Vic radioed, scanning the shoreline for Nat. Too many people, obscured by face masks and helmets, to recognize her.

"Fielder here, WPU." Chase's voice crackled back. "Setting a fire break on the western flank. Wind's pushing that way."

"Copy," Vic said, relieved to hear a familiar voice. "Standing by for evac."

"Stay frosty, Water Patrol."

Vic grinned. She loved this job.

Then—an explosion rocked the shoreline. Fiery debris rained down onto the water.

"What the hell was that?" Milt shouted.

"Phee! Look to starboard." Vic pointed to a red two-man speedboat tearing out of a narrow inlet beyond the fire.

"Shit," Phee yelled. "Follow them!"

"Aye, aye." Vic yanked the wheel and the Whaler banked sharply. She gunned the engine, emergency lights flashing.

"Water Patrol in pursuit," Phee radioed. "Unidentified vessel fleeing the scene."

Vic swore under her breath. "That's a go-fast."

Phee frowned. "So?"

"Twin 400-horsepower engines. That's cartel level."

Milt swore.

"Arm up," Phee ordered and radioed all channels. "Suspects possibly armed and dangerous. Heading northwest. Requesting backup."

Juanita unlatched the weapons case, handing rifles to Phee and Milt.

"Vest on!" Phee snapped.

"Can't. Hands full." Vic locked eyes on the escaping craft. At these speeds, focus was everything. The speedboat zigzagged, churning the lake's glassy surface into chaos. The roar of the engines filled Vic's ears. She braced, instinctively adjusting to the roll and pitch as the Whaler skimmed the waves. She stayed tight on their tail, pushing the Whaler harder.

"Come on, you bastards," she growled, coaxing the boat into the perfect intercept position. "Turn."

The speedboat ahead zigzagged erratically, its wake churning the placid lake into a frothy mess. Trying to lose her.

"Not today," she muttered, adrenaline flooding her veins. The Whaler responded like an extension of herself. For a fleeting moment, she wondered what her father would think of her now.

You always did love a good chase, Victory, she could almost hear him say.

Only then she'd been chasing tuna.

A sudden burst of water off the bow—too precise for a rogue wave.

Gunfire.

"Shots fired," Vic snapped.

Another bullet ripped past.

"Hold fire," Phee ordered, her curly hair whipping in the wind. "Civilian boats ahead." She gripped Vic's shoulder. "They're veering east. Aiming for Gull Bay Harbor."

Vic's stomach knotted. "That's packed with tourists."

"Cut them off," Phee shouted.

"Hold on." Vic angled sharply toward shore, pushing the engine to its limit.

Phee's expression sharpened. "Vic, they're slowing down. I think—"

"I see it." Vic circled in a tight arc, using the speedboat's wake to propel the Whaler forward. "They're going to ground her."

The speedboat skidded up onto the rocky shoreline of a deserted cove. Two men scrambled out, disappearing into the tree line.

"Damn it." Phee keyed her mic. "Suspects beached at Cove Point. Retreating on foot."

A shot cracked. Milt grunted and clutched his arm. "I'm hit!"

Phee shouted over the radio, "Shots fired. Officer down. Requesting immediate backup and medical assistance."

Vic instinctively swung the Whaler away from the shoreline and into deeper waters, throwing a protective wake.

"How bad, Milt?" she called.

"Grazed. Hurts like hell."

"Hang in there. Five minutes."

Vic gripped the wheel and pushed toward Gull Bay at top speed. The suspects were gone, but the pursuit wasn't over.

Not by a long shot.

And neither, she suspected, was whatever had ignited that fire.

❖

Nat barely registered the steady stream of radio chatter as teams reported in from the fire line, her focus narrowing to one chilling transmission: *Shots fired. Officer down.*

Her pulse slammed. All around her, officers were arming up. A helicopter soared overhead, heading northeast—toward the direction the Whaler had taken in pursuit of that speedboat.

Vic was out there.

Was she involved? Was she hurt?

"Dispatch, DEC Evans. Status and location?"

The response came almost immediately. "10-33, Cove Point. All available units responding."

Nat clenched her jaw. Cove Point—miles away. She paced, dividing her attention between the smoldering remains of the boathouse and her radio.

Stay here or go? The fire was under control, but the investigation was just beginning. She paced, staring into the smoldering ruins of the boathouse. If this was more than arson—if the suspects were still out there—she needed to be at the command post.

But if Vic was hurt…

"Come on, come on," she muttered, willing more information to come through.

After minutes that felt like hours, her radio crackled again.

All units stand down. Suspects at large. Officer transported to Lake George Regional Hospital.

Nat exhaled hard, tension momentarily loosening. Someone was hurt, but alive.

"Shots fired?" Meg appeared at her side. "What the fuck is going on here?"

Nat shook her head. "I don't know. This wasn't just a fire."

"You think our fire is connected to that speedboat that took off?"

"Starting to look that way."

Meg scanned the scene. "The fire marshal's on her way. Wants a full lockdown of this area."

Nat barely heard her, still listening for more news on the injured officer.

Megan's gaze sharpened. "Hey. What's going on with you?"

Nat hesitated, then sighed. "That call—officer down. The Whaler hasn't checked in."

Megan nodded slowly. "You think it's them."

"I don't know."

Megan studied her, then jerked her chin toward the charred remains of the boathouse. "Fire's contained. We're just waiting on the marshal's assessment. Go, Nat. We've got this."

Nat hesitated. Leaving went against every instinct she had, but her gut pulled her in another direction.

Chase jogged up. "We're good here, Nat. What's the word on the officer?"

"No details yet. I'm headed to the hospital."

Chase nodded. "Go. We'll keep you posted."

Nat didn't wait for more. She sprinted to her truck, throwing it into drive before the door had even fully closed. Too many emergency runs to the ER lately. Too many people she cared about ending up on a hospital bed.

Please be okay, Vic.

The hospital waiting area was the usual flurry of controlled chaos. Rangers, deputies, paramedics—so many familiar faces—milling about. She searched frantically, breath burning in her chest.

Then…at last. Vic paced near a cluster of deputies.

Alive. Whole.

Relief hit so hard Nat had to pause for a breath.

Vic looked up, her eyes stormy.

For a moment, neither moved.

Then Nat pulled her aside, her voice low but urgent. "Are you hurt?"

Vic exhaled. "I'm fine. Milt took the hit."

"How bad?"

"Docs are with him now—looked superficial, but he...he was bleeding pretty good."

Vic's voice cracked slightly. She was pale, shaking.

Shock. Adrenaline crash.

Nat gripped her arm. "You need something warm."

Vic shook her head. "I'm good."

"No, you're not." Nat glanced around. "Where's Phee?"

"With Milt."

"Stay here. I'll get coffee. This could be a long wait."

Vic sagged slightly. "Thanks."

Nat returned a moment later with two steaming cups and handed one to Vic. "We'll have to reschedule."

Vic frowned. "Reschedule?"

"Our meet tonight. Reports to file."

"Right," Vic said, a flicker of disappointment in her eyes. "We'll need to secure the boat the suspects abandoned. Sweep the area again."

"Yes." Nat hesitated. She should go. Instead, she touched the top of Vic's hand, all the contact she allowed herself. "Be careful out there, Vic. These guys already fired on us once. They won't stop now."

"Roger that," Vic said.

Nat exhaled. She couldn't leave her like that, with so much unsaid. Keeping her voice low, she said, "You're still coming to the lodge tomorrow for the Fourth, right?"

"Wouldn't miss it." Vic looked as if she wanted to say more, but merely shrugged. "I'll look for you."

Nat forced herself to go, when all she wanted was to stay.

CHAPTER NINETEEN

Nat leaned against the weathered porch railing of Thunder Ridge Lodge, the flickering bonfire casting golden light over the common area. The campers bustled about, their chatter mingling with the sharp crackle of kindling. Marty's full-throated laughter rang out as they directed a group of teenagers stacking wood.

A loon called across the lake, the sound a familiar thread woven through years of memories—nights spent here as a teenager, later as a young ranger overseeing evening events.

And then there had been Vic, the bright-eyed camper, fearless and full of boundless energy, always the first to climb, to dive, to take a dare. Life had weathered some of that shine for both of them, but what remained in Vic was something stronger—steady, passionate, relentless.

The woman Vic was now wasn't just someone she admired. Vic was someone she wanted.

The memory of their kiss sent a shiver through her, heat curling low in her stomach. She could still feel the softness of Vic's lips, the way it had taken everything in her to pull away. The promise of more still called to her.

"Earth to Nat." Sarah leaned on the rail next to her, holding out a glass of wine. "You looked about a million miles away. Everything okay?"

Nat accepted the drink, taking a slow sip before answering. "Just…thinking about the past. Remembering the first season we were all here."

Sarah sipped her wine, their shoulders brushing. "Mmm. We were all younger then."

Nat laughed. "Nice way of saying we're getting old."

Sarah grinned. "Older. Wiser." She studied Nat for a beat, then arched a brow. "So…what's going on with you? Still dancing with the hot new deputy?"

Heat crept up Nat's neck. No point pretending—not to Sarah, not to herself. "I suppose denial is useless?"

"That ship has sailed." Sarah laughed, bumped Nat's hip with her own. "An apt metaphor considering the subject. Come on, spill. Have the two of you gotten past the 'desperately want each other but too much in your heads to do anything about it' stage?"

Nat sighed, swirling her wine. "I can't speak for Vic, but I'm working on it."

"Why does it take working on it?" Sarah asked. "Last time I looked, you were both unattached and, as I may have mentioned, about to incinerate any time you were in the vicinity."

Nat sighed. "It's all so…complicated."

"Love usually is," Sarah replied softly.

The word struck like a match dropped into dry leaves. Love.

Nat's heart raced. "I didn't say anything about love."

Sarah snorted. "Didn't have to. It's written all over your face every time you look at her."

Nat let out a slow breath, staring into the firelight. "That's what terrifies me."

Sarah stayed quiet, waiting.

Nat swallowed. "The way she makes me feel…like I'm standing on the edge of a cliff, knowing that one step could change everything."

Sarah tilted her head. "And what exactly are you afraid of?"

Nat hesitated, gripping her glass. "What if we sleep together, and that's all it is? I'm not sure I could handle that."

"Do you think Vic is a player?"

Nat thought about Phee. About the casual ease Vic had with people, how she attracted attention without trying. But Vic—Vic had kissed *her*. Wanted *her*—as hard as that was to believe.

She exhaled. "No. I don't think she is."

Sarah smiled. "Then take the first step."

Nat stared into her wine, the deep maroon surface reflecting the firelight. "Maybe. Maybe you're right."

"Usually am," Sarah said dryly, and Nat laughed. "The equivocating—that doesn't sound like the Nat I know. Since when do you hesitate to go after what you want?"

Nat shook her head, frustration curling inside her. "Ever since Vic showed up, I feel...off-balance. Like I'm not quite myself."

"Or maybe," Sarah mused, "you're finally letting yourself be more than just Ranger Evans. Maybe you're finally allowing yourself to *be*."

Nat gripped the railing. Forcing herself to look inward. To ask the questions she'd avoided answering for so long. "I've spent so long taking care of everyone else—the land, the campers, the community—I wonder if I've been using that to avoid taking care of myself."

"Don't beat yourself up too much." Sarah squeezed her arm. "There's nothing wrong with caution. As long as you don't cheat yourself out of happiness."

The crunch of tires on gravel saved Nat from more soul-searching. Her breath hitched as a familiar Jeep pulled into view, Phee behind the wheel and Vic beside her. Vic climbed out, moving with her usual easy grace. Memphis bounded from the back seat, tail wagging furiously.

Nat couldn't even pretend not to be watching her. An irrational pang plagued her as Vic leashed Memphis, Phee laughing at something Vic said. Phee was confident. Outgoing. Someone Vic worked with, someone who understood her world, someone her own age.

Someone who made more sense.

"They look good together, don't they?" The words, tinged with bitter regret, left her mouth before she could stop them.

Sarah followed her gaze. "They look like friends. Good friends, sure, but nothing more."

Nat shook her head, unconvinced. "They have so much in common. My world and Vic's are light years apart."

Sarah snorted. "And you think you can't understand Vic's world?"

Nat started to protest—but then Vic looked her way and smiled.

Just a simple smile. But it hit her deep, a spreading warmth that challenged the whispers of doubt.

Sarah nudged her. "Tell me something—do you want to understand her world?"

Nat's throat tightened.

She watched Vic. Watched the way she moved, the way she smiled. Something inside cracked open just looking at her.

"Heaven help me, I want to understand every part of her."

❖

The warm summer breeze carried the scent of pine and campfire smoke, mingling with the anticipation tightening in Vic's chest. She'd known Nat would be there, and she planned to say what needed saying before the night was over. No more avoiding. No more wondering. No more pretending the kiss they had shared hadn't ignited something she couldn't ignore.

Right now, though? She just wanted to look.

Nat walked down the slope to the campfire, altogether gorgeous in faded jeans and a pale blue tank that showed off her toned shoulders.

Phee nudged Vic's shoulder. "You intend to stand there all night, or are you gonna go talk to her?"

"In a minute." Vic felt heat rise to her cheeks.

Phee smirked. "Good. Because you look like you're about to combust."

"I'm going."

A minute passed.

Phee snorted. "You see drug runners with high-powered rifles and chase them without a second thought. But you're dragging your feet with a woman you want?"

Vic grimaced and looked away. "I'm just waiting for the right time."

"Time's not always your friend. Just do it."

Time *was* the problem, wasn't it? Nat thought their age difference was a problem—as if years alone was an insurmountable barrier. She thought Vic might not even be around after the summer—as if the future was already decided. As if life was a predetermined road, and nothing could change. And what did any of that matter if they let time just slip away?

Vic exhaled, squaring her shoulders. "Right."

Phee scooped up Memphis, "Then do it. Take a chance, O'Brien."

Take what joy life brings your way, Victory.

Her father's voice, strong and clear.

I'm listening, Dad.

Heart hammering, Vic headed toward the firepit, where campers jostled each other in the warm glow of the bonfire. The air was thick with woodsmoke and the sweet scent of roasting marshmallows. Nat turned, saw her, and smiled. For a moment, time stretched—uncertain, electric—and Vic knew.

This was it.

Vic took a slow breath and stepped closer. "Hey."

"Hey, yourself," Nat said. "Memphis is looking good. And you, by the way."

Vic laughed and tucked her hands into her pockets. "I don't mind coming in second to that guy."

"Mmm, never second," Nat said. "Where is he?"

"Phee has him."

Nat's expression remained steady, but shadows swam in her eyes. "Ah. Yes."

That instant of uncertainty spurred Vic's resolve.

Phee had been right.

No more time to waste.

"I was hoping to steal a moment with you," Vic said.

Nat's gaze flickered over her face. "You can have more than that."

"Walk with me?"

Nat hesitated. Vic held her breath. Then, with a nod, she fell into step beside Vic, away from the fire. The laughter and chatter faded into the rustling of wind through the trees.

When they stopped, Vic faced her, pulse hammering. "There's been something I've been wanting to tell you."

Nat arched a brow. "I'm listening."

Vic took a breath. "It's about my parents."

Nat's expression softened. "Tell me."

Vic tilted her head back, staring at the stars like she had so many times from the deck of the *Nightingale*.

"My dad was a fisherman's son. He went to sea when he was a teenager, never finished high school—not that he let me get away with that." She laughed, then exhaled. "My mom worked at the village diner. Dad swore he'd loved her since he was twelve."

Nat smiled. "A romantic."

"That's what she always said. He said he was just smart enough not to let her go." Vic's throat tightened. "When he was twenty, he finally asked her out. She said no."

Nat frowned. "Why?"

Vic met her gaze. "She was twenty-two years older than him."

Nat inhaled sharply. "Oh."

"Yeah. She told him to find someone his own age. Someone who could give him a big family."

"And of course he listened."

Vic chuckled, the warmth of the memory easing some of the

ache in her chest. "Not for a second. He kept showing up, wearing her down. Finally, she gave in. Said he was the handsomest man she'd ever seen—but it was his determination that did it. She said he was a man she could count on."

"Your parents sound wonderful," Nat said.

"They were. Two years later I came along—a surprise. They didn't think they would have any."

"Hence your name."

Vic nodded, looking back toward the fire where campers huddled together, carefree in a way she barely remembered feeling. "I used to think happiness was something you could hold on to forever. That if you worked hard enough, you could keep it."

Nat's gaze sharpened. "And now?"

Vic exhaled slowly. "Now I know it's more like catching lightning in a bottle. Fleeting. Unpredictable. But beautiful when you have it." She hesitated. "They had ten years together. My dad called them their glory days. And he wouldn't have traded a second of it, because he had her, and she gave him me."

Nat brushed her fingers over Vic's arm. "Oh, Vic—I'm sorry you lost them."

"I think I'm incredibly lucky." Vic turned into Nat's touch, her pulse spiking. "I told you this because I'm like my dad, Nat. When I know what I want, I don't walk away." Her voice dropped. "And I want you."

Without a word, Nat gently took Vic's hand and led her from the fire's warm glow into the cool shadows of the trees. Vic followed. Whatever happened next was up to Nat. She'd opened her heart, revealed her secrets. Only Nat could decide where they went next.

Nat turned, her hand still wrapped around Vic's, her eyes shimmering with an intensity that made Vic's knees weak. "Vic, I—"

Vic closed the distance, cupping Nat's face, giving her the chance to pull away.

She didn't.

Vic kissed her.

Soft at first. Testing.

Then Nat's arms slid around her waist, pulling her closer, deepening the kiss, and Vic felt it—the urgency, the hunger, the surrender. Desire surged, and in that perfect, stolen moment, only the two of them existed.

Nat eased away. "You make a very…compelling argument, Victory."

Vic pressed her forehead against Nat's, breathless. "I've wanted to do that for days."

"I've been wanting you to." Nat's fingers curled against Vic's back, gripping her like she wasn't ready to let go. Then, quieter, "What is it you want, Vic? Besides this?"

Vic cupped the nape of Nat's neck. Kissed her again. "To be close to you. Tonight. Tomorrow. As long as you'll have me."

Nat let out a slow breath. "I can't stop thinking about you." She swallowed hard. "It's like you've taken up residence in my head, and I...I don't want you to leave."

Vic's heart pounded. "Nat—"

Nat silenced her with a finger against her lips. "I need to say this."

Vic stilled.

Nat's voice was barely above a whisper. "You terrify me, Vic O'Brien. The way you make me feel...intense and overwhelming and absolutely wonderful. I've spent so long convincing myself I was fine just the way things were. But you..." She smiled ruefully. "You waltzed right through those walls like they were made of paper."

Vic tightened her hold, sensing the shift. She'd made her choice. She could wait for Nat to make hers. "We don't have to rush. We don't have to do anything you're not ready for."

Nat shook her head. "I want this." Her voice gained strength. "I want you. But I can't promise more than that."

Not yet.

Vic pressed her palm to Nat's cheek, reveling in the rapid beat of her pulse beneath her fingertips. "Then take me home, Nat."

Nat inhaled sharply, studying Vic's face as if memorizing it. And then, with quiet certainty: "Let's go find Memphis."

CHAPTER TWENTY

The soft glow of the moon slid over across Vic's lap as Nat drove down the mountain. Vic absently stroked Memphis's silky fur, his warm weight a comforting anchor amid the butterflies dancing in her stomach. She stole a glance at Nat—at the elegant slope of her nose, the determined set of her jaw as she navigated the midnight roads with ease.

Vic swallowed. "This is ridiculous, but I'm nervous. Are you?"

Nat's gaze flickered to Vic, and she smiled. "A little. But mostly, I want to be here with you. Tonight. No thinking ahead."

Vic squeezed Nat's hand, holding on to the quiet certainty in her words.

"Me too," she murmured. "One night at a time. That feels right."

Nat sighed. "I just don't want to hurt you."

"You don't need to worry about me, Nat," Vic said. "I'm pretty good at knowing what I want."

Nat chuckled. "I've noticed."

Vic slid her hand onto Nat's thigh. "I'm glad this is a short trip."

Nat covered Vic's hand, thumb stroking over her knuckles. "Do not move that hand any higher. I need to drive."

Delighted, Vic leaned in and pressed a kiss to the shell of Nat's ear.

Nat exhaled. "*Vic.*"

Grinning, Vic eased back, keeping her palm on Nat's leg. "I'll be good."

Nat didn't look convinced. "I already know that."

Vic's stomach clenched. "Glad you didn't forget."

Nat's glance burned into her. "What I *am* wondering is why it took me so long to get you back in my bed."

"Then maybe hurry, so I don't go up in flames here."

"Five minutes, baby," Nat murmured. "Just think good thoughts."

"If I think any harder, I'll explode," Vic muttered, clenching her free hand. She wanted to go slow, to savor, but her body had shifted into another gear.

Memphis stretched and yawned.

"I should take him to the cabin."

"No," Nat said instantly. "He stays with us."

"You're sure?"

Nat squeezed her hand. "We're all lucky to be here."

Vic leaned back against the headrest, curling her fingers in Memphis's fur. He nuzzled her palm, tail thumping. This was exactly where she wanted to be—hand in hand with Nat, Memphis by her side, surrounded by the wild beauty of the Adirondacks. Not a picture she'd ever had in her mind, but one that fit better every day.

"Yeah, buddy," she whispered, "we are."

Nat parked in the drive, but neither of them moved. Nat turned to Vic, her eyes catching the glow of the porch light, and leaned in—slow but sure. Vic barely had time to catch her breath before Nat kissed her. Heat surged, flooding every nerve. She melted into the kiss, surprise giving way to pure, unfiltered joy.

When they finally pulled apart, Vic grinned, breathless. "I could kiss you all night."

Nat chuckled, low and throaty. "I like the way you think, Victory. Let's start there…" Her gaze flickered to the cramped space of the car. "But maybe not *here*. I don't think Memphis would appreciate being squished in the middle of all this."

Vic glanced down at the dog, happily wedged between them, his tail wagging furiously. "Not so sure about that."

"I think we can find a more comfortable spot inside." Nat tilted her chin toward the house. "And I'd say we've waited long enough."

Vic climbed out into the cool night air, heart racing. Nat quickly rounded the car and grasped Vic's hand. Their fingers intertwined effortlessly. A perfect fit.

Memphis bounded ahead, but Vic lingered, struck by the weight of the moment. This wasn't just a casual visit. This was something more. Something she hadn't expected—hadn't even known she wanted.

Until Nat.

Nat changed everything.

At the door, Nat fumbled with her keys, and Vic's heart clenched. That small flicker of hesitation—Nat wasn't as sure of herself as she pretended. Without thinking, Vic took the keys. "Let me."

Nat tilted her head, surprised. "Is that the way it's going to be, then?"

Vic held her gaze. "If that works for you."

Nat stroked her jaw, ran her thumb over Vic's lower lip. "You work for me. Let's go see what you've got."

Vic's legs trembled as she opened the door and stepped aside to let Nat pass. She followed, met by the familiar scent of pine and woodsmoke, mingling with Nat's subtle scent.

Nat led the way upstairs, her hand never leaving Vic's. Memphis followed close behind, nails clicking against the hardwood stairs. With each step, Vic's anticipation grew, a delicious tension coiling in the pit of her stomach. She'd been with Nat before—had held her, tasted her, given herself over completely.

But this time, everything was different.

Inside the bedroom, Nat nudged Vic toward the bed. "Wait right there."

She returned with a blanket, laying it on the floor.

"Your spot," she murmured, scratching Memphis behind the ears. He circled twice, sighed, and flopped down.

"Now, where were we?" Nat turned back, gaze dark with promise, and pulled her shirt over her head. Moonlight danced over the long, lean muscles of her stomach and the full curves of her breasts.

Vic's mouth went dry.

"Like what you see?" Nat asked in a husky whisper.

Vic nodded, words impossible.

With slow, deliberate movements, Nat unzipped her jeans, easing them down her hips with deliberate slowness. Watching Vic watch her, she murmured, "Your turn."

She knelt, reaching for Vic's boots.

Vic leaned back on her elbows, eyes closed, arousal flaring as Nat stripped away each layer—boots, socks, jeans, shirt—until only her briefs remained. Cool air brushed over her skin, but heat roared beneath it.

For a second, Vic tensed. Scars. Imperfections. She never thought much about them—until now.

Then Nat looked at her.

Really looked at her.

Like she was something to savor.

The heat in her gaze erased every doubt.

"You're beautiful." Nat brushed her fingers down Vic's torso, raising goose bumps in their wake. "Every inch. Every story written on your skin. I want all of it."

Vic's heart pounded. "You can have anything you want."

She pulled Nat into a kiss that burned away the last of the space keeping them apart. The fire caught, then roared.

Clothes vanished into a pile on the floor.

Nat pressed Vic's shoulders, her playful glint darkening into unmistakable hunger. "Lie down. And watch."

Vic obeyed.

Nat straddled her, slow and deliberate, every movement teasing, torturous.

God, Nat was beautiful. How did she get so lucky?

Vic ached to touch, to explore every inch of Nat's body, but she forced herself to stay still, to let Nat set the pace.

And Nat took her time.

She mapped every sensitive inch, teasing, tasting, until Vic was a live wire, trembling under her hands. "Tell me what you want."

Vic's control snapped.

"You." She shuddered. "I want you."

Nat smiled and pressed her lips to Vic's collarbone. "You can. Later."

Then Nat took her apart. Slowly. Thoroughly.

Vic wasn't falling—she was crashing. Lost in the heat of Nat's mouth, in the slick slide of their bodies. Nat's fingers danced over Vic's sensitive skin, building the ache within her higher and higher.

Vic arched, gasping, her body a taut wire.

"Nat," she whimpered, "I'm so close."

Nat's laughter was low and throaty. "Not yet. I want to savor this."

Vic moaned, twisting the bed sheets in both hands. "I can't. God, please."

Nat's mouth covered her, hot and knowing.

Vic shattered, Nat's name on her lips.

Pleasure ripped through her, sharp and endless, stealing her breath, her thoughts, her name.

Before the aftershocks faded, Vic flipped them, pressing Nat into the mattress, and kissed her. Her turn to explore, to discover Nat's sensitive places. When Nat trembled and gasped, she dipped lower, gently circled her clit.

"More." Nat dug her fingers into Vic's shoulders and thrust, silently demanding more.

Vic slipped inside, and Nat's eyes slammed shut.

"Look at me," Vic whispered.

Nat's lashes fluttered open. Fear, want, surrender. Trust.

Vic kissed her, took her higher, and watched Nat explode.

When the last tremor passed, they lay tangled together, slick with sweat, breath mingling.

Nat traced lazy patterns on Vic's back. "You have all of me."

Vic's breath stopped.

Everything she'd ever wanted.

Everything she'd ever needed.

And just like that, she knew.

CHAPTER TWENTY-ONE

Vic stirred, the familiar scent of pine and lavender pulling her back to the night before. Instinctively, she reached for Nat, drawing her closer. She rarely had the chance to see Nat unguarded like this, and drank in every detail—the loose strands of hair splayed across the pillow, the relaxed curve of her lips, the swell of her hips beneath the thin sheet. Memory rushed back, potent and visceral—the heat of Nat's skin against hers, the slow unraveling of restraint, the whispered confessions under cover of moonlight.

She'd promised to take things slow, but there was no use pretending anymore.

She was in love with Nat Evans.

Not what she'd planned.

Not even what she'd thought she'd needed.

But now?

Now she couldn't imagine waking up anywhere else. Couldn't picture a future that didn't have Nat in it. The thoughts lodged like ice in her throat. What if Nat's picture didn't include her?

Beside her, Nat stirred, lashes fluttering as she blinked awake. Her slow smile sent warmth unfurling in Vic's chest, melting her uncertainty.

"Morning," Vic murmured.

Nat stretched, her gaze traveling over Vic's face. "You're still here."

The wonder in her voice made Vic's heart ache. How could Nat not know how special she was? She cupped Nat's cheek, brushing her thumb along her jaw. "Where else would I be?"

Nat sighed, her smile rueful. "I don't know. I half expected to wake up alone, convinced last night was just a dream."

Vic pressed a kiss to Nat's palm. "Not a dream. I'm right here."

Something flickered in Nat's expression—vulnerability, quickly masked. She shifted, pressing closer, her breath warm against Vic's lips. "Show me."

Vic kissed her—slow, lingering, wanting to say with touch what words couldn't. She wrapped one arm around Nat's waist, thrilling to the way their bodies fit, like the last missing piece of a puzzle. A sense of completeness she hadn't realized she'd been searching for.

She mapped Nat's body, tracing soft skin and firm muscles, memorizing every touch that made Nat sigh or gasp. She wanted to linger, to savor, but the way Nat trembled beneath her touch nearly undid her.

"I love touching you," Vic murmured.

"Vic," Nat whimpered, her fingers tangling in Vic's hair. "Please…"

With Nat whispering her name like a plea—or a benediction—Vic gave in, falling deeper into something she no longer feared.

She kissed a path down Nat's neck, relishing the thundering pulse beneath her lips. For moments that stretched like hours, there was only Nat. The softness of her skin, the taut lines of her legs as she wrapped them around Vic's, the scent of her desire. The world existed only in touching her, tasting her, taking her higher until she crested with a sharp cry.

Afterward, tangled together in the morning light creeping in through the blinds, Vic brushed a kiss over Nat's forehead.

"You're incredible," she whispered. "I can't stop wanting you."

Nat smiled, but uncertainty flickered in her eyes. "This is real, right?" Her voice was soft, almost hesitant. "You and me?"

Vic's chest tightened. She caught Nat's chin, tilting her face up. "This is real. More real than anything I've ever known."

Nat exhaled, her expression softening. She tucked her face into Vic's neck, sighing. Vic held her close, vowing—silently but fiercely—to prove it.

One day at a time.

❖

Vic pulled Nat into the shower, warm water cascading over them. She stilled, mesmerized by the damp strands of hair curling against Nat's shoulders, the shimmering droplets clinging to her lashes, and the rivulets trailing down the elegant line of her throat.

Nat arched a brow. "Something you wanted?"

Vic grinned, running her hands along Nat's waist, savoring the way her muscles tensed beneath her palms. "Everything."

"Good answer." Nat laughed, low and husky, and grabbed the shampoo. "Here, let me."

Vic turned so Nat could work her fingers into her hair. She sighed, leaning into the touch as Nat massaged her scalp, firm but gentle. A simple thing—mundane, even—but it unraveled her. "Mmm. That feels amazing."

"You're easy to please."

"Only when it's you." Vic turned, the soapy water slicking their skin. She cupped Nat's face, grazing her cheekbones with her thumbs. "I mean it, Nat. You're…everything."

Something flickered in Nat's expression—a softness, a tenderness she wasn't trying to hide. She threaded her fingers through Vic's hair, holding her just a second longer before she rinsed away the soap. The teasing glint in Nat's eyes grew darker, and she pulled Vic into a slow, deep kiss, the kind that made Vic's knees threaten to give out.

Time always seemed to disappear when Nat touched her. She closed her eyes while they lingered, touching, tasting, stealing seconds before the day intruded.

When the water finally cooled, Vic reluctantly drew away. "I should check on Memphis. Make sure he hasn't redecorated your bedroom."

Nat laughed, drawing the towel over her torso. Vic followed the movements, her throat going dry.

Nat caught her staring and grinned. "Go. Work awaits."

"It's going to be a very long day," Vic muttered, stepping naked into the bedroom, the sound of Nat's laughter chasing her.

Memphis waited with an expectant expression, tail thumping, just outside the bathroom door. Pulling on her clothes, she told him, "Yes, you're going too. Everyone in the department would complain if you didn't show up."

As Vic sat to lace her boots, Nat came out with the towel wrapped around her torso. Vic groaned. "Do you seriously want to go to work today?"

"Patience is a virtue," Nat said lightly.

"Not my long suit," Vic grumbled, pausing to kiss her again on the way to the door.

Nat gripped her shoulders, the towel falling to the floor, and pulled her close. "Kiss me like that again, and we'll both be late."

Memphis whined softly.

"Damn it," Vic muttered. "He needs a walk."

Nat gently pushed her away. "Take him out. I'll make coffee."

"I'll be back in a few," Vic said, her voice slightly husky.

Vic leaned against the back porch railing as Memphis explored the back yard as if he'd never seen it before, the crisp morning air filling her lungs. Her heart thrummed wildly, imagining more intimate time with Nat, but a nagging uncertainty clawed at her ribs. "What am I doing, Memphis? I'm falling so hard, so fast. What if it's too much?"

Memphis looked up, tongue lolling, utterly unconcerned.

Vic sighed. "Yeah, yeah. One day at a time. But God, I'm already in love with her. How do I show her she can trust this—trust us—without scaring her away?"

Memphis didn't answer, but Vic already knew.

One step at a time. One night. One morning. One kiss.

She could be patient. She could be steady.

She had to be.

❖

The bell above the diner door chimed as Vic stepped inside with Nat, the aroma of fresh coffee and sizzling bacon reminding her how hungry she was. The place was packed—locals nursing steaming mugs at the counter, groups crowded into booths piled with stacks of pancakes and platters of eggs, and off-duty LEOs swapping stories over end-of-shift breakfast.

Phee, sitting with Charlie in a corner booth, waved them over with a faint smirk already curving her lips.

Vic hesitated. Would Nat want to sit with them? Would this—whatever *this* was between them—extend to something as normal as breakfast with friends?

"We can grab another table," she offered.

"No, let's go over." Nat's voice was easy, without hesitation. "Can't pretend we don't see them."

Vic relaxed at the way Nat hadn't hesitated. She hadn't seemed worried about what Phee or Charlie might think. As they wove through the tables, Vic lightly touched the small of Nat's back—an unthinking, automatic gesture. When Nat didn't pull away, Vic rejoiced. Nope. Nat didn't seem worried about what Phee or Charlie might think.

Maybe, just maybe, this *was* real.

Charlie grinned as they slid into the booth, Vic next to Phee, Nat beside him. "You two are up early."

"Ditto," Nat said, reaching for a menu.

"Good morning," Phee said brightly, her sharp gaze flicking from Nat to Vic. "Enjoy the festivities last night?"

Vic felt heat creep up the back of her neck.

Nat casually nodded. "Campfires at the lodge are always fun."

Phee propped her chin on her hand. "You missed the fireworks. The ones out on the lake, I mean."

"Mmm." Nat accepted the coffee Charlie poured from a carafe sitting on the table. "Thanks. Knowing Sarah and Chase, I imagine they were spectacular."

Vic frowned. "Fireworks? In the forest?"

"They set them off from a floating dock in the middle of the lake," Nat said. "Low altitude, self-extinguishing. No risk of errant sparks that way."

Vic said to Phee, "Memphis was pretty wiped after his first full day without the bandages. I figured he needed an early night."

Beneath the table, Nat softly brushed her thigh.

Phee, never one to let a moment sit too long, nudged Vic's shoulder. "I was surprised to see you both at breakfast, honestly. Thought you'd be *busy*."

Vic coughed into her coffee.

Charlie chuckled. "Phee."

"What?" Phee spread her hands. "I'm just saying, it's nice to see O'Brien looking...well-rested."

Nat arched a brow, sipping her coffee. "You're awfully invested in our sleeping habits, Gomez."

Phee grinned. "Only because it's *so* much fun watching you two pretend you're not completely—"

Charlie kicked her under the table. "Don't you have eggs to eat?"

Vic shot him a grateful look as the server arrived. She and Nat placed their orders, the conversation shifting to summer events—the upcoming regatta, the inevitable tourist influx, the patrol schedules.

Over a second round of coffee, Charlie leaned forward, his

expression shifting into business mode. "So, Vic...I've got some news that might interest you."

Vic stilled. "Oh yeah?"

Charlie nodded. "Remember my buddy in the Manhattan sheriff's department I mentioned? Well, seems he's got an opening for an experienced captain in their Water Patrol unit. We're talking patrolling the harbor and the river. Year-round work, real tactical operations—not just seasonal lake patrol."

Vic gripped her cup tightly, willing Charlie to silence.

Phee added, "You'd be *policing*, O'Brien. Doing real work, real investigations. You're good at it."

The world tilted slightly.

Vic chanced a glance at Nat, but Nat's expression was unreadable. She just sipped her coffee, her posture giving nothing away. But then, Nat was a master at keeping her feelings close.

Vic's stomach flipped. A job on the harbor? Out on the water year-round? It should've been a dream offer. But everything had changed, hadn't it? At least for her.

"That's...interesting." Vic cleared her throat. "Although I'm pretty happy with the work I'm doing up here."

Charlie, oblivious to the sudden weight in the air, waved that off. "I told him all about you, and he's really interested. Said your experience would be perfect."

The words barely registered. Vic's thoughts whirled. For so long, she'd imagined a job like that. A command position. More action. More water. And yet...

Images of mornings tangled in bed with Nat, of Memphis sprawled at their feet, of laughter over late-night beers with the crew held so much more possibility. She already had a place in the world.

Somewhere she belonged.

"You should consider it," Nat said.

Vic's stomach dropped. She stared at Nat. Was Nat serious? Could she just say *go* without a second thought? Could she say good-bye as if they were strangers?

Nat's expression remained carefully neutral, a wall Vic couldn't see through.

"Well, I'd have to consid—"

"It sounds like an amazing opportunity," Nat said abruptly. "The kind of thing you've always wanted, right?"

The coffee in Vic's stomach turned to lead.

Charlie nodded enthusiastically. "Exactly. It'd be a hell of a step forward."

Vic forced a smile. "Maybe."

But Nat's words echoed in her head.

You should consider it.

Did that mean Nat didn't see a future here? That she didn't see them as something lasting?

Vic found Nat's hand under the table, squeezing gently.

Nat squeezed back—but her smile didn't quite reach her eyes.

The server arrived, setting down plates of eggs and toast and pancakes. The conversation shifted back to easy chatter, and Vic breathed a little easier. But the atmosphere had changed. Grown cooler.

Vic ate mechanically, nodding when appropriate, her mind miles away.

She'd wanted that job once.

But now the thought of leaving Lake George—leaving Nat—made her chest ache.

And yet, Nat had encouraged her to go.

Hadn't she?

The rest of breakfast passed in a blur of conversation. Nat's fingers brushed hers once or twice, but each time, there was hesitation.

Vic didn't know what to do with that.

By the time they left the diner, a knot of uncertainty had taken root in her chest.

She wasn't sure how to untangle it.

CHAPTER TWENTY-TWO

I'll grab a ride back to the station with Phee," Vic said to Nat outside the diner, "and swing by the cabin for Memphis on break."

Nat nodded. "If that works, I've got a pile of paperwork waiting for me at the office."

Vic hesitated, then kissed her—a quick, chaste press of lips that left more unsaid than spoken. Nat's fingers lingered against Vic's wrist—just a breath too long—before she let go and walked away without a word.

"All set?" Phee asked brightly.

"Sure," Vic said, tracking Nat as she disappeared.

She barely registered the drive to the station, letting Charlie and Phee chatter about some fishing tournament they'd signed up for. Nat's cool expression haunted her. Inside, she cut through the usual hum of activity and hurried to the locker room for her gear. A minute later, the door opened, and the scent of Phee's apricot shampoo reached her.

She braced, already knowing what Phee was going to say.

"So," Phee drawled, leaning against the lockers with coffee in hand, "you gonna tell me what the hell that was at breakfast?"

Vic closed her locker with a little more force than necessary. "What *what* was?"

Phee scoffed. "Oh, come on. One second you were all starry-eyed. The next, you looked like you'd been sucker-punched." She took a slow sip of coffee, eyes narrowed over the rim. "In my experience, a splinter hurts a lot less if you pull it out before it festers."

Vic exhaled, rubbing her jaw. "Charlie's job pitch."

"Mm-hmm. Thought that might be it." Phee crossed one ankle

over the other. "And let me guess—Nat encouraging you to think about it threw you."

Vic grimaced. "Yeah. Just when I thought—well, I thought maybe we'd gotten somewhere—she practically pushes me to go."

Phee let out a low whistle. "Oof. That's rough."

"Thanks," Vic muttered. "That helps."

"I mean, I'm just saying," Phee said more gently, only sympathy in her eyes, "that's Nat for you. She's not the type to ask someone to stay."

Vic's stomach twisted. "Why the hell not?"

Phee shrugged, as if the answer was obvious. "Because if you go, she won't have to deal with the fact that she wanted you to stay."

The words landed like a punch to the gut. Frustration gnawed at her. "How am I supposed to deal with that? I can't even make sense of it."

"Look, O'Brien," Phee said patiently. "I've known Nat for years—she's wired for self-preservation. And she cares about you. Probably more than she's ready to admit." Her expression softened. "Honestly? If you didn't matter, she'd have brushed off Charlie's pitch like it was nothing."

"Like I said—that makes no sense." Vic shook her head. "If she cares, why encourage me to leave?"

"If there's one thing about Nat, it's that she's unselfish to a fault." Phee shook her head. "She thinks she's doing the right thing, pushing you toward something great. But that doesn't mean it's what she wants."

Vic exhaled sharply, balling one hand into a fist. "Hell. I'm falling for a woman who'd rather push me away than ask me to stay."

Phee whistled low. "You said it, not me."

A sharp rap on the locker room door cut off Vic's response.

Charlie called in his all-business voice, "Briefing room. Now. DEA called—big operation brewing. All hands on deck. Task force meeting at DEC headquarters in an hour."

Vic and Phee hurried out, following Charlie down the hall.

"DEA?" Vic asked. "What's going on?"

"They're running a joint op with DEC and local agencies. Something's going down in the park, and they need WPU backup on the lake."

Vic tensed. "Why hold the meeting at DEC?"

Charlie's expression darkened. "Because whatever's going down? It's in their jurisdiction."

❖

At DEC headquarters, the conference room buzzed with tension. Officers from multiple agencies filtered in, some carrying files, others murmuring about what kind of operation warranted a meeting of this scale.

Vic sat with the other deputies near the back, spotting Nat at the head of the long table, surrounded by rangers.

DEA agents, clustered at the front—all crisp suits and sharp-eyed stares. Some spoke in hushed tones with DEC officers. Others, like the tall man with close-cropped graying hair, scanned the room, sizing up personnel like they were pieces on a chessboard.

Charlie leaned over.

"That's Special Agent Monty Reeves," he murmured. "Been with the DEA twenty-plus years. Hardass, but good at what he does. If he's here, this is big."

Vic filed that away and focused on Nat. Their eyes met—just for a second—before Nat looked away with an unreadable expression. The quick dismissal blindsided her, but she forced her attention to Reeves as he stepped forward.

He cleared his throat, and the room fell silent.

"We'll keep this brief because time isn't on our side," he said. Deep voice, gravel-rough—the voice of a man used to being listened to. "We have intel on an off-grid meth operation deep in the Adirondack Preserve. They've been running under the radar for months, but a recent drone sweep pinpointed a probable location."

He gestured to a satellite image on the monitor, laser-pointing to a dense forest with a small clearing near a winding river, barely visible through the thick canopy.

"We suspect they're using this site as a mobile lab," Reeves continued. "Production, packaging, and distribution—all happening out of temporary structures that can be dismantled and moved within hours. That's how they've stayed ahead of us."

Charlie let out a low whistle. "Mobile meth lab on protected land. That's bold."

"Bold," Reeves agreed, "but not unprecedented. These aren't street-level dealers cooking in basements. This is a well-run operation supplying major distribution channels across state lines." He folded his arms. "Which is why we're shutting it down."

Vic studied the map—no trails or access roads. "How are they moving product?"

"By water," Reeves said. "Loading product onto boats, then ferrying it to remote drop sites along the river and lake and transporting it to locations accessible by road. It's a controlled system. Tight. Efficient. Hard to track."

Which explained why the DEA needed WPU. Vic exchanged a glance with Charlie and Phee. WPU as backup. More waiting.

Phee whispered, "These are the slimeballs who shot Milt. They need a rude awakening."

"We're planning a coordinated raid at dawn, two days from now. DEA takes point. DEC navigates." He glanced at Nat. "Your people know the terrain better than our GPS. WPU locks down the water routes."

Vic's pulse quickened. High-stakes operations were nothing new, but this was her lake. *Her* territory.

Nat nodded, looking resolute. "What level of resistance are we expecting?"

Reeves didn't sugarcoat. "Armed. Potential for violent engagement is high."

The muscles in Nat's jaw tightened. The room filled with murmurs as officers shifted in their seats.

Vic's gut churned. If things went south, the DEC would be right in the thick of it.

Phee muttered, "Perfect. Just what we need. A bunch of desperate meth heads with guns."

Reeves went on, not a flicker of unease in his eyes. The red laser dot crawled over the map. "Ground teams move in from the north and east, cutting off overland escape routes. Aerial surveillance monitors movement on the river, WPU secures the lake. No one gets out."

Nat tapped her fingers against the table, eyes on the aerial image. "What intel do we have on personnel?"

"Six to eight core crew members, more during transport. Organized. Disciplined. And we already know they're willing to fire on law enforcement."

Vic tensed. Armed suspects, rugged terrain, and water access—this had all the makings of a clusterfuck.

Reeves let the weight of that sink in before nodding to Nat. "DEC Evans, your team leads the approach."

Nat nodded, calm and composed, but Vic saw the flicker of something else in her gaze. Not fear. Calculation.

"We'll approach from the north," Nat said. "Steep terrain, dense canopy, but manageable. It's not drone-friendly, so if they're using UAVs for perimeter security, they'll have blind spots. We'll move in under cover, get eyes on the structures before your team advances."

"Good." Reeves turned to Charlie. "Sheriff, we need your people on the water an hour before first light."

Charlie nodded. "We'll be ready."

Reeves clicked off the laser pointer and closed the aerial map. He looked over the room. "This operation is zero tolerance. The suspects are flooding communities with poison. We shut them down. No half measures."

The air in the room grew heavier.

Vic's gaze flicked to Nat. She wasn't looking at Reeves—she was looking at her.

As soon as Reeves rejoined Nat, officers congregated in groups, discussing assignments. Vic worked her way through the crowd toward Nat, but before she could reach her, Reeves clapped a hand on Nat's shoulder.

"Need you for a few minutes, Evans."

Nat flicked a quick look at Vic. "I'll contact you later."

Vic nodded, unease gnawing at her as Nat disappeared down the hall with Reeves.

Phee nudged her. "This looks like fun."

Vic exhaled slowly. "This op could turn ugly fast."

Phee sighed. "Yeah."

Vic set her jaw. "We'll get it done."

Nat and her team would be first in...

And first to draw fire.

CHAPTER TWENTY-THREE

The porch light flickered as Vic climbed the steps to Nat's house, each creak of the weathered wood tightening the knot in her chest. She gritted her teeth, willing her pulse to steady, but her heart still slammed against her ribs. She hesitated, her hand hovering over the knocker, steeling herself for the conversation ahead. Thirty-six hours, and no word from Nat. Two days of silence stretched like a frozen river. She'd tried to give Nat space, tried waiting for the knock on her door that never came—but she couldn't wait any longer. Not with the mission set to commence before dawn.

She rapped twice, the sound of metal on wood sharp as a gunshot.

The door swung open.

Nat stood there. Barefoot, her Henley slightly wrinkled, a pair of sweatpants slung low on her hips. The crisp scent of pine and woodsmoke curled around her, mingling with something softer— lavender soap and the lingering trace of something that was simply Nat. Her hair was mussed, like she'd run her hands through it one too many times, and the shadows beneath her eyes told Vic she hadn't been sleeping well, either. But her face, despite the weariness, was cool, composed. Guarded.

No warmth. No welcome.

"Vic. I wasn't expecting you."

"I know." Vic searched her face, looking for something— anything—that suggested Nat wanted to see her. But there was nothing. "Can I come in? There's something I need to talk to you about."

Nat hesitated for a moment before stepping aside. "Sure."

Vic brushed past her, and for one agonizing second, their arms nearly touched. Nearly. The air vibrated with tension. Normally, Nat's space radiated welcome. Tonight, the silence stretched thick and heavy, like neither of them knew how to cross the distance.

Nat crossed her arms. "What's on your mind?"

Vic exhaled, trying to keep her voice steady. "The raid. And…" Her throat tightened. "The job offer Charlie brought up at breakfast the other day."

Nat's lips pressed into a thin line. "What about them?"

Vic swallowed. Now that she was there, Nat so close and yet so distant, she wasn't sure where to start. The mission? The way her gut twisted with unease? Or the offer that had suddenly become something bigger than just a career move?

She took a deep breath. "I can't shake this feeling that something's off about this op. Some factor we're not considering." She shook her head. "And the job…I don't know *what* to think about it."

No reaction. Not even a flinch that either topic bothered her.

"The raid's been meticulously planned," Nat said, her voice even. Too even. "And the job—" Her gaze flickered away, just for a second. "It's a hell of an opportunity. You should seriously consider it."

Vic tensed. Cold. Logical. Detached.

"Is that what you want?" Her voice tightened. "For me to take it and just leave?"

Nat's jaw twitched. Something raw, unguarded flashed across her face. Then it was gone.

"What I want doesn't matter," Nat said, moving toward the kitchen—putting more distance between them. "This is about your career. Your future."

Vic's heart twisted.

"Of course it matters." She followed, desperate for some kind of break in Nat's defenses. "Nat, I thought we were…I thought this was something."

Nat exhaled sharply, reaching for a mug like she actually wanted tea, like this was all so casual. But her hands trembled slightly when she grabbed the kettle. "We agreed to take things slow. Slow means accepting things can change."

Frustration welled in Vic's chest. "Taking things slow doesn't mean pushing me away. What's changed?"

"The job offer changes things." Nat shrugged. "I'm just being realistic. You signed on here as a summer hire while you sorted out what you wanted to do next, where you wanted to go with your life. Am I wrong?"

"No. but—"

"And now you have a great opportunity in front of you—a huge jump in responsibility, salary, chances for advancement. A new life, new people. All of it. You shouldn't let anything hold you back."

"Anything? Or anyone?" Vic's voice caught.

Nat stiffened. "You have a big decision to make, and we have a critical mission in a few hours. There's no time for this."

Vic pressed, sensing Nat's walls growing higher. "Is that what this is about? You're afraid I'll choose you over the job, so you're making the choice for me?"

Nat's eyes blazed. "I'm not making any choices for you, Vic. Just the opposite. I'm encouraging you to do what's best for your future. Isn't that what a…friend should do?"

Friend. Vic flinched, the word hitting like a bullet. "I thought we were more than friends, Nat. I thought…"

"You're turning this into something it isn't," Nat cut in, tone sharp. "We're two adults who've shared some enjoyable moments. I've told you and told you I couldn't make promises…" She shook her head. "In another month, you might be gone."

Vic felt like the air had been sucked from her lungs. She stared at Nat, searching for any sign of the warmth and connection they'd shared. But Nat's face was a mask of cool indifference.

"I see," Vic said finally. "I guess I'll go, then."

At the threshold, she opened the door. And hesitated. Once she walked through, this would be the end.

She turned back. One last chance.

"Be careful on the raid, Nat. Please."

Nat's eyes softened for a heartbeat. Then the mask slipped back into place. "You do the same."

Vic swallowed hard. This couldn't be how it ended. Not like this.

Before she could think better of it—before fear won, before Nat shut her out completely—she shoved the door closed.

Nat's eyes widened. "Vic, what—"

Vic didn't bother to think anymore, just moved. Three steps. Then she cupped Nat's face and kissed her, hard and deep. Like she could force the truth past Nat's barricades.

For a second, Nat resisted.

Vic stilled, her lips a breath away. "Tell me to go."

Nat shuddered and clutched Vic's shirt, dragging her closer. "I can't, damn you."

Vic whispered, "Tell me again we're just friends."

"I can't." Nat clasped her nape, kissed her. "I can't."

The hopeless ache in Vic's chest eased. As long as tomorrow promised another chance, tonight would be enough. Vic kissed her again. "We've only got a few hours left before we mobilize. Spend them with me?"

"You make it sound easy," Nat whispered, fingers lacing through Vic's hair.

"Maybe it is." Vic kissed her. Waited.

With a nod, as if having reached a decision Vic couldn't decipher, Nat pulled her by the hand toward the stairs. Vic managed to kiss her while stopping on every step to remove an article of clothing. By the time they reached the bed, most of their clothes were gone. Naked, they tumbled down, wrapped around each other.

Vic memorized every gasp, every shudder, every whispered plea—afraid that come morning the walls might be back up. As they lay tangled in the sheets, she traced lazy patterns on Nat's bare shoulder, resisting the urge to push, prolonging the fragile moment.

She kissed Nat's temple and sighed.

"Go to sleep," Nat said murmured. "We'll need to be up in a few hours."

As Nat slumbered, Vic lay awake, staring at the ceiling, at a crossroads. Much as she had been when her dad died. This time, though, the future was not set in stone. The job in New York City loomed—excitement, money, bigger waters. Could she make that be enough if Nat wanted nothing more than the stolen hours they'd shared?

How long could she wait?

She hadn't been able to bring her dad back or resurrect the life she'd known, but she could change the road ahead.

Her choices could change her life.

❖

Nat woke in the dark, instantly aware of Vic beside her—the warmth of her body, the steady rise and fall of her breath—a comfort she could get lost in. She struggled not to move. Not to reach for her. But the urge to press closer, to bury herself in the haven of Vic's arms, to pretend that morning would never come, was nearly unbearable. She'd freeze this moment if she could, suspend time and hold on to this fragile happiness forever. But the cold reality of the impending raid crept in like a chill. And when the mission was over—what then? So few weeks remained before summer ended, and along with it, Vic's seasonal position.

She ached at the idea of letting Vic go, of standing aside while she walked away into the rest of her life—because she might. Vic wasn't tied here, wasn't bound to this place, this life, the way she was. Vic was young, with a future stretching wide before her. And Nat wouldn't be the anchor weighing her down. She couldn't be.

Twenty-plus years and a lifetime of protecting her heart stood between them.

Vic might not be hers to keep.

And God, that hurt.

She turned her head slightly, just enough to see the soft rise and fall of Vic's chest, the curve of her mouth relaxed in sleep. Her stomach clenched, and she inhaled deeply, breathing in Vic's clean, sea-salt scent that seemed to have settled into her very pores. How easily Vic had slipped beneath her defenses, how deeply she'd burrowed into the parts of her she'd long thought untouchable.

God, Vic was beautiful. And not just in the way that made her breath catch—though that was part of it. In the way she kissed her, touched her. In the way she held her—like she was something worth treasuring. Like she was something worth waiting for.

In the way Vic looked at her in the quiet moments…like she was worth loving.

A sharp, aching tenderness bloomed inside her, wedded to a fear so visceral it left her breathless. Because Vic made her feel safe in a way she hadn't realized she craved. And that?

That was dangerous. Safety meant surrender. Safety meant trust.

And trust meant risk.

Nat curled her fingers into the sheets, swallowing against the painful knot forming in her throat. This wasn't supposed to happen. She wasn't supposed to let herself want this. Want her.

But maybe…maybe it had already happened. Maybe she'd never had a choice at all.

Vic stirred beside her.

"Vic?"

A small frown creased Vic's brow before her lashes fluttered open, her eyes sleep-hazy and searching.

"I'm awake," Vic rasped, her voice still rough with sleep.

Nat hesitated. Didn't want to say what came next. But there was no time left. No time to let herself pretend.

"Did you sleep?" she asked.

"Some." Vic's fingers brushed against Nat's wrist, a fleeting touch, as if testing whether the distance was still there.

Nat drew away. Pulled the wall back up. "You should go take care of Memphis. He's probably wondering where you are."

Vic sighed, pushing up onto one elbow, studying her, like she was trying to memorize every detail. "He had his favorite dolly with him in his bed, and I haven't been gone that long."

When Nat didn't answer, Vic sat up fully, dragging a hand through her tousled hair. Her movements were sharper now, her frustration bleeding through. "I'll leave him at the station today. Angie's on the desk, and she'll take him home with her if I'm delayed."

That word. Delayed.

Not hurt. Not missing. Just delayed.

The stone in Nat's chest grew heavier. Vic would be on the lake, the last line of defense—not the first in. That should have reassured her.

It didn't.

Nat clenched her jaw, forcing back the fear. Vic would be fine. She had to be.

"Good. I'm going to shower. I'll see you—after."

"Wait," Vic said softly, catching Nat's arm.

Nat turned, but before she could form a word, Vic's lips were on hers—urgent, imploring, a kiss that felt like a plea. Vic cupped her face, thumbs brushing over her cheekbones with a tenderness Nat didn't know what to do with.

She should have pulled away.

She didn't. Couldn't.

She leaned in, clung to her, drowning in the kiss. Letting herself have this, just for a little while longer.

When they parted, Vic whispered, "Be careful out there, okay?"

Nat nodded, not trusting her voice. Didn't trust herself to say anything at all.

Vic searched her face, her eyes dark with something unspoken. Then she exhaled, giving Nat's hand a small squeeze. "Promise me you'll be safe out there. That you'll come back to me."

The words struck like a hammer blow—because that was the problem, wasn't it? Vic spoke like there was something to come back to.

Like they weren't standing on opposite sides of a countdown, waiting for the inevitable good-bye.

Nat's throat tightened, the weight of the promise heavy on her heart. She knew the risks. They both did. But with Vic looking at her like this—so open, so vulnerable—she could believe. Just for a little while.

"I promise." Nat summoned all the confidence she could muster. "We've got a solid plan, and the best teams backing us up. No matter what happens, we'll be ready."

Vic nodded, but the way she inhaled—sharp, uneven—said she wasn't convinced.

"I know," Vic whispered, her voice was soft, but steel underneath. "I just…I can't lose you, Nat. Not now."

Nat broke then. Just a little.

She pulled Vic into a fierce hug, burying her face in the crook of her neck. Held on tight, as if she could imprint the moment into her skin, keep it locked inside forever. As if holding her close now could somehow make up for all the ways she'd have to let go later.

"You won't lose me," she murmured. It wasn't a promise. It was a prayer.

Vic let out a shaky breath. "Go." Her voice was rough, but steady. "Go and kick some ass. I'll see you when it's all over."

Nat forced a smile, though her heart felt splintered right down the middle. She surged forward and poured everything she couldn't say into one last kiss. The time had come to answer the call to duty.

"Say hi to Memphis for me." Her voice barely wavered. "And be careful out there."

She turned for the shower.

She didn't look back.

CHAPTER TWENTY-FOUR

The wharf at Bolton was already alive with movement when Vic pulled into the parking lot, her pickup kicking up a spray of gravel. The early morning air was thick with diesel, the tang of lake water riding the crisp breeze. The Whaler bobbed at the dock, its powerful engines idling while the crew moved about securing gear, checking comms, and running final diagnostics. A well-oiled machine, every movement precise, every step routine. No wasted motion, no chatter that wasn't mission-critical. Just like it should be.

Everything looked normal. Felt normal. But it wasn't. Not for her.

She sat, clenching the wheel a second longer than necessary, before she shut off the engine. The gnawing weight in her chest hadn't let up since she'd left Nat's house. She was off. Restless.

Last night had been…something. The way Nat had kissed her, the way she'd held on, like she wasn't ready to let go—but then she *had* let go. Pulled back. Kept her walls up even as she whispered a promise.

I'll come back.

A promise that haunted Vic now.

How long? How long before Nat decided once and for all that Vic wasn't who she wanted? Maybe she should just make the break now—take the damn job in New York and get out at the end of the summer. A swift cut bled less.

On the peer, Phee shaded her eyes and looked her way.

Right. She had a job to do. Until everyone was back safe, her only thought needed to be the mission. She grabbed her gear and jogged toward the boat, the familiar rush of adrenaline buzzing low in her gut—the potent mix of excitement and razor-sharp focus that only came before an op. She needed that focus now.

"I was worried you'd gotten lost," Phee teased, her curly hair whipping in the wind. She looked at ease, but Vic sensed the tension beneath the grin Phee shot her way.

"Like I'd let you have all the fun without me." She tossed her bag onto the deck.

Phee snorted, but a flicker of relief crossed her face. She clapped Vic on the shoulder. "Glad you're at the wheel. It's gonna be a hell of a day."

"Wouldn't miss it." Vic shifted the weight of her vest, adjusting the straps. Focusing on the task. On what was in front of her. What she couldn't focus on was Nat, already deep in the forest, moving into position with the DEC team.

The uneasy coil in her stomach tightened. This was the waiting part. The worst part. The part where her brain filled the silence with every bad outcome imaginable.

The radio on her vest crackled to life. "Evans to WPU One. Do you copy?"

Nat's voice shot through Vic like an electric charge, but her hand was steady as she pressed the button. "Copy, Evans. WPU One set to roll. You moving?"

"Affirmative. Two teams, approaching from north and east. Terrain's tight, but visibility is good. No movement yet." Nat sounded solid. Controlled. But Vic caught the edge of tension underneath. Not fear—just awareness.

Vic exhaled slowly. "Copy that. Eyes sharp up there."

A beat of silence. Then, softer, low enough that no one else would hear, "You too, O'Brien."

The line went silent.

But the ghost of Nat's touch, the weight of her promise, the ache of uncertainty? That didn't fade so easily. She should have said something last night. Should have pushed harder instead of letting Nat pull away. Should have told her…what? That this wasn't just a summer fling? That she didn't want to say good-bye in the fall? That every time Nat whispered her name in the dark, something inside her shifted, deepened, rooted?

But she hadn't said any of that.

And now, all she could do was wait.

Please be safe.

Please come back to me.

"There's nobody better in these mountains, Vic," Phee said softly.

Vic gritted her teeth, stifling the urge to argue. She knew that. Knew it down to her bones. But that didn't mean it sat easy. "I know. I do. But I can't shake this feeling…" She shook her head. Swallowed the words she didn't know how to say. "I just—" She broke off, steadying herself. "I care about her, Phee."

Phee pursed her lips. "Yep. That's it. That's the look. Someone's got it bad."

Heat crept up Vic's neck, and she turned back to her gear, making a show of double-checking the fastenings on her vest.

"Shut up," she muttered.

"Too late for that." Phee scanned the Whaler, checked her watch. "We're set. Let's get this party started."

"Aye, aye, Chief." Vic, instantly in work mode, stepped toward the helm, slipping into the familiar rhythm. This, at least, was simple. This, she could control. The Whaler rocked gently beneath her boots, the steady purr of the engines a low, reassuring hum. She scanned the horizon, instinctively noting the texture of the lake—small rolling waves, a light hop from the wind picking up out of the northwest. The sky remained clear for now, but there was a heavy quality to the air, the kind that signaled a possible shift in weather later.

Flipping on the radar display, she checked their plotted course. They'd be running a steady patrol line along the lake's eastern shore, keeping all possible escape routes under surveillance. The position of the other WPU boats blinked green on the screen—one unit stationed at the mouth of the inlet, another holding near the state marina. Everything was set.

She adjusted the throttle slightly, and the Whaler responded smoothly beneath her fingertips. Solid. Reliable. Just like she needed to be.

Phee opened channel wide. "WPU One to all patrol units—confirm positions and status."

A brief crackle, then another deputy's voice. "WPU Two, holding position at Eagle Point. Conditions stable."

Another voice followed. "WPU Three, patrolling east channel. No movement."

Vic scanned the water. Everything was as it should be. Controlled. Methodical. Locked down tight.

And yet that gnawing unease remained, coiled tight in her ribs.

She thought of Nat—of the dense, unforgiving terrain, of the armed suspects they were about to engage. Of how damn far away she was from it all.

Vic tightened her grip on the wheel. She couldn't be in those woods, couldn't be beside Nat. But here? Here she could make damn sure nothing slipped past them on the water.

"Alright," she muttered under her breath. "Let's do this."

She pressed forward on the throttle, guiding the Whaler toward their patrol zone.

Nat was doing her job.

Time for her to do hers.

❖

The radio crackled to life, and Vic jerked to attention.

"WPU One, this is DEC ground team." Nat's voice came through—tinny and distant, but steady. "Approaching target location. ETA five minutes."

Vic's heart pounded, a steady drumbeat against her ribs. Nat's team was close. Too close. The tension in her chest coiled tighter with every second. The water, the mission, the hum of the boat beneath her—it all faded. Only one thing mattered.

"We should be out there with them," she muttered, clenching the wheel. "I…we should be watching their backs."

She should be watching Nat's back.

Phee shot her a sharp but not unkind look. "Probably every one of us out here wants to be up on that mountain right now, and there are times we would be. But today is not that day. Today our job is to secure the lake and hold the line against retreat."

Vic exhaled hard. "Yeah. But, man, waiting down here and listening to Nat and the others about to engage? It's eating holes in my stomach."

Phee nodded, grim. "I hear you."

The minutes dragged. The Whaler's steady engine hum barely registered, drowned out by Vic's racing pulse. She tightened her grip on the helm, scanning the lake, the shoreline—every potential point of egress. Her imagination ran wild, conjuring up a thousand worst-case scenarios, all of them ending with Nat injured while she was too far away to help.

To stop the merry-go-round of disasters, she forced herself to focus: Nat, marshaling the campers through a raging storm to safety. Nat, cool and commanding at the plane crash. Nat, in a dozen other situations—steady, strong, whole.

Another patrol boat checked in. "WPU Two holding position at Eagle Point. No movement."

"Copy that, Two," Vic answered, keeping her voice steady despite the storm raging inside her.

The radio crackled again. Nat's voice. Tight. Controlled. But with an edge.

"Visual confirmed. Target structure dead ahead."

Vic forced herself to breathe. They were in position. Not long now.

Nat again. "Single-story, camouflaged with natural cover. Partial thermal read—picking up at least six heat signatures inside, possibly more."

A brief pause. Then, sharper: "Smoke venting near the rear. Active burn. Could be the cooking lab."

Another crackle, followed by a slight shift in tone. "Perimeter scan. Makeshift logging site to the west, abandoned equipment. ATV at the south wall. No other visible transport."

A beat. Then urgency. "Eyes on movement—south side, near a stack of crates. Armed subject. Possible lookout."

Silence for half a second. Then, measured, precise: "Team holding. Standing by for breach."

"DEA moving in." Reeve's authoritative tone cut through the airwaves. "DEC, maintain perimeter."

Vic's fingers curled against the helm, her body wound tight. This was it.

Silence. A beat too long.

Then the sharp, unmistakable *crack-crack-crack* of semiautomatic fire ripped through the early morning.

Vic's breath seized. The lake, the boat—everything disappeared. Only the radio. Only Nat's voice.

"Shots fired! Shots fired!" Sharp. Urgent.

Gunfire erupted in the background—a rapid burst, then another.

"Return fire!" Reeve's command, clipped and controlled.

Nat again: "DEC, close ranks."

More shots. Too many. Each crack landed like a punch to Vic's gut. Her breath caught, picturing Nat diving for cover, dirt and leaves flying.

"10-33, officer needs assistance," another voice cut in, the emergency distress call turning Vic's blood to ice.

The gunfire didn't stop.

Vic gritted her teeth, jaw clenched so hard it ached. "Phee— permission to advance."

"Hold position," Phee snapped. "WPU Three, report!"

"WPU Three holding position. Nothing moving on the water," came the clipped response.

"WPU Two?"

"Nothing yet."

Vic's focus crystallized—sharp, cold. Hands steady, she locked eyes on the mouth of the inlet.

"All vessels, hold fast," Phee ordered, already checking the FLIR camera feed, scanning the shoreline for movement. "If anyone tries to run, intercept."

The radio crackled—garbled words, static swallowing part of the transmission.

Then Nat's voice. Strained. "Movement on the west side. Multiple suspects fleeing on foot."

"There," Phee muttered, pointing at the feed. A cluster of dark shapes shifting in the trees. "Could be runners. Heading downriver."

"They might be going for boats," Vic said.

"All units," Phee ordered, "converge on the inlet."

Vic jammed the throttle forward. The Whaler roared, slicing through the water like a blade. The islands to her right blurred into patches of green. She ignored the sting of wind-whipped spray lashing her face.

"WPU One, we have eyes on a vessel," WPU Two reported. "Headed downriver."

Phee cursed. "They're running for it."

Vic gritted her teeth. "Not if I get there first."

❖

Gunfire ripped through the forest.

Nat pressed against a thick pine, breath sharp, pulse hammering. The rough bark bit into her shoulder as she strained to listen.

"Targets retreating! I repeat, targets retreating!"

A distant roar—ATV engines revving hard. Then the high-pitched whine of outboard motors. Nat mapped the escape route in her mind.

"They're heading for the river. Moving fast."

Headed toward Vic. The thought hit hard, swift, unbidden. An image flickered in her mind—Vic's fingers tightening on her wrist before they parted, the weight of that last kiss.

Stay safe out there.

"Copy that, Evans." Reeves, voice tight, clipped. "Move in. Maintain cover."

"Copy." Nat's gut twisted. She adjusted her grip on her rifle, nerves twanging. The forest was a blur of shifting shadows, snapping twigs, the low murmur of voices over comms.

Then a blast tore through the night.

A concussive shock wave slammed into her, knocking the air from her lungs. Heat seared the air. She was airborne before she even registered it—then the ground rushed up to meet her.

Impact. Hard. Bones rattling.

Her ears rang, the world swallowed by high-pitched static. Shrapnel rained down—splintered wood, twisted metal, debris from what used to be the lab.

Instinct took over. She rolled behind a fallen log, gasping for breath. Smoke choked the air, thick and acrid. She blinked away grit. The target building was gone—a smoldering ruin, jagged shards of wood and metal all that remained. Flames clawed at the wreckage, black smoke curling into the night.

"Lab's gone." Her voice came out rough. "Status report—all units check in."

Fragments of responses crackled through:

"Johnson here. Minor cuts."

"Alvarez is down…looks like a broken leg."

"Martinez checking in. All clear."

Nat shoved down the thrumming pain threatening to immobilize her. Adrenaline kept her moving.

"Chase, regroup at extraction. Johnson, stay with Alvarez." She shook her head to clear the dizziness, pushing through the haze. "Watch for stragglers."

Her left arm throbbed—sharp, insistent. She glanced down. Blood, dark and slick, soaking her sleeve. A jagged piece of shrapnel jutted from her bicep. She exhaled, pressing a hand over the wound. Later. The suspects were running. They needed to be stopped. And she had to make it back to Vic.

She'd promised.

Gritting her teeth, she pushed the pain aside. She spotted Meg, made her way to her.

"Get a medic out here. Stay with the wounded."

Meg hesitated. "You're hit. You need to—"

"Just a scratch." Nat was already back on comms. "Runners heading for the river. All teams converge on extraction."

She moved. Fast. Pushing through the debris-strewn forest, boots crunching over charred branches. Smoke curled thick in the air, laced with the acrid stench of burning chemicals. Ahead, the suspects were making their break.

Her arm screamed in protest. She ignored it. *Focus. Keep moving.*

Vic was out there. The fight was headed her way.

I'm coming. Trust me.

A sharp snap—wood breaking underfoot.

Nat stilled, every muscle locked tight. She raised her weapon.

"Nat?" Martinez's voice. Low, steady.

"Here."

He emerged through the smoke, rifle up. "Area's clear. No sign of the runners. Looks like they scattered after the blast."

Nat exhaled slowly, lowering her weapon. "Copy. We'll sweep once secured. Let's get to the river." She switched back to comms. "Evans to command—lab is destroyed. No suspects in custody. Runners heading for the river. In pursuit."

"Understood." Reeves again, voice taut. "WPU, be advised: potential incoming."

Somewhere out there, she was waiting.

Nat clenched her jaw, eyes locked on the path ahead.

Let her be safe.

❖

The explosion hit an instant before the shock wave rocked the Whaler. A column of trees, splintered wood, and rock erupted skyward near the river, mushrooming into the night.

"They blew the lab!" Vic shouted.

Phee, jaw set, scanned the inlet through binoculars. "Hold here."

Vic bit back a protest, muscles jittering. She wanted to move. Now.

The radio crackled. Nat's voice—tense, but steady. "Suspects on foot, heading downriver. In pursuit."

Alive.

For a second, Vic's head swam. Relief hit her like a gust of wind, whipping through her, loosening a knot in her chest.

The state police chopper pilot radioed in. "Two outboards heading downriver."

Phee clamped a firm hand on Vic's shoulder. "WPU One, intercept. Go."

Finally.

Vic shoved the throttle forward. The Whaler surged ahead like a sleek, deadly predator.

In the distance, patrol boats, lights flashing, converged like a swarm of angry hornets. She scanned the shoreline, only half listening to the constant radio chatter, straining to spot the suspects.

"There," Phee shouted, pointing toward a narrow inlet.

A cigar-shaped speedboat shot out, veering hard.

Phee on comms. "WPU, all units. Shift to intercept."

A chorus of *copy* in response.

Vic gunned it. The thrill of the chase honed her senses to a razor's edge. The Whaler roared, closing fast. The suspects' boats were quick, but not fast enough.

The speedboat cut toward a DEC patrol boat.

What the—

A man in the boat braced—rocket launcher on his shoulder.

"Phee!"

The radio flared, static-laced panic bursting through.

"WPU Two—taking fire! Repeat, we're—"

An earsplitting explosion split the dawn.

Vic's head snapped up. A flash—then another concussive blast.

A fireball swallowed the silhouette of WPU Two. The patrol boat vanished into a roiling column of black smoke.

"Shit!" Phee grabbed her radio. "WPU Two is hit! Diverting to assist!"

Vic wrenched the wheel, banking hard as she pushed the throttle forward.

The radio crackled—garbled distress.

"We're going down. Mayday—"

Vic braced. *Hold on. Hold on.*

Dead ahead, the wreck of WPU Two listed, flames licking at the stern. In the water, dark shapes thrashed—two, no, three bodies.

"Deck crew—lifelines ready!" Phee's voice was steel.

Vic eased back on the throttle, maneuvering through the chop.

"Starboard side," Phee directed.

Vic locked on the struggling deputies. One had their arm hooked around another, barely keeping them afloat. The third—motionless.

Too still.

Get to them. Get them out. Keep moving.

Phee and Juanita tossed a lifeline to the officer fighting the weight of their gear.

"Grab on!" Juanita called.

A wave surged, obscuring them. For a breathless second, Vic lost sight—

Then the line went taut.

"Got one!"

Phee and the crew hauled them aboard.

"Matt's unconscious!" the first officer gasped.

No time to think. Vic dove.

The cold punched the air from her lungs. Water closed over her head, dark, numbing, relentless. Her vest inflated, forcing her up. She kicked hard, zeroing in on the floating deputy. His life vest kept him up, but he wasn't moving.

Vic gritted her teeth, wrapped an arm around him, and swam.

The weight dragged at her, but she fought forward. Straining. Kicking. Pushing.

She found the lifeline. Forced her numb fingers to hold on.

"We got you," Phee yelled, reaching for Vic's vest, pulling her up.

Coughing, Vic hoisted herself over the side. Sprawled on the deck, gasping. "Is he breathing?"

Phee, checking him over, grim. "Barely."

Vic dragged herself, leaning on the railing for half a second before— The chase. The runners. The boats.

Where—

The radio flared. "WPU Three in pursuit. Suspects heading north. Two vessels, no lights."

Vic snapped upright. "Status on the chopper?"

"Air unit en route. ETA two minutes."

The heavy thump-thump-thump of rotor blades grew. A dark shape streaked overhead, sweeping the lake with a blinding searchlight.

"There." Phee pointed.

Two speedboats, barely visible against the moonlit lake, tore toward open water.

Engines snarled, sending white spray skyward.

"They're running!" Juanita yelled.

Not today.

Vic gunned the Whaler, joining the chase.

"WPU Three engaging—boxing them in."

Vic's heart pounded. The chopper's light raked over the speedboats, illuminating their fiberglass hulls.

A figure moved. Twisted.

A voice over the radio: "Gun, gun, gun…"

A sharp burst of suppressing rounds from the chopper. The shooter scrambled for cover. The second boat veered, trying to cut across the lake.

"Not happening," Vic muttered. She angled hard, cutting off their escape.

WPU Three bore down from the opposite side, closing the pincer. Nowhere to run.

The chopper circled, spotlight locked.

A voice through the loudspeaker—commanding, unyielding: "Slow your vessel. Hands where we can see them."

The first boat cut speed. The driver raised his hands. The second boat hesitated—a fatal mistake.

Vic turned hard, sending a wave slamming into their hull. The boat rocked violently, nearly flipping. The driver fought for control, but WPU Three was already there.

A half-second pause. Then the whine of engines winding down.

Surrender.

"Suspects in custody," WPU Three reported.

The radio crackled. "Evans to WPU—status?"

Nat.

Vic inhaled sharply. Safe.

Her stomach unclenched. She grabbed the radio. "Suspects in custody." A pause. "We're good. You?"

A beat.

"Still here."

Phee draped a warming blanket over her shoulders. "Let's get these guys to the medics." She squeezed. "And next time, don't be a hero."

Vic let out a breathless laugh. "Aye, aye, Chief."

CHAPTER TWENTY-FIVE

The hospital parking lot was chaos.

Red-and-blue strobes sliced through the early morning haze, flashing across the pavement, bouncing off the mass of parked cruisers, unmarked SUVs, and emergency response vehicles. Law enforcement churned everywhere—so many uniforms that they spilled past the entrance, clustering in tight groups, murmuring in low voices. Some still caked in dirt and sweat, others nursing minor wounds—bandages hastily wrapped, bruises darkening in the dim light.

Vic climbed out of the sheriff's van, rolling the tension from her shoulders. Her body ached, but adrenaline still buzzed under her skin, refusing to let go. She spotted a cluster of DEC rangers by the doors, Chase among them, arms folded tight as she spoke with a deputy from another unit. Further up, Reeves stood near the entrance, conferring with a pair of DEA agents, his sharp gaze flicking over everyone who passed, missing nothing.

Vic searched for Nat. Why wasn't she with Reeves or the DEC team? She headed for Chase, tamping down the unease. Before she reached her, the ER doors slid open, and a fresh wave of personnel spilled out.

There.

Nat strode out of the ambulance bay, still in her smoke-and-mud-encrusted uniform, left arm wrapped in thick white bandages. The sleeve of her tactical jacket had been sliced away by medics, the jagged edge stark against her skin. She arrowed to Reeves, who gestured to her, expression grim.

Vic clenched her jaw. *Wounded.* She could have lost her out there—with still so much unfinished, so much unsaid.

As if sensing Vic's presence, Nat looked up. For a moment—just a moment—their eyes met across the sea of officers. Vic stilled, hoping for something—a flicker of recognition, a sign that what they'd shared a few hours before had meant something.

But Nat's expression was closed. Unreadable. Then she turned away. No hesitation. No pause.

Like nothing had ever happened.

Vic froze as Nat fell into step beside Reeves and disappeared through the ER doors. She didn't look back.

Vic's stomach knotted, pulse drumming hollowly in her ears. The exhaustion she'd been holding at bay crashed over her like a rogue wave, dragging her under. Was that really all they'd ever have? Moments stolen in the dark, lost as soon as duty called?

Was that all she was ever going to be to Nat?

A cold breeze cut through the humid air, raising a chill against her damp skin. She exhaled, steadying herself.

Whatever answer she'd been waiting for, she wasn't getting it today.

Maybe it was time to stop waiting at all.

❖

Nat sat at her desk, staring at the same open file she'd been pretending to read for the past twenty minutes. The words blurred together, exhaustion turning official jargon into nothing but a jumble of black ink and bureaucracy.

The dull glow of her desk lamp cast long, angular shadows against the walls, leaving her spotlighted in a ring of gloom. The DEC station was silent, the lot outside her windows empty except for her Jeep. She hadn't meant to stay this late. But going home meant facing the silence there too.

She scrubbed a hand down her face. Maybe she was hiding.

A knock at the door made her flinch.

She straightened, heart kicking up before she forced herself to relax. "Yeah?"

The door creaked open, and Meg stuck her head in, eyebrows raised. "Figured I'd find you here." She stepped inside, closing the door behind her. "Your Jeep's been parked outside since the raid. Haven't seen it move."

Nat exhaled, leaning back in her chair. "I've been busy."

Meg snorted. "Yeah, I bet. Buried in after-action reports? Meetings with Reeves? Dodging reporters?"

Nat narrowed her eyes. "All of the above."

Meg studied her, then nodded slowly. "Sure. That makes sense."

Something in her tone made Nat's spine stiffen.

"Unless," Meg continued, too casually, "you've actually been hiding."

Nat's hands curled into fists before she could stop herself. "I don't hide."

Meg lifted a brow, unbothered. "No? Could've fooled me."

Silence settled, thick as the humidity before a storm. Nat glared at her desk, jaw tight. She didn't want to do this. Not now.

Meg sighed and dropped into the chair across from her, stretching out like she had all the time in the world. "So, you saw Vic outside the hospital."

Nat's pulse skipped.

Saw her. Didn't speak to her. Didn't let herself. The adrenaline surge of the raid draining away but the memory of her fear for Vic still fresh and raw. Fear that had almost been incapacitating when she'd needed all her focus. When lives had depended on her.

"She wasn't hurt," Nat said, keeping her voice neutral. "That's all that mattered."

Meg hummed. "Right. And now that you know she's fine, you've been..." She gestured loosely. "What? Relaxed? Feeling totally at peace?"

Nat clenched her jaw.

Because no. She hadn't been able to relax—not even after seeing Vic standing outside the ER, alive. Whole.

She'd told herself the fear eating at her insides was unnecessary. That she could let it go.

But she hadn't. Fear was a subtle enemy, preying on her irrational mind. Impossible to will away. So she'd walked away instead.

And Meg, damn her, knew it.

Nat exhaled sharply, fixing Meg with a glare. "Did you stop by just to interrogate me?"

"Thought I'd warn you." Meg rocked back in her chair, studying her nails. "The news people have been sniffing around. They're trying to get more details about the explosion."

Nat frowned. "The boat explosion?"

"Yeah." Meg looked up. "You heard what happened, right?"

Something about her tone made Nat's stomach twist.

"I…" She faltered. "I mean, I know the WPU lost a boat. Chase said everyone got out."

Meg's head tilted, eyes sharp. "She didn't say how?"

A slow, uneasy chill slid down Nat's spine. "No. We were more concerned with our injured."

Meg's lips parted slightly, then she shook her head, as if realizing something. "Jesus, Nat. No one told you?"

"Told me what?"

"WPU almost lost three deputies—one is still in the ICU. Near drowning." Meg sat forward, gaze locked on her. "Vic dove into the lake after their craft exploded to go after the one who was drowning."

The words hit like a punch to the gut.

"What?" Nat's voice barely sounded like her own.

"She pulled him out before the flames spread. It was on the radio chatter, but I guess in all the chaos…" Meg trailed off.

Nat sat as if turned to stone.

Vic could have died out there.

And no one had told her.

Why would they?

She'd given no one any reason to think Vic mattered to her in any special way. Not even Vic.

The cold fear unfurled in her chest again, creeping into every corner of her ribs, her lungs, her heart.

What if she'd lost her?

Not just the hypothetical what-if that had been gnawing at her since Vic had arrived and turned her world upside down. Not the vague fear of emotional pain—but a real, solid, horrifying possibility.

What if Vic had died, and she'd never said a damn thing to her? Never told her that she—

She sucked in a sharp breath, gripping the edge of her desk as her stomach lurched.

Meg watched her carefully. "You okay?"

Nat swallowed hard, nodding once. Lying.

"Nat." Meg's voice was softer now. "You're not okay."

"I'm fine," Nat bit out. Habit. Reflex. Defense.

Meg leaned forward. "You don't always have to go it alone."

Nat stared past her, buffeted by a stark awakening.

This—this was the cost of safety, wasn't it?

Keeping her walls up. Keeping Vic at arm's length. Telling herself it was for the best.

Pretending she didn't care—so much so that no one thought to tell her what Vic risked. That Vic might need someone—need *her*—after a life-threatening experience like that.

The truth settled like lead in her gut.

She'd built her life around protecting herself. Around not taking risks, not letting herself need anyone too much.

And yet, she had walked away from Vic outside that hospital and felt like she was tearing in half.

Now, knowing what could have happened—knowing that she could have lost her without ever truly having her...

She couldn't breathe.

Meg must have seen something crack in her expression, because her voice gentled. "You should talk to her."

Nat's throat was too tight to answer.

"Think about it," Meg said, walking to the door.

Then she was gone, leaving Nat alone in the dim glow of her office, swallowed by the weight of everything she hadn't said.

For the first time in years, she wasn't sure if she was keeping herself safe—or if she was just breaking her own heart.

CHAPTER TWENTY-SIX

Thirty-six hours since the raid. Since the gunfire, the chemical stench of the lab, the adrenaline that had left her wrung out and vibrating at the same time. Since watching Nat glance over her as if she was a stranger.

She hadn't heard from Nat since.

Vic peeled off her uniform shirt, wincing as the stiff fabric dragged over a bruise she hadn't realized she'd earned. Just another to join the collection of aches—some fresh, some old—that lived in her body like ghosts. Vic tossed the shirt into her locker, the clang of metal sharp in the near-empty room. She'd tried not to notice the silence. Tried to tell herself it was nothing. Nat was a lieutenant, a DEC officer—she had reports to file, statements to sign off on, a dozen bureaucratic tasks that kept her buried in paperwork. Still, she knew—really knew—what silence felt like when it was deliberate.

"Got plans tonight, Vic?" Phee asked as she breezed into the locker room.

"Nah." Vic pulled out a T-shirt featuring a school of dolphins advising to *Swim Against the Stream*.

Phee opened her locker, dumped in her gear. "Talked to Nat?"

Vic yanked the tee over her head. "Nope."

Vic ignored Phee's stare and rolled her shoulders like it might shake loose the tension twisting her up inside.

"She's probably buried in reports," Phee said, changing into a sleeveless white tank. "Charlie's been grousing that Reeves is still sorting the after-action statements and wants everything in triplicate. State attorneys are breathing down their necks."

Vic nodded. Made sense. Of course Nat had to be there. Of course she was too busy to check in.

Probably.

But a part of her, the part that had watched Nat back away every time they got close, whispered it wasn't just work keeping Nat away.

"She's got a lot on her plate," Vic murmured, forcing her voice to stay even.

Phee studied her, then shrugged. "I'd say give it time, but…you don't seem like you want to."

Vic huffed out a laugh, bitter and short. "Time for what?"

For Nat to come around? For her to finally admit they had something real? For Vic to keep waiting, holding her breath, hoping Nat would decide this was worth it?

Wasn't happening.

And that was the part that stung the most—not that Nat had walked away, but that she had never really been there to begin with.

The understanding she hadn't wanted to face settled inside her, slow and cold.

She'd been fooling herself.

She'd fallen—hard, fast, with no brakes and no second thoughts. But Nat?

Nat hadn't.

Maybe Nat cared, maybe there was something there, but it wasn't enough. It hadn't been enough the night Nat had walked away from her porch, or the night she'd chosen distance over honesty.

And it wasn't enough now.

Vic swallowed, the taste of resignation bitter. She wasn't going to be that person. The one waiting for a door that would never open. The one hoping for something that wasn't hers to have.

A calm settled over her, cooling the anger that had been simmering beneath the surface. She knew what she had to do.

Vic grabbed her duffel and slung it over her shoulder. "I gotta go."

Phee raised a brow. "That so?"

"Yeah," Vic said, turning toward the door. "Need to talk to Charlie about a job."

Phee's lips parted, surprise flickering across her face. But she didn't press, didn't ask what Vic meant by it.

Vic didn't look back as she walked out.

The only way now was forward.

❖

The rich aroma of freshly brewed coffee filled Nat's kitchen as she poured the steaming liquid into two mugs, her hands steady, though a slight tremor lurked just beneath the surface. The warmth seeped into her fingers but did nothing to calm the storm inside.

Three days. Three long, torturous days since she'd last seen Vic. Since that moment in the hospital parking lot when she'd walked away—afraid, uncertain, a coward. Relieved Reeves gave her an excuse to avoid the morass of emotions roiling inside.

That ended now.

She took a slow, measured breath. This was it. No more hesitating. No more hiding behind excuses and fear.

This was about laying her heart bare—about taking a chance on something real. She hadn't even said the words out loud, not even to herself. But the time for running was over.

"You can do this," she whispered to herself. "It's just Vic."

Who was she kidding? This wasn't just Vic. Vic wasn't *just* anyone. She was the woman who had slipped past every defense Nat had ever built, the woman she couldn't stop thinking about, the woman she was in love with.

There: Step one. Admitting to herself what she'd been avoiding for weeks. She loved Vic O'Brien. Against all odds, against every expectation—or absence of it—she'd fallen.

The truth, equal parts terrifying and exhilarating, lifted a weight from her heart.

Gripping the mugs tightly, Nat stepped outside into crisp morning air that bit at her cheeks. The forest stretched out before her, vibrant and alive, the scent of damp earth and pine filling her lungs. She followed the familiar path to Vic's cabin, each step punctuated by the crunch of pine needles beneath her boots, the sound echoing the rhythm of her thoughts.

What if Vic didn't want to see her? What if she'd waited too long?

The memory of Vic's eyes—wounded, filled with disappointment—spurred her on. She had to make this right. She wouldn't let fear win this time.

Not now. Not when there was so much at stake.

And yet, despite the nerves coiling in her stomach, a strange sense of rightness settled in her chest. This was what she needed to do. This was the moment that mattered.

She hesitated only a moment in front of Vic's cabin, her heart hammering against her ribs, before pushing doubts aside and striding across the porch. She knocked—one, two, three sharp raps, each one a promise not to fail.

Her pulse pounded so loudly she was sure Vic would hear it inside the cabin.

Seconds stretched into eternity before the door swung open.

Vic stood barefoot in the doorway in a frayed navy-blue tank top and gray sweatpants cut off just above the knee—the sexiest, most unintentionally devastating set of sleepwear Nat had ever seen. Tousled hair, golden skin kissed by morning light—Vic was breathtaking.

For a moment, Nat forgot how to breathe.

Then Vic's expression shifted—from surprise to guarded wariness.

Nat thrust one of the mugs toward her, willing herself not to linger on the way Vic's muscles shifted under smooth skin, or the soft indent of her collarbone, or how the loose fabric of her shorts clung to the dip of her hips.

"Nat?" Vic's eyes widened for a second, then narrowed. Cautious. And for just an instant, vulnerable. "What are you doing here?"

That flicker of uncertainty made Nat's heart ache. Feeling ridiculously foolish, still holding out the mug, she said, "I…I brought coffee."

"Um…thanks." Vic's fingers brushed Nat's as she took the offered mug.

The brief touch sent a familiar flutter of excitement through Nat's chest.

Vic hesitated, her gaze flicking over Nat's face, searching. Waiting.

Nat steadied herself. "I have something to say."

Vic didn't move. Didn't step back. Didn't invite her in. Her eyes, usually so warm and inviting, now held a guarded distance that made Nat's stomach clench.

The silence stretched, thick and heavy, before Vic finally exhaled. "About what?"

Nat swallowed. No more rehearsing. No more running.

"About us."

A host of emotions crossed Vic's face—hope, doubt, pain, all tangled together.

Nat held her breath. What if Vic simply closed the door? Shut her out for good?

"I've missed you," Nat whispered. "These past three days… they've been hell. But I needed time."

Vic's grip on the doorframe tightened. "If you're about to tell me…" she started, her voice laced with anger and resignation. "If you're about to say we can't do this, you don't have to bother. I get it. I—"

"Just listen," Nat interrupted. "Can I come in?"

The pause was endless.

Then, with a sharp exhale, Vic stepped aside. She didn't invite Nat to sit, retreating instead to the far side of the small room, as if unsure where to put herself. The silence stretched, thick and unrelenting.

Vic leaned against the counter, arms braced on the worn wood surface, and finally said, "I'm listening."

Nat set her mug on the small table by the window and took a deep breath.

"I know I hurt you," she said, voice steady despite the storm inside her. "And I'm sorry for that. I've spent three days trying to find the right words, and I still don't have them."

Vic let out a sharp breath, her eyes narrowing. "You've been practicing?"

"God, yes." Nat rubbed her forehead. "But now that I'm here, everything I planned to say sounds wrong."

Vic's jaw clenched. "Then just say it."

No turning back now.

"The truth is, I've been scared," Nat admitted. "Terrified, actually. I've never felt anything like this before, what I feel for you. The things you make me feel. I've tried to convince myself I would be fine with something temporary, something *safe*. But I can't."

Vic's arms dropped to her sides, her expression unreadable. "What exactly are you saying, Nat?"

Nat met her gaze. "I'm saying that I love you."

Vic sucked in a sharp breath. Hope. Anger. Longing. All there.

"You think you're the only one who's scared?" Vic's voice trembled, frustration and need warring in her eyes. "I put myself out there, Nat. Over and over again. I waited. And you pushed me away."

"I know," Nat whispered, stepping closer. "And I'm so sorry."

Vic shook her head, looking away. "Do you have any idea what it's been like? Watching you run hot and cold? One minute you're here, and the next you're shutting me out completely?" She held up a hand, stopping Nat's protests. "You'll risk your life in a heartbeat for me—for anyone...hell, even an injured moose—but you won't take a chance on us." Her voice broke, but she powered on. "I want all of you, Nat. Your heart, your fears, your joy. All of it. Because I love you. And for me, that means all in. But if you can't give me that, then I'm done waiting. I'll be out of here by tonight."

Nat's breath caught.

"Are you done?" she asked softly.

Vic's shoulders sagged. "Yes. I'm done."

Nat stepped forward and cupped Vic's face in both hands.

"You're not moving out," she whispered, thumb tracing the edge of Vic's tense jaw. "Unless it's up to my house. Because I'm all in too."

Vic's lips parted, but no words came.

"You have all of me," Nat whispered. "If you still want me."

Vic's breath hitched, her hands hovering uncertainly at Nat's waist.

One more rejection, and this was over. Nat could see it in her eyes.

"I didn't come here to say I didn't want you," Nat said, laughing hollowly. "You must know by now I do, even if I *am* too old for you and too scared inside to deserve you." She pressed her fingers to Vic's lips when Vic started to speak. "Wait...please. When we were both out there in the middle of that firestorm a few days ago, I was terrified I'd lose you. I've been so afraid of losing you since the moment I saw you, when I first felt things I'd never expected to feel, I've been trying to stay safe. You're right. I've been pushing you away. I've been a coward."

"Damn it, Nat." Vic trembled. "You're the most fearless woman I've ever known."

Nat kissed her, just a fleeting touch. "I came down here to tell you I'm more afraid of a life without you than I am of risking you'll leave one day. I love you. Right now. For always. If you can take a chance on me—on my fears and hang-ups and everything else—I'm yours. All of me."

She kissed Vic again, pouring every ounce of longing, fear, and love into the touch. Vic stiffened for a split second before melting into the embrace. Nat deepened the kiss, and the tension that had been coiled tight in her chest for so long unraveled, replaced by a warmth that spread through her entire body. When they finally broke apart, both breathless, Nat rested her forehead against Vic's.

"I love you."

"Can you say that again?" Vic asked, wrapping her arms around Nat's waist.

"I love you in a way I've never loved anyone, and I'm done running from it. I'm in," Nat whispered. "All in."

A slow smile broke across Vic's lips, a soft, disbelieving laugh slipping free. "Yeah?"

"Yeah," Nat murmured. "For always."

Vic let out a shaky exhale and whispered, "I love you too."

Nat ran her hands along Vic's arms. "We should talk about that job in New York. I can't leave here, but you could commute or—"

Vic kissed the corner of her mouth, her voice soft and steady. "One—I hate cities. Two—I already have a job that gives me all the excitement I'll ever need. And three? I adore you, I want you every second of every day, and I want to be *with* you for every day to come."

From his bed in the corner, Memphis slowly thumped his tail.

Nat laughed. "Well, then, it seems we all agree. I'm sure with your experience, you won't have any trouble finding a job. You could probably even captain one of the big tour boats."

"Too slow for me." Vic grinned. "Besides, I already have a job. Come fall I won't be a rookie any longer. Charlie hired me full-time."

Nat raised a brow. "Sure of me, were you?"

Vic shook her head. "Sure of what I wanted. I was preparing a winter campaign to wear you down."

Delighted, Nat shook her head. "Why I thought for even a second I could resist you, I'll never know."

"Say it one more time," Vic whispered, her lips brushing Nat's ear. "Please."

"I love you." Nat pushed Vic back step by step toward the bed. "I love you, and right now, I want to show you just how much."

Vic's eyes darkened. "Yes."

"Yes, what?" Nat teased.

Vic laughed, her laugh melting into a soft gasp as Nat pressed her down onto the mattress. "Yes, now."

Nat tugged away Vic's clothes, shed her own, and lay down beside her. "You're beautiful."

"So are you." Vic pulled Nat into another kiss that seared Nat's soul.

Nat stroked Vic's shoulders, her breasts, the long stretch of her abdomen, reveling in the sounds she coaxed from Vic when she dipped lower. Vic echoed each caress, each teasing stroke until, trembling and breathless, they crested together.

As they lay tangled in the aftermath, sweat cooling on their skin, the fears that had plagued Nat for so long seemed distant and insignificant. Now there was only peace.

"What are you thinking?" Vic asked softly, trailing lazy patterns on Nat's back.

Pressing her face to the curve of Vic's neck, Nat laid her hand over Vic's heart. "You are all I'll ever want. My heart is yours."

"Your fearless heart," Vic murmured, pulling Nat closer, "is all I'll ever need."

About the Author

In addition to editing over twenty LGBTQIA+ anthologies, Radclyffe has written over seventy romance and romantic intrigue novels, including a paranormal romance series, The Midnight Hunters, as L.L. Raand.

She is a three-time Lambda Literary Award winner in romance and erotica and received the Dr. James Duggins Outstanding Mid-Career Novelist Award from the Lambda Literary Foundation. A member of the Saints and Sinners Literary Hall of Fame, she is also an RWA/FF&P Prism Award winner for *Secrets in the Stone*, an RWA FTHRW Lories and RWA HODRW winner for *Firestorm*, an RWA Bean Pot winner for *Crossroads*, an RWA Laurel Wreath winner for *Blood Hunt*, a Book Buyers Best award winner for *Price of Honor* and *Secret Hearts*, and a 2023 Golden Crown Literary Award winner for *Perfect Rivalry*. The first book in the Red Sky Ranch romance series, *Fire in the Sky*, is a 2024 GCLS romance award winner. She is also a featured author in the 2015 documentary film *Love Between the Covers*, from Blueberry Hill Productions. In 2019 she was recognized as a "Trailblazer of Romance" by the Romance Writers of America. She was named a Woman of the Year by *The Advocate* (2021), included in the Out100 (2022), and was selected for *Curve*'s Power List (2025).

In 2004 she founded Bold Strokes Books, one of the world's largest independent LGBTQ publishing companies, and is the current president and publisher.

Find her at facebook.com/Radclyffe.BSB and follow her on Twitter @RadclyffeBSB.

Books Available From Bold Strokes Books

A Thousand Tiny Promises by Morgan Lee Miller. When estranged childhood friends Audrey and Reid reunite to fulfill their best friend's dying wish, the last thing they expect is a journey toward healing their broken friendship and discovering a newfound love for each other. (978-1-63679-630-7)

Behold My Heart by Ronica Black. Alora Anders is a highly successful artist who's losing her vision. Devastated, she hires Bodie Banks, a young struggling sculptor, as a live-in assistant. Can Alora open her mind and her heart to accept Bodie into her life? (978-1-63679-810-3)

Fearless Hearts by Radclyffe. One wounded woman, one determined to protect her—and a summertime of risk, danger, and desire. (978-1-63679-837-0)

Stranger in the Sand by Renee Roman. Grace Langley is haunted by guilt. Fagan Shaw wishes she could remember her past. Will finding each other bring the closure they're looking for in order to have a brighter future? (978-1-63679-802-8)

The Nursing Home Hoax by Shelley Thrasher and Ann Faulkner. In this fresh take for grown-ups on the classic Nancy Drew series, crime-solving duo Taylor and Marilee investigate suspicious activity at a small East Texas nursing home. (978-1-63679-806-6)

The Rise and Fall of Conner Cody by Chelsey Lynford. A successful yet lonely Hollywood starlet must decide if she can let go of old wounds and accept a chance at family, friendship, and the love of a lifetime. (978-1-63679-739-7)

A Conflict of Interest by Morgan Adams. Tensions rise when a one-night stand becomes a major conflict of interest between an up-and-coming senior associate and a dedicated cardiac surgeon. (978-1-63679-870-7)

A Magnificent Disturbance by Lee Lynch. These everyday dykes and their friends will stop at nothing to see the women's clinic thrive and, in the process, their ideals, their wounds, and a steadfast allegiance to one another make them heroes. (978-1-63679-031-2)

Big Corpse on Campus by Karis Walsh. When University Police Officer Cappy Flannery investigates what looks like a clear-cut suicide, she discovers that the case—and her feelings for librarian Jazz—are more complicated than she expected. (978-1-63679-852-3)

Charity Case by Jean Copeland. Bad girl Lindsay Chase came home to Connecticut for a fresh start, but an old, risky habit provides the chance to save the day for her new love, Ellie. (978-1-63679-593-5)

Moments to Treasure by Ali Vali. Levi Montbard and Yasmine Hassani have found a vast Templar treasure, but there is much more to the story—and what is left to be found. (978-1-63679-473-0)

The Stolen Girl by Cari Hunter. Detective Inspector Jo Shaw is determined to prove she's fit for work after an injury that almost killed her, but a new case brings her up against people who will do anything to preserve their own interests, putting Jo—and those closest to her—directly in the line of fire. (978-1-63679-822-6)

Discovering Gold by Sam Ledel. In 1920s Colorado, a single mother and a rowdy cowgirl must set aside their fears and initial reservations about one another if they want to find love in the mining town each of them calls home. (978-1-63679-786-1)

Dream a Little Dream by Melissa Brayden. Savanna can't believe it when Dr. Kyle Remington, the woman who left her feeling like a fool, shows up in Dreamer's Bay. Life is too complicated for second chances. Or is it? (978-1-63679-839-4)

Goodbye Hello by Heather K O'Malley. With so much time apart and the challenges of a long-distance relationship, Kelly and Teresa's second chance at love may end just as awkwardly as the first. (978-1-63679-790-8)

Emma by the Sea by Sarah G. Levine. A delightful modern-day romance inspired by *Emma*, one of Jane Austen's most beloved novels. (978-1-63679-879-0)

One Measure of Love by Annie McDonald. Vancouver's hit competitive cooking show *Recipe for Success* has begun filming its second season, and two talented young chefs are desperate for more than a winning dish. (978-1-63679-827-1)

The Smallest Day by J.M. Redmann. The first bullet missed—can Micky Knight stop the second bullet from finding its target? (978-1-63679-854-7)

To Please Her by Elena Abbott. A spilled coffee leads Sabrina into a world of erotic BDSM that may just land her the love of her life. (978-1-63679-849-3)

Two Weddings and a Funeral by Claudia Parr. Stella and Theo have spent the last thirteen years pretending they can be just friends, but surely "just friends" don't make out every chance they get. (978-1-63679-820-2)

Firecamp by Jaycie Morrison. Going their separate ways seemed inevitable for two people as different as Fallon and Nora, while meeting up again is strictly coincidental. (978-1-63679-753-3)

Coming Up Clutch by Anna Gram. College softball star Kelly "Razor" Mitchell hung up her cleats early, but when former crush, now coach Ashton Sharpe shows up on her doorstep seven years later, beautiful as ever, Razor hopes the longing in her gaze has nothing to do with softball. (978-1-63679-817-2)

Fixed Up by Aurora Rey. When electrician Jack Barrow and artist Ellie Lancaster get stuck on a job site during a blizzard, close quarters send all sorts of sparks flying. (978-1-63679-788-5)

Stranded by Ronica Black. Can Abigail and Whitley overcome their personal hang-ups and stubbornness to survive not only Alaska but a dangerous stalker as well? (978-1-63679-761-8)

Whisk Me Away by Georgia Beers. Regan's a gorgeous flake. Ava, a beautiful untouchable ice queen. When they meet again at a retreat for up-and-coming pastry chefs, the competition, and the ovens, heat up. (978-1-63679-796-0)

Across the Enchanted Border by Crin Claxton. Magic, telepathy, swordsmanship, tyranny, and tenderness abound in a tale of two lands separated by the enchanted border. (978-1-63679-804-2)

Deep Cover by Kara A. McLeod. Running from your problems by pretending to be someone else only works if the person you're pretending to be doesn't have even bigger problems. (978-1-63679-808-0)

Good Game by Suzanne Lenoir. Even though Lauren has sworn off dating gamers, it's becoming hard to resist the multifaceted Sam. An opposites attract lesbian romance. (978-1-63679-764-9)

Innocence of the Maiden by Ileandra Young. Three powerful women. Two covens at war. One horrifying murder. When mighty and powerful witches begin to butt heads, who out there is strong enough to mediate? (978-1-63679-765-6)

Protection in Paradise by Julia Underwood. When arson forces them together, the flames between chief of police Eve Maguire and librarian Shaye Hayden aren't that easy to extinguish. (978-1-63679-847-9)

Too Forward by Krystina Rivers. Just as professional basketball player Jane May's career finally starts heating up, a new relationship with her team's brand consultant could derail the success and happiness she's struggled so long to find. (978-1-63679-717-5)

Worth Waiting For by Kristin Keppler. For Peyton and Hanna, reliving the past is painful, but looking back might be the only way to move forward. (978-1-63679-773-1